# THE STORY OF
# DAMON AND PYTHIAS

The Incidental Music for the Production of Damon and Pythias was Written by Professor M. WINKLER and is Published and Sold by the Carl Fisher Music House, Cooper Square, New York.

THE CHARACTERS OF DAMON AND PYTHIAS, AS PRODUCED BY THE
UNIVERSAL FILM MANUFACTURING COMPANY.

# THE STORY OF
# Damon and Pythias

BY

## ALBERT PAYSON TERHUNE

ADAPTED AND ILLUSTRATED FROM THE PHOTO-PLAY
CONCEIVED AND PRODUCED BY THE UNIVERSAL
FILM MANUFACTURING COMPANY

"Greater love hath no man than this, that
a man lay down his life for his friend.
JOHN 11: 53.

**WILDSIDE PRESS**

# FOREWORD

The pages of history and the traditions of the " long ago " furnished no scene that should count for more in man's relation with his fellows, as day by day he lives his life, than the one laid in Sicily and furnished by DAMON and PYTHIAS.

Its elaboration in the play of that name by John Banim found a welcome in the public heart, and later the friendship of these two was made the basis for a society, established in the City of Washington, February 19, 1864.

This society has developed into one of the great Fraternities, with membership rapidly nearing eight hundred thousand splendid men, known as the " Order of Knights of Pythias." That Sicilian scene is so human, so filled with lessons that mean for mutual, community and universal good, that the devotees of that great Order gladly encouraged every effort to disseminate the lessons to be found therein.

It teaches and will develop the spirit of fraternalism — a spirit that should have a place in the heart and life of every well-meaning individual.

As an entirely and distinctive business enterprise, wholly separate and apart from the Order referred to, The Universal Films Company has reproduced

# FOREWORD

the wondrous grouping of the scenes that faithfully
represent many incidents in the lives of these, our
prototypes, and to aid in the better understanding
and appreciation thereof. This publication, the
first presentation in book form of the lives of these
men, by Albert Payson Terhune, with its human side,
its realistic settings, its poetry, its tenderness, its
strength in characterization, and touching pathos
will illumine the subject and hold the thought, and
from it all life will be enriched and humanity bene-
fited by the films and by the publication of the story of
DAMON and PYTHIAS.

*Walter B. Ritchie*

*Past Supreme Chancellor*

LIMA, Ohio, December 12, 1914.

# CONTENTS

# THE STORY OF
# DAMON AND PYTHIAS

## CHAPTER I

### THE FRIENDS

THE late afternoon sun bathed the Sicilian hillside in soft rays. It tinged with shell-pink a villa of glistening white marble, midway of the verdant slope. Through the foliage, purple-patched with grapes, that covered the pergola of the garden, a single beam slanted down upon the figure of a man who sat beside a playing fountain.

From the white toga he wore, with its broad badge of purple upon the breast, his rank as a senator of Syracuse in the year 480 B. C. was proclaimed.

A woman and child — his wife and little son — sat near him; but of their presence he seemed oblivious. One hand shading his eyes, he was lost in a reverie. Now and again his other hand clenched upon his knee, as though at some thought which he found displeasing.

But if he paid no heed to the two who shared his occupancy of that Eden-spot, the eyes of the woman, at least, turned often upon her lord's averted head.

She marked his locked jaw, the restless opening and shutting of his hand; signs of a bitter mental struggle going on within him; and her experience and love enabled her to read these as a frown of tender concern deepened between her brows.

At last, with a murmured word to the child, she rose and crossed to where the Senator sat.

" Damon, what is it? " she asked softly.

At the light touch on his shoulder, the man roused from his meditation with a guilty start.

" Hermion, I — I crave your pardon! " he stammered, quickly.

Looking up into the dark, lovely face that bent so solicitously over him, he laid his hand on hers.

" For a moment my thoughts were wool-gathering," he explained, lamely.

" What is it? " she repeated in the same anxious tone, not deceived by his pretense at lightness. " You are troubled with something — can you not confide in me? "

" It is nothing," he reassured her, with a forced smile. " Sit here beside me. Nothing is wholly bad in life, with you to share it."

Instead, she sank on the turf at his knee.

" You are my husband," she said simply; " and I have tried to be a dutiful and obedient wife; but if I have failed, you shall tell me wherein my fault has lain. Have I broken the laws laid down for womankind? Have I touched wine? Have I been meddlesome in the affairs of others? Have I ever spoken before men, save in your presence and at your wish? These things I know I have not done. But perhaps in some other way I have displeased you —"

He checked her with a grave headshake.

" You are a wife without a fault," he declared, his deep, sad voice softening into a gentleness that accorded oddly with his stern face.

" Then is it your child's health that disturbs your peace of mind — but no, that cannot be." A tear trembled on the long lower lashes of her violet eyes. " It is six weeks since you ordered me to bring him here, away from the heat and dust of the city, which you thought were causing him to grow pale. And now he is the very picture of sturdy, blooming health, as you yourself must see —. It is as I feared — the root of your melancholy brooding. However once it may have been, time and that familiarity, which we are told brings indifference to a long-held treasure, have worked their change upon your heart; and now — you do not love me."

He took her dusky head, bound with its coral-hued fillet, between his hands. " Not love you! " With a low cry, he folded her head to his breast in a rush of passion.

" If I could find words to tell you of my love! " he breathed, looking off over his clenched arms as though to ward away some unseen thing that threatened to snatch from them the treasure they held.

"But they would be but words.   And so useless to make you understand!   You are my life — all that makes it worth the living, is bound up in you and in that fair child, yonder, which you have given me."

With a sigh of content, her doubts on this point set at rest by the vibrant sincerity in his voice, Hermion raised her lips to his.

"But now I have distressed you," he reproached himself after a pause, rising to pace restlessly to and fro.   "Wretched actor that I am, not to have been better able to conceal my feelings!"

"You could not hide your moodiness from me, Damon," she told him with a sad little smile; "even if this were the first time you had shown it.   I have noticed, of late, how abstracted you have become. Every time you have come out here to visit little Xextus and me, I have seen your eyes turn back to the city, while your features grew hard.   It — it was that made me think some fairer face than mine perchance having attracted you,— that your heart was *there*."

He halted, to gaze through the vista between two columns of the peristyle in which he stood, upon the white house-tops of the town that lay touched with mother-of-pearl by the sunset glow in the valley beneath.

"Ay, my heart is there," he said, musingly. "Not in the keeping of any one of that city's thousands, but in the city itself."   He sighed, wearily.

" And oh, Syracuse, city of my birth, how you wring
that heart of mine at times ! "

She watched him; and of a sudden buried her face
in her hands.

" Oh, what suffering I am forced to undergo," she
moaned, " by the fate that makes me a statesman's
wife ! And there are those down there, I suppose,
who envy me ! If they but knew what I endure, not
the lowliest of them but would pity me, instead.
Harassed, daily, hourly, by what apprehensions,
dreads ! Oh, Damon, Damon ! " she broke off,
catching at his robe and drawing him to her. " I
am afraid ! "

He seated himself beside her, taking her again in
his sheltering embrace. " Afraid — of what? " he
questioned gently, as to a dark-affrighted child.

She shook her head impatiently. " How can I
put all the fears, the terrors that assail me, into one
word? I *am* afraid — that is all. Of something,
I know not what; but," and she laid a hand upon
the garment that fluttered above her heart, " something I feel, here, is menacing our happiness."

" No, no ! " he soothed. " Nothing will harm
you, or me — please the gods ! "

Glancing up, she surprised the stern lines in which
his face was chiseled as he still sat looking down,
above her head, at the distant town.

She turned hot eyes upon sun-kissed Syracuse.
" Oh, I hate that city ! " she exclaimed, fiercely.

" And I, too, hate it," he responded, between his set lips "— sometimes. For the crass indifference of its masses, as well as for the corruption and dishonor of its ruling classes, that each day is bringing it nearer its ruin, and," his voice dropping, " that of any honest man, as inevitably, who tries to stay the disaster."

" That was what you brooded upon? " she asked, half-fearfully, as she nestled closer. " You fear an impending danger, too? "

" No, no! " he repeated his reassurance. " Nothing threatens us."

He added to himself the grim word " Yet! "

" Then of what were you thinking just now? " she persisted. " Perhaps it was of Pythias, your friend —? "

He shook off his air of somber gravity, and glanced toward the sundial.

" True," he answered; " for on Pythias my thoughts did turn. It is strange that he is not yet come, when it is already past the hour he set for his visit."

His eyes swept the garden. The child, playing among its fluted columns, was the only living thing in it that met his gaze.

" Shall I send Xextus to look for him? " questioned Hermion. " He loves Pythias; and the eyes of Love, they say, are keen. From the knoll that tops the slope behind us, perhaps he might spy him on the road winding up from the city ——"

But before the order could be given, the garden rang with a glad treble shout. In a scamper of short tunic-skirts and sandaled feet, the lad, halting in his play, had run straight as a dart toward the doorway of the *tablinum* of the villa that gave into the garden, wherein stood the stalwart, armored figure of a man.

" Pythias ! " cried the boy; and found breath to utter no more; as he swung aloft to the shoulder of the laughing giant who caught his joyous onslaught, and thus repelled it, in his strong arms.

" Ho, now, my hero-baby ! " the arrival laughed up at the squirming, big-eyed figure perched beside his plumed helmet. " And can you guess the prize that is held by this citadel you've so boldly stormed ? "

He forgot that the lad, from his coign of vantage upon his shoulder, could look down along his back, and thus obtain an unobstructed view of the contents of the right hand he was guardedly holding behind him.

" Give them to me, Pythias ! " crowed the child, kicking his heels in impatient delight against the burnished breastplate of his captor. " Oh, *give* them to me — quickly ! "

The man thus wildly importuned, glanced up with

a start of surprise and caught the direction of his
companion's eyes.

With a deep, full-throated laugh, he swung the
boy to the ground.   From behind him, he brought
forth a miniature shield, which he gave into the small
hands that were eagerly upstretched to receive it.
Then followed a sword — its blade of lead, and
with point and edges so blunt as to render the weapon
harmless to a juvenile wielder.   And, last of all, a
helmet was produced before the lad's joy-wide eyes;
a helmet, plumed and steel-studded as was the giver's
own and,— wonder of wonders! — so exact a replica
of that bigger headpiece as to bear a visor that was
moveable.

So cunningly wrought a plaything must have
meant the labor of weeks on the part of some silver-
smith, and in consequence had entailed a goodly
drain on its donor's purse.   Setting the casque upon
the child's bronze curls, and so completing his mock
armament, the man swung the tiny, warlike figure
about.

"Now, sir, salute your mother and father," he
ordered, "as a soldier should!"

Smiling at them past the child who was standing
in stiff salute with the hilt of the mimic sword presented to his lips, the visitor advanced upon his
grown-up watchers.

He bowed over the woman's hand.   And, then, in
a stride, he stood before the man.

Their right hands gripped; as our greeting is from man to man to-day. What passed in that clasp was not discernible to the eye; but in the eagerly smiling affection with which each regarded the other's face, the warmth of the friendship that existed between them was plainly revealed.

Both were of noble proportions; the blonde head of the soldier had the advantage of perhaps an inch over the other's prematurely whitened locks, but this and the warrior's mightier breadth, as well, were off-set by the power of intelligence that shone from the statesman's countenance. It would have been odd if a pair so well matched should not have been drawn by the call of like to like, into friendship.

But the years that had passed since their first meet-ing had steadily disclosed the fidelity, courage and honor that were at the core of each of the two friends' character, and had long since ripened their feeling of mutual respect into an enduring love.

Now, as he looked into the other's face, reading there the shadow of care that underlay its expression of pleased welcome, the soldier's free hand clapped Damon's shoulder in rough sympathy.

"I have heard how the election went to-day," he said. "Philistius was raised to the presidency of the senate; so that means you were defeated."

"Defeated," nodded the togaed one, the tired smile still playing about his lips. "The vote was three to one — we were a hopeless minority. But," he went on, " how heard you this, Pythias, when you are but to-day returned from the fighting in the South? And how have the wars used you? Not ill, so far as eye may see."

The other was scanning his features anxiously.

" The city is full of the talk of the royalists' victory to-day; I had been deaf not to overhear it," he said. " I hastened here to you as soon as I could, to tell you that you must not take this too much to heart, Damon."

" The mere result is not what grieves me, since I expected it," the statesman answered; " it is what must follow on the result."

With a shrug, he turned away, signing his guest to seat himself.

" But I bring you news," announced Pythias, with a return to his former light-hearted manner, as he found a place on the marble brim of the fountain between Damon and the latter's wife. " News that will cheer you out of your despondency."

" News? " his friend repeated, curiously.

" The best in all the world to me. And so it will be to you, Damon, I am sure. And to you, Hermion, who are also my friend."

Regarding the warrior's radiant countenance, Damon turned to his wife with a smile.

" We will first hear what this good news of Pythias is," he said. " And then he and I will talk alone upon another matter."

## CHAPTER II

### IN THE CITY

"YOU hear them shout your name?"

"Yes, but I am wondering if such a demonstration, following so close on the heels of what to-day befell in the Senate, is altogether wise."

The speakers stood on a certain street-corner of Syracuse, at the moment that the trio we left back at the villa on the hillside were seated around the fountain in its garden.

One of the two on the corner of the street — a man with a bronzed, wind-bitten visage and of mighty stature — was a soldier.

The other was likewise clad in the helmet and breastplate of a warrior. He was hatchet-faced. A pair of hawk eyes looked piercingly out from above his Roman nose. For the rest, his face was thin-lipped, lean-jowled, of a puttyish-gray complexion. The silver buckles that fastened his lambrequin of Tyrian purple to the points of his shoulders did not come within a foot of his strapping companion's. But somehow — perhaps it was from the commanding gleam that shot forth from those steel-gray eyes of his — he seemed the larger of the two.

His name, even then, was being roared in the nearby market place.

As the seas break first upon the rocks with a boom! to be followed by the hiss of falling spray, so the guttural mob-yell rose, with the last syllable sibilantly prolonged, thus:

" Dion-ysius-s-s ! "

Again, from another quarter, the rough-lunged shout thundered between the echoing house-sides of the narrow streets.

" Dionysius — *Triomphe!* "

The thin lips of the man thus hailed twitched. He had spoken in jest; his apprehension at the wide-spread proclamation of his name through the city being voiced with a fine tinge of sarcasm. But the gentle irony of his utterance had been wholly lost upon the thick-skinned son-of-battle at his side. Now, the latter turned to regard his chief.

" Not wise? " he repeated, staring. " And what have you, Dionysius, the almighty warlord, to fear from the puny tailors, jewelers, and wineshop-keepers who might — if they dared! — raise their voices in protest at your rule? Are not a picked company of your warriors, with me at their head, stationed here in the city? And scattered through the mob, at every street-crossing and alley-turning from east to western gates, are not a horde of your followers among the thousands waiting, in readiness to do your will —"

" But unarmed," quickly interposed the other, the catlike smile still curving his cameo lips. " Unarmed. You forget that, my Procles. And so of what avail is their willingness to fight my fight; when they stand without the wherewithal to do so? "

Turning, the soldier flung out a long arm toward the turrets of a fortress behind them.

" There are your arms," he answered, with grim eagerness. " Yes — *yours;* if you will but utter the command, and let me to my work. In one bold dash only, I pledge you, my handful of ironguts shall win that citadel and all in it —"

Stepping back to regard him from under uplifted brows, the general raised his hands in a gesture of effeminate horror.

" You would attack the city's garrison? " he said. " And from within the town itself, where we are held to be its friends? But this is treason! "

The warrior stood tensely watching him, in no way deceived this time by the mock sobriety of the other's speech; which, indeed, could not have cheated a child, accompanied as it was by a frank widening of the satiric smile upon the hatchet features.

" Give the word," he answered through his clenched teeth, " and you shall see how quickly I will obey."

The other's gaze traveled toward the fort to which his companion had pointed. High against the heavens, his sharp eyes made out what to another

would have been only an indistinguishable speck; —
the form of an eagle. Its outstretched wings and
fiercely majestic head tipped with gold by a ray of
the setting sun that shot just then through a cloud-
rift, the bird circled directly above that armory's battlements. It seemed to mean an augury to the
watching leader. The smile had given way on his
countenance before a look of hard purpose, as he
turned back.

" I have tasted blood to-day," he said, squaring
his shoulders; and, with the motion, the mantle of
his former sneering suavity dropped wholly from
him. " They thought they had me worsted — the
dogs! " he went on half to himself, his eyes narrowing bitterly. " But I have whipped them to their
kennels. It is not a year since I was flung down,
disgraced, from the high office to which at last I had
climbed. Too bold, in that I impeached the magis-
trates for what I deemed treason in accepting the
terms of surrender from a foe I would have crushed
still further to wring a heavier indemnity from them
for our own gain —' an exceeded authority,' that was
the charge by which they caused my downfall. Not
a year ago! And now I have won back my power,
but in redoubled measure. I have worked! worked!
worked! as no man ever before me has worked. To
bribe the controlling vote of the Senate, on one hand;
to gain the trust and following of the army, on the
other. It has meant sleepless nights. It has meant

the surrendering of every pleasure to unending toil.
But I have done it. They did not know the man they
sought to break. They do not know me yet. But
they shall, to their cost, ere I am done."

He leveled his right arm past his lieutenant, carried out of his wonted taciturn astuteness by his own
fierce review.

"Go!" he rasped. "The garrison I *will* take.
Its arms, and store of food and gold shall equip these
men of mine against a future time of need — That
is," he added, his voice descending from its pitch of
passion to the thoughtful key of one who is accustomed, as a successful strategist, to weigh every plan
down to its smallest detail, " that is, if the men under
you are as eager as you say you are, yourself, to attempt the attack. You have sounded them?"

Procles nodded, with a reassuring smile.

"And they are ready," he answered. "Your
gold, that I distributed among them this noon at your
bidding, has whetted their appetite for more. The
heaped-up, yellow contents of those coffers back there
is the goal on which the greedy eyes of every rascal
of the lot are set. How willingly at your command
they would storm that, or any other stronghold,
wherein lies so rich a treasure for their sacking, you
have only to hear them acclaim you to know — as
now!"

Fainter, the rioters having passed into some
farther thoroughfare, the triumphantly chorused

roaring of the name "Dionysius" came again to their ears.

"Be off!" curtly ordered the lean-visaged chief. "Tell them what I say — the citadel falls. But first lead them here. There may be one or two who, at the last moment, would hesitate at the actual striking of so bold a blow. And all depends on the unexpected effect of their solid, fearless rush. I think a few words of encouragement from me may be of help. Bring my wolf-pack here, and I will speak to them."

The soldier saluted, and set off upon his errand. At the next turning he passed a man,— the train of his toga draped over one shoulder across a heroic stomach that quaked, jellylike, as he walked,— who was approaching along the narrow, chariot-rutted street.

The rotund one halted before the armored figure of Dionysius who barred his way; Dionysius whose head was turned at that moment to look measuringly up along the ledges on the pedestal of a statue behind him; a pedestal which might serve as steps to the platform of the monument and from which a view of all the wide space, at the intersection of those two streets, could be commanded.

"I salute you, Dionysius," the pedestrian hailed in a furry, fawning voice.

The other, turning, nodded an indifferent greeting. He contemplated the speaker without any par-

SCENE ON THE ESTATE OF DAMON.

CALANTHE AND PYTHIAS.

ticular fondness; sweeping him from the sleek black curls that framed his smiling, oily-skinned face, to the plump bare calves that bowed under the hem of his robe with the task of supporting the vast girth above them. The granite eyes beneath the burnished helmet's visor held only the coldly appraising look of one who regards a chattel.

"Damocles," the general questioned, "why has not Philistius accompanied you?"

"He follows!" The answer came with placating haste. "He but tarried at the banquet, given by his admiring friends in honor of his well-merited election, to join in a last pledging of his name,— a cup to each letter. Ten cups, only, in all."

Dionysius' mouth-corners were twitching. Looking beyond the fat sycophant, he had spied a lean figure, clad also in the toga of senatorial rank, and with a fringe of white hair surrounding the bald crown of his head, coming toward them along the winding thoroughfare.

"Ah, Philistius!" he hailed, his voice vibrant with mockery. "Let me add my congratulations! So you wined and dined thus early, I learn! A cup to each letter? Royal honors! Those whose votes elevated you to your high place, I presume, companioned you in this feast of celebration? Yes. To be sure. A little getting together, to decide which one shall be given some well-paid office, which this, or that. Quite right. But you will not forget," with a sudden biting lack of levity in the masterful voice, " whose gold paved the way for it all. Yet I do not begrudge you your pickings," he carelessly went on. " Enrich yourselves, all of you, at the public's cost, while you may. It is on a higher goal my eyes are set."

From the head of the street just then, a wild shout went up; louder, because much nearer, than any of those which the wind had borne that way before.

" The soldiers are at hand, and with them the curious rabble," the commander told the two. " It would be wisest, perhaps, in view of what I am about to say, if you were not seen here with me. Go, then, to the square before the Academy and await my coming."

As the white-robed pair departed, the street rang with the clash of arms. Pouring forward, a shield-and-sword-brandishing, shouting, semi-drunken band, into the alleylike thoroughfare, the chosen bodyguard of Dionysius swept toward him. They were bearing with them, bumped and jostled against the housesides, as chips on a surging wave, a body of the idly inquisitive citizenry; as their chief had announced.

And, as one such chip out of the many is oft-times tossed aloft by the breakers, so now there rose upon a doorstep the wild-eyed figure of a blonde and pimply-chinned young man. He shook his fists above the heads of the crowd.

" Fools! " he exhorted them. " Will you stand

quietly by, and see them carry out the purpose which they have shouted; grinning in your very faces? You will see our treasury fall into their thieving hands — and not lift a finger to stop them? What if they are armed, and you are not? We outnumber them, twenty to one. Fall on them, with me! Or do you want a tyrant's rule? This is treating you to a taste of what you will have in store, once that iron-shod despot, Dion —"

A soldier, springing out from the rest, checked the socialist's words with a leveled sword-point at his throat.

But the fanatic raved on:

" Be men, to-day or slaves forever! I call on you to —" The soldier drove the weapon forward. It bit deep into the orator's throat.

Without a second glance behind him at the figure of the unknown youth, fallen curiously limp across the doorstep, the slayer leaped down among his fellows.

A welcoming roar burst from them as, crowding round the statue's base, they looked up at the short, square-shouldered form of Dionysius himself who stood upon its platform.

Dionysius signed for silence; and it came.

" My friends," spoke the gaunt-cheeked general, smilingly pointing toward the citadel's turrets, " they tell me there is a goodly sum of new-minted money there. Also, that the treasury is but ill-defended.

How true that last may be, I do not know.  But this
I do:   I think I may claim the friendship of the man
who to-day has been chosen president of the senate.
If any assault you might make upon that garrison
were to fail, I am sure I could put forward the word
that would spare any one of you from punishment.
I can say no more.   But perhaps I have no need to
add anything further, to speed you on to that golden
storehouse — ? "

With an affirmative shout, mixed of laughter and
cheers, the guerilla mob surged forward up the
street, its eyes fixed with one covetous accord upon
the battlements of the fortress.

Dionysius, descending from the monument, walked
in their hurried wake to the public square two corners ahead.

" Philistius," was his first greeting of the pair he
had sent on there before him, " I wanted to ask you
in what manner your election was received this morning within the senate chamber? "

The leader-elect of that body shrugged.

" How could it be received? " he said, smiling.
" We outnumbered them so completely as to drown
their hisses with our cheers, even as our votes
drowned theirs."

" But there must have been some expression upon
some face," the other persisted, impatiently; " the
face for example of one to whom the outcome meant

bitterer disappointment than to any other there. I
mean Damon. Did he rail against the decision, or
sit gnawing his knuckles, instead, in glum dejection?
Or how took he the result?"

"He must have expected it," indifferently replied
Philistius.

"I watched him," put in Damocles, with a true
courtier's instinct perceiving what the general wanted
to know, and eager to please him. "I marked how
his brows drew together, as with bodily pain. His
lips pressed tight shut, his hands clenched at his sides.
He rose from his place without a word. He had not
joined the groans of his party. But it was as though
a full ten years had been added to him; so drooped
his shoulders, so bowed was his head, as he passed
out through the doors."

"Good!" the soldier approved, vindictively. "I
am glad if it roweled him. It was he who led the
attack upon me, a year ago. He is still my enemy.
And, by Pollux, I am his — for I do not forget.
He shall learn, and soon, that this triumph of to-day
is but a single step in my march."

He addressed Philistius.

"What think you, now? Would the senate be of
a mind to disband, and name me ruler if it were
asked of them — say, on the morrow?"

"Nay, be patient," protested the president.
"That will come in time. We must not risk all, nor

hasten matters unduly. There are still those upon our side who need to be talked into a stiffer backbone for so bold a move."

The other nodded, the eager light fading from his eyes. " I can wait," he said, in the grimly laconic tone of one who has proved his right to the palm of Patience.

" There are some of that number of whom Philistius speaks," the greasily opulent Damocles informed him, " who will be waiting, even now, at my house to meet you and hear your plan discussed. Let us walk there."

But if the general heard him, he gave no sign. Crossing the square in front of them were a bevy of maidens. All of them were fair to see; but one — the center of the group, and, so, apparently their leader or mistress — was fairest of all.

" Come, Dionysius," said Philistius, starting off.

" Yes, yes," the warlord answered vaguely, his eyes still following the girl. " In a moment, brothers, in — a — moment."

# CHAPTER III

PYTHIAS' BETROTHAL

PYTHIAS, in the garden of the hillside villa, meantime was trying, in a fit of wholly unwonted embarrassment, to tell the great tidings that filled his brain.

"But I think I can guess what your news is," Damon was saying. "And indeed, Pythias, you are right in believing that whatever good-fortune falls to your lot brings equal joy to me."

The soldier laughed, with a schoolboy's zest.

"See if you *can* foretell what my tidings are!" he invited. "You could not do it, I am sure, in a week's trying. But, go on — what think you is the confidence?"

The other smiled at him in fond assurance.

"Why, what could it be but one thing? To me who am acquainted with your valor, and seeing you freshly returned from battle, as now, it is no difficult matter to apprehend what good news to yourself, and to those who have your interests at heart, you bring back. Your prowess has won you promotion. You have been given a higher rank in the army than you held before."

" No! "

Pythias was laughing at him, boyishly.

" It has nothing to do," Damon questioned, his forehead crinkling, " with a triumph won by your feats of arms? "

" Nothing! "

The blonde warrior laughingly shook his head.

" That is," after an instant's thoughtful pause he corrected himself, " it may be that some tale of the successes that have met my efforts in the field, being borne to her ears, helped to sway her heart toward me.   She has told me she admires bravery in a man.   She —"

The other checked him with brows incredulously uplifted.

" She? " he repeated.   " What mean these ' shes ' and ' hers ' in your speech, Pythias?   Explain yourself! "

But, by this time having guessed what the other's tidings were to be, the smile had returned to his lips as he watched the soldier.

" Well, there you have it! " declared Pythias, spreading out his hands, an embarrassed flush suffusing the tan of his handsome face.   " Such is my news. I love, at last; and, praise Venus, am loved in return. But by what a maid!   Damon, she is fair — fair," he launched, with a rush of lover's eloquence, into a description of his adored one, " as the rosy dawn itself.   Such laughing eyes she has!   Such dimpling cheeks! She is like some young daughter of the goddess of laughter, sent down to earth to show us dreary mortals what joyous life may be. Not the Graces themselves could outvie the poetry of motion in her going. Light as thistledown —"

"Pythias turned orator!" murmured the states- man in wonder. "But who is this Divinity, may one inquire?"

"She is Calanthe," Pythias replied. "And if you but knew her, you too would chant her praises with- out ever wearying. She is the daughter of Arria (a widow of means whose house is in the street of the Three Arches). It was while I was on furlough, three months ago, that first I met her. Before a dozen words had passed between us, love had en- tered my heart; and 'twas the same with her. She promised to name me the day she would be mine, when I returned again from the wars. And she had kept her word, within this same hour. We are plighted to take the marriage vow, a fortnight from to-morrow."

Damon, rising soberly, took the other's hand.

"I wish you as much happiness, as I have found in wedlock with this sweet woman, here. The gods granting me that prayer, you will not need to sacri- fice to them for any further favor."

His friend, grown serious likewise, looked from one to the other of the pair before him.

"Indeed," he said, "I would ask for nothing

more than that. That I may know throughout my future married life the same rich content you have found in yours — I echo your great wish."

Damon, with a deepening of the gravity on his countenance, turned to the woman who sat on the fountain's marble brim beside him.

" Leave me to talk for a while with Pythias," he gently ordered.

But even when Hermion had departed into the villa, Damon was silent. He took up his slow pacing back and forth once more, with hands clasped behind him. Watching his frowning profile, his friend's look of concern returned.

" Damon "— laying a hand again upon his shoulder to stop him in the midst of his restless walk, and so swing him about to gain a full look into his face, " what is preying upon your mind? "

The senator reseated himself upon the brink of the fountain.

" I did not speak of it before her," the soldier went on, still regarding him from under a worried frown, " for fear of rousing her alarm —"

" She suspects, I fear," Damon, glancing toward the doorway behind them, broke in musingly, half to himself. "— But she does not *know*, not yet. That is why I sent her away."

" Know? Suspect? " repeated the warrior, in stark mystification. " *What*, will you tell me? Perhaps, because I speak of noting its effect upon you, you think I, too, suspect the cause of your uneasy mind. But, I assure you, I do not! What has gone amiss with you in my absence?"

The other looked up at him grimly.

"You told me," he answered with meaning, "that you had heard the result of the election to-day."

Sitting down beside him, his friend held him off by both shoulders.

"New silver among those locks, at the temples," he read aloud the inventory which his shrewd gaze made. "A fresh network of wrinkles beside the eyes. A brow deeper-furrowed by at least three added creases. Man, you have aged five years in the six months since I saw you last! And all for what? Because of a change in our country's politics? A change that will be forgotten in less than a decade in another change, as that will be lost to memory in another, and so on — as the history of affairs of state, since first they began, has ever proven. You surely have not been so foolish as to brood over such a trifling matter! If nothing more than that has destroyed your peace of mind, be advised by me: Think no more of it. You take far too seriously the office you hold."

"The office I hold!" echoed the other reflectively; and so sat for a space in thought. With a slow smile, he turned at length to his well-meaning adviser.

"Pythias," he said, leaning forward and speaking

with forefinger illustratively laid across one palm,
" you are a general in the army of this country of
ours. You have sworn, on accepting your commission, to defend with your life its gates, should they
be attacked by some enemy. Suppose hostile hordes
were at hand, to storm those same gates. That they
were even now swarming over the walls, to put to
the torch all this fair land of yours and mine. Has
that, thus far in the history of nations, not been
done, and then forgotten in succeeding time of peace,
which in turn has been blotted from the minds of men
in red war's new coming? What would you do,
then? Throw down the sword and shield you had
vowed to your country's defense, and run to save
your own life — because you knew the incident would
be forgotten in a few years? "

" No! " flared the other. " No, by Mars! You
know me better! "

The statesman rose, with a shrug.

" Exactly so," he responded, resuming his restive
pacing as before. " I, too, took a vow, when I ac-
cepted my commission as a servant of the people.
It was to defend our country's welfare. Not, as in
your case, with brawn. But with brain. And now
an enemy *does* threaten us. One viler than any bar-
barian tribe that might be sent to scale our walls,
since it is from within the walls themselves the menace comes — at the hands of traitors. And you call
this a trifling matter; one I ought to take less to

heart? When I see the land I have pledged myself
to protect so endangered? And myself too weak to
redeem that pledge? For, Pythias, you would have
an army at your back to repel that other attack.
And what have I? We are so few — so pitifully
few," he clenched his hands in impotent anguish;
" we who hold our patriotism higher than the highest
bribe could reach — as against the number we oppose. You do not guess why I am near to the brink
of distraction. But think of yourself in my place,
and you will quickly understand. I must — I *will*
hold to my vow, no matter what the cost! "

He halted to gaze, as before, down upon the
roof-tops of the town in the far-off vale. But
now his eyes, as they rested upon it, held a zealot's
fire.

" One deed only can end it! " he breathed. " And
that deed I must take into my own hands. I have
seen it coming. For that reason, I sent her and the
child out here into the country on pretext of the little
one's health. But in reality it was to have them
safe out of harm's way, when the time comes to
strike the blow —"

" Damon, are you mad? " queried the soldier, half
starting up and gazing at him, aghast. " If I catch
your meaning — but, listen to me: this must cease.
Promise me you will do nothing rash. I must have
your word that you do not even contemplate —"

The other checked him with a warning gesture.

A servant, sent back by Hermion to bring in the little boy, had emerged just then from the villa.

He was a man of middle age, whose dark, humble eyes were set in a lean, war-seamed face. The green of the slave-tunic blending in the foliage against which he stood at the rear of the garden while he looked for his small charge, lent an added obscurity to his presence.

Turning back to his guest, Damon waved an inviting hand toward a bowl of fruit on a nearby pedestal. Pythias shook his head. The other, following the soldier's gaze, looked around again to ascertain whether the servant had carried out his errand and gone.

But Xextus, playing among the pillars of the peristyle — pillars which he called his soldiers — and being of no mind to give up his sport so soon, had turned, at the head of his slender white, marble legions at the approach of the slave; brows martially beetling under the toy helmet, mimic sword akimbo, to repel the attack of the invader.

The slave had given back a step before the tiny, militant figure. All the color drained from his cheeks, he was looking, not at the child, but through him, as though upon some dread vision he saw there.

Damon, watching, understood what was passing through the fellow's thoughts. His own sped back to a street in Rome, through which he had been

walking, the business of state that had taken him
to that city being completed, on his way from the
Forum to his lodgings in the Palatine, on a day three
years before.

Midway of the street before him, he had seen a
small group gathered near the deadwall of a building.   It had comprised three young men, in the in-
signia of Roman officers, and another, of their own
age, whose robe, gathered in the expansive folds of
a fop's, revealed him to be a gentleman of leisure; as
readily as did his over-ringed white hands.

Damon had perceived that one of the soldiers was
just then adding a fresh spot of red to the two or
three that already marred the white skirt of his
tunic, as he held the hem of that garment to a thumb
which had apparently been wounded by an accidental
scratch.

" And we contend that the blood of a slave is of
no different color than yours or ours," another of
the officers had been saying, loud enough for Damon
to overhear as he drew nearer.   " But come; the
question is soon settled.   You have a few sesterces,
perhaps, my good Pyrrhus, with which to back your
opinion in the matter."

" It is impossible that a slave's blood could be of
the same hue as a patrician's," the coxcomb had made
answer with disdainful assurance.   " But I will
wager on it, gladly.   A sestertium * that I am right."

* $400 in our currency.

Damon had halted. He had come close enough to the group by that time to see over their heads. And thus he had made the discovery that it contained yet another member. It was this same slave upon whom his gaze now rested, that he had then seen standing with his back to the wall, hemmed in by the knot of disputants. Ashen cheeked, then as now, the wretch had been staring in dumb, sick-eyed terror at the short swords of two of the three officers.

"Stay a moment," the soldier with the bleeding thumb had objected. "We have not yet decided who pays for your slave. We shall open him well, in order to leave no doubt in your mind. Shall we agree that you are to stand his loss, along with the wager, if your judgment is proved wrong? And we to reimburse you for him, in case we are the losers?"

"That will be another sestertium," the dandy, in smiling confidence, had nodded his agreement to the terms. "I paid that much for him to Draco, the dealer, last summer — but he has proved worth the price. I would hesitate to lose so good a servant, were it not that, with the two sestertia which I am about to receive from you, it should not be a difficult matter for me to find another as good. Strike, Hecale, and you, Gracchus,— and let us have the matter put to the proof!"

Damon had stepped forward.

"Your pardon, sirs," he had apologized quietly for his intrusion.

The three officers, at sight of his senatorial toga, had given way before him respectfully. The fop, however, had shown no such deference for the stranger's rank. Turning, he had looked the in-truder up and down with haughty eyes.

"Why," he had begun, coldly, "I, myself, can see no reason why you should be granted pardon for breaking in upon a conversation that does not pos-sibly concern —"

"A desire to be of service to you," Damon had bowed, in unsmiling response, "by settling the dis-cussion I have overheard you engaged in, is my ex-cuse. It entitles me, I think, to forgiveness for the interruption. Your friends, these soldiers, are right. The blood that runs through the veins of that vassal," tapping his breast, "is the same as mine. Its color is no different from any other fel-low-being's. I would not advise you to touch him with your swords, since "— and Damon had placed a bag of gold pieces in the hand of the astonished ex-quisite —" since, on the payment to you of twice what I have heard you say he cost you, he now be-longs to me."

Beckoning the slave to his side, Damon had been about to walk on.

"I am not a slave-dealer!" the young dandy had checked him, in a tone of scornful wrath.

"Nor are you a fit master for any slave," the older man, turning to face him, had answered with laconic sternness. " Nor fit to hold knightly rank. A true knight does no man wrong."

He had passed on down the street. The servant whose life he had saved had followed at his heels and had thenceforth loved him as a dog its master.

. . . . . . .

Now Damon spoke with quiet, but obedience-compelling, firmness to the child.

" Xextus, go into the house with Lucullus," he directed.

The lad, dropping his pose of playful menace before the servant, turned at the voice of paternal authority. The slave had got back his grip on himself. Stepping forward, with a bow of apology to his master and the latter's guest for his intrusion upon their occupancy of the garden, Lucullus picked the child up in his arms and convoyed his burden of protestingly wriggling small boyhood into the villa.

Damon, turning back from watching their departure, saw his friend frowningly regarding the ground at his feet.

" But enough of my troubles,"— the statesman, with a self-condemnatory headshake, went on in a tone of assumed lightness —" This is a bright day for you, Pythias — do not let me cloud it by bothering you with my cares."

Pythias rose, the troubled wrinkle still between his brows.

" It is not as bright a day for me as it was, I cannot but admit," he answered ruefully. "To come back this way and find you so sore distressed, grieves me —"

"Do not let it grieve you," the other interrupted, laying his hand in turn upon his shoulder with an affectionate smile. "It has been good to see you. But I have made you spend too much time away from your Calanthe. I would not have you think ill of me. So, if you are in haste to return to the city —"

"But 'tis a strange thing," the soldier broke in, "how love works in one. It is all new to me. But, though I left her not an hour ago, I *am* a-hunger at this moment for another sight of her, as though it were a week since we parted."

"I will summon Hermion," his host responded, with an understanding nod, "that we may both take leave of her. For I shall accompany you on your journey. I must know," he continued, with a return of his former seriousness, as he looked down again upon the town "— what is going on there."

Pythias stepped to his side.

"But remember," he charged, "I have asked you to pledge me that you will make no rash move. You *must* be careful, Damon. Not alone for yourself — for I know too well how little you would think of that — but for the sake of all of us who love you, you will attempt nothing desperate. ' *Caution!* ' "

## CHAPTER IV

### HE WHO COVETS

UP the winding, chariot-rutted road ran Calanthe, pursued by her maidens. The gay breeze, borne from the blue waters of the Mediterranean, whipped her gold bronze curls into her laughing eyes, whence she shook them free; and lifted the silken folds of her snow white draperies, till they snapped smartly about her tiny, sandaled feet and slender ankles.

She turned, both hands clasped to her wind-tossed locks and called gayly to her companions.

"Sluggards, heavy-footed ones!" she mocked. "What is it that weights your steps? Calanthe outstrips you all; and despite the strong breezes and the hills to climb, is not a bit the worse for breath. Come, come, vie with her fleetness, lest she call you old — and that before you have found your lifemates!"

A slender maid, whose sleek, jet-black head was closely bound with golden fillet, darted up the slope in pursuit. With gay, little outbursts of mirth the remaining four gave chase. Beauty, grace, gayety, and the unbridled spirit of happy youth, on the green

36

hills outside Syracuse, while below, in the heart of the city, craft, hatred and the shedding of blood ruled supreme.

"Calanthe, do not be so willing, nay anxious to be rid of us, on this, one of the last days of your freedom," gasped Eunice, the leader of the pursuing band, grasping the flying folds of her companion's tunic.

With a little shout of dismay, the fleet Calanthe tripped and fell to the green sward. Her maids swooped down upon her and held her prisoner, while she pleaded in vain.

"Always do those filled with conceit tumble to earth, before they have soared too high, sweet," censured Eunice, pressing close a tiny red garland that encircled the brow of the captured one.

"And now that you have tasted the dust, we will set you free, on the sole account that, in so short a time, you will be bound for always and never again taste freedom!" chaffed another.

"Who speaks of freedom and those bound?" indignantly demanded the tortured one. "'Tis but the lack of that same prison cell and those iron chains, that tips your tongues with smarting language. Who would not be bound in the arms of him who is beautiful and beloved by all the city? Who would not inhabit a cell, with a lover whose voice is liquid music, whose eyes are fiery pools with wondrous depths to be sounded?"

Flinging her rose garland into the face of the open-mouthed Eunice, Calanthe sprang from the ring of admiring maids and darted toward her mother's garden.

Down at the foot of the hill, a figure, lean but squat, with helmet and breastplate catching the low-slant rays of a late sun and red-striped mantle wrapping its ill-shaped knotty legs in obedience to the wind, plodded its upward path.

With the grim, sardonic persistence that character-ized all his acts, Dionysius was in pursuit. Men of state, his hirelings, awaited to thresh out the ways and means to a throne — the overthrow of a popu-lace — ruled city,— the introduction of a crown. And he, whose brow the crown was to grace, gasped and fought for breath, as he pursued, uphill, the lithe, fascinating form of a Grecian maid.

The ascent accomplished, he leaned upon the stone gate and surveyed the roof-tops of the city he had just left. With a sudden victorious gesture, laden with vindictiveness, he flung aloft his right arm and extended it, as in a sort of benediction, toward Syra-cuse — a benediction that was grooved with curses; then he turned, and, with a slight pressure, swung in the gate and stepped into the garden of Arria, mother of Calanthe.

Treading a graveled path, brilliantly bordered with a variety of blooms, Dionysius came upon a shaded, green-carpeted grove of silver birch trees.

In the center, a fountain of shell-pink marble, flecked with gray held crystal clear waters, that reflected the slender, white tree trunks. And around the basin sported Calanthe and her maids.

"It is not fitting that we be so joyous and without sacred calm, having but just come from the temple, where we offered sacrifice to insure your happiness in coming marriage," expostulated Eunice, suddenly dropping to the ground in sedate determination.

"You talk as though my marriage were but the approach to my tomb!" pouted Calanthe. "I will not have it so. My heart is brimful of joy and hope and my head abuzz with divine ideas of what happiness will be mine. Come, let us dance! Come, Eunice! See, I plead so prettily, dear one."

Thus cajoled, Eunice sprang to her feet and lifted her slender arms above her head.

"This time it shall be the dance of lilies," she ordained. "Pure, cold, sedate, like a sheaf of the blossoms themselves. Gather some to be borne on our arms — a symbol of our chastened spirits."

"No — not lilies," objected Calanthe. "They are beauteous blooms for altar or casket — But for love! For love, sweet Eunice, there must be roses; pink and creamy yellow, for the love that not yet has flamed; but red, crimson-red for a love like mine. Is it not so, my maids, that the red, red rose betokens love?"

"It is indeed!" interposed a rasping voice.

" But who has brought such worldly knowledge to
so sweet an innocent as Calanthe? "

Eunice, in sudden fright, dropped her perfumed
burden of pink and crimson and darted to Calanthe's
side. With a harsh laugh Dionysius, a jarring, in-
congruous note in the gay garden, stepped into view.
One by one the other maids shrank behind the trembling figure of their leader.

" Why this fright? Why this fleeing as from a
monster? I was but looking on, in profound admiration of your dancing."

Dionysius for whom men sold their souls, whose
raised hand in battle drove hordes of brave soldiers
to their deaths, was plainly aggrieved at the uncon-
cealed horror in the pretty eyes of the huddled group
before him.

Her first dismay allayed, Calanthe woke to the
realization that before her stood her lover's general.
She knew the utter awe in which this man was held.
She felt that if she were to help Pythias at all, her
first duty was not to offend his superior. Taking
Eunice by the hand, she pulled her forward.

" Look you, Eunice, 'tis Dionysius, the overlord of
our army! " (" My Pythias " was trembling on her
lips, but with a sudden burst of diplomacy she substituted " our army.") " It is an honor to be visited
in our little garden, by one whose name rings through
the streets of Syracuse! "

With a sudden, forced humility, the maids bent

CALANTHE AND HER MAIDS.

"OH, MY PYTHIAS. YOU WILL NOT GO?"

low before the armored figure. Then, as silently, rose to their feet and stood grave and abashed. The warlord took off his helmet. A stray shaft of sunlight fell on his head, accentuating the hollows under the high cheekbones, the sunken, gimlet eyes and the knotted tautness of the mouth corners.

" It is not thus that I would see you," he observed. " So suddenly has the light gone from your eyes and the laughter from your lips. Be gay again and let me feast my weary eyes on the grace of your steps and the music of your mirth. Will you not bid me be seated, fair Calanthe? "

" In this grove we have not a bench, my lord, but if the fountain edge will —"

" The fountain edge shall be my seat. And you will sit beside me? "

Calanthe twisted her pretty hands in sudden terror. Half unconsciously she fell back a step toward Eunice, who was looking on, resentment plainly graven on her lovely face. This intruder! What right had he to invade the privacy of a maid's garden? A warlord in pursuit of a dancing gazelle! Indeed it was a strange combination and not at all to her liking. She went forward and slipped an arm about Calanthe's waist.

" Do you know when first I saw you, Calanthe? " questioned Dionysius, an amused gleam transforming the cold steel of his eyes. " 'Twas but a half hour since, outside the entrance to the Academy. Grave affairs of state were weighing on my shoulders. Senators stood by to beg my indulgence and ask advice. A parcel of fools, not yet convinced of my supremacy, were about to be convinced by means best known to my satellites, when suddenly there burst upon my vision a dream of loveliness and youth — yourself, Calanthe! "

Eunice's hold tightened about the slender waist of her loved companion. Calanthe, a sullen crimson spreading, as spilled blood, under the velvet whiteness of her flesh, closed and opened her hands convulsively. Dionysius laughed.

" Think you 'tis often that generals of invincible armies push to one side the powerful ones and pursue to mountaintops a tiny maid, unused to the life and gayeties of cities? "

Calanthe dropped in a quivering, disconcerted heap, at his feet. With a sudden gesture he stooped and lifted her by her little icy hands.

" Do not hide your beauty, sweet one," he besought; not restrained by his openmouthed audience of awestruck maidens. " It has ne'er been my good fortune to look upon such rounded damask cheeks, such snowy shoulders or such luscious lips. From whence comes your wondrous loveliness, Calanthe? "

" Oh, my lord, you do but joke with me." Calanthe's voice was choked with fear and indignation. " I am but a poor subject for your brilliant speeches; and for beauty I am badly off. Why, the face of

ιny of my maids, reflected in this fountain, casts to
the heavens a far more glorious image than my
own."

" It is not true," murmured the overlord, pressing
too closely her imprisoned hands. " Your fingertips
are chilled, child. I would cast a wager they were
not so before my approach. Come, look into my
eyes with those violet orbs that drew me hither.
Have no fear. All my power fades before your
glance and my stern will shall be clay to your pretty
fingers. Come, look!"

With an intimate gesture, Dionysius tilted up the
dimpled chin and smiled into the frightened face.
Calanthe broke from his grasp and turned as if to
flee.

Suddenly came thoughts of Pythias, resplendent
in war regalia, strong, erect, beautiful as the sunlit
day. This man was his overlord. If he wished to
confer favors, he, and he alone, held the power to
do so. If he wished to overwhelm and disgrace, he
had but to raise a finger.

A poor helpmeet would she be for her lover, if at
the first distaste, she escape the mighty one and thus
destroy his chances, when their relationship should
be discovered.

" Your pretty words are overwhelming," she said.
" And my poor brain is stunned with the honor.
Pray let us converse on other matters, for the mo-
ment, till I get back my calm of everyday existence.

Think you that there will be more battle to call our army again to the front?"

"Battle? Army? What coarse words to issue from the velvet lips of a sweet flower like yourself! What know you of battles and armies, tender one? Your converse should be of butterflies and blossoms, of sunshine and sweets. Speak not again of battle. The clash of swords is a memory that grates my ears, when I am seated here in your perfumed paradise. What do you know of battle, child?"

"Alas, but little! I would know more, but no one will speak to me of it. It would be wonderful to see the fire of men's spirits as they dash into the fray. To hear the dull roar of trampling hoofs and chariot wheels. To note the blood-red quivering nostrils of the steeds, urged into the thick of the fighting; and the harsh clang of sword on shield, when it fails to penetrate. It mounts to my brain like wine — and it is just the imagining of my foolishness."

Dionysius glanced through half-shut lids. His under lip was caught in sudden misgiving, lending his face the expression of a swooping hawk.

"That is not the imagining of either a foolish, or an adroit, mind. You have been spoken to by a soldier who has seen battle. Your soul has caught the war-fire from his. Was it the spark of love that performed the ignition? Who was he who inspired you?"

"Your surmise is incorrect, my lord. But often

have I heard my elders speak of ancestors great in
battle. The spirit is in the sons of our family, from
their sires, and grandsires. But I, alas, a girl, can
share none of it and sit, an alien, on the outside rank,
to listen — and that is all."

" I think there is something secreted from me.
In that tender breast is locked a something I am
ignorant of."

Dionysius clamped his pointed chin between a
nervous thumb and forefinger. It was a gesture
well known to his associates and feared by his under-
lings.

" But since you ask of present battle news and the
possibility of our army being again called forth, fair
Calanthe, I will say that I know not what conditions
are at Agrigentum. For days past, my ambitions
have been resting here, in Syracuse. By nightfall,
however, there should be word. Now come, enough
of this grave talk. Your snowy brow is furrowed
and your cheek is faded ashen. If you would
please me, dance. Entrance me, as you did when,
unseen, I saw your golden sandals flashing in the
dying sun, as you lifted your rosy feet in gay meas-
ures. Dance, Calanthe — dance for me — and en-
thrall me ! "

" Dance with your love roses," whispered Eunice.
" The aged fool need not know that they signify
the twined hearts of Pythias and you. Dance for
him, with the love of Pythias shrouding your soul;

and the mountain of conceit will take unto himself the radiance of your glance."

" I will! " agreed Calanthe, bounding to her feet and gathering with a wild suddenness the scattered garlands.

For a moment she poised on the tips of her toes, arms thrown aloft, twined with crimson blooms. Her head thrown back, revealed the perfect line of throat melting into bosom. Dionysius watched with greedy eyes.

As the dance grew more and more violent he leaned forward, from the fountain edge, his thin lips compressed and twitching at the corners, his eyes narrowed and pierced by a lustful gleam, his nostrils dilating and contracting spasmodically.

Faster and faster spun Calanthe, till she was but a blur of silken whiteness, gold and crimson. Then, in a final burst of abandon, she flung far the scarlet garland and fell to earth, a panting, radiant, laughing sprite.

For the space of a second Dionysius sat motionless, while a dull flood of color surged under his sallow skin and sought his temples. There it pounded at his brain until his breath came in quick, hot gasps. Uttering a sound half triumph, half goulishness, he snatched the pulsing Calanthe from the ground, pinioned her in a vise-like grip and fastened his dry, burning lips to her mouth.

Eunice and the maids gasped in horror to see their

mistress so assailed; yet made no advance to rescue her from the arms of the vandal.

Calanthe needed no aid. At first contact her heart had stood still in her breast. Then the sickening terror of it gave her strength, superhuman strength, and she fought and kicked and bit her way to freedom.

Once out of his grasp, outraged, quivering with anger, she raised her hand and cut him sharply across the mouth.

"Now go!" she commanded, imperious in her fury. "Warlord, general, commander of men, that you are, you have for once stepped too far. Leave this garden and do not enter it again, whether there be pretext or whether there be none. Go!"

Dionysius bent to take his helmet from the fountain edge, his eyes still fastened on the indignant maid before him. As if in insolent retort, he pulled down one corner of his purpling mouth and laughed. It curdled the blood of his victim, but she stood, taut and defiant, her hand still indicating the white stone gate.

And a moment later, through this same gate, slouched Dionysius, the warlord of Syracuse, to be greeted by Damocles and Philistius, who had come in search of him, alarmed at his long absence.

"What has kept you, Dionysius?" queried Philistius, a hint of petulance in his tone. "There were several awaiting you at the house of Damocles, to discuss, in serious vein, that which you so keenly desire — and you came not."

"Hold," muttered the general. "I have been much worried and distressed. I —"

He cast a crafty look back over his shoulder, where could be dimly seen a white-robed, closely huddled group, through the silver birches.

Philistius followed the look and grinned. Damocles, unknowing and slow to comprehend, looked from one to the other in blank bewilderment.

"What is this secret understanding? This exchange of shoulder-shrugs and lifted eyebrows? Is there that afloat that would not interest me?"

Philistius pointed expressively to the distant garden and tapped Dionysius on the shoulder.

"There must be other maids as fair," he suggested significantly. "For this one is the property of none other than our famed Pythias. Calanthe, daughter of Arria and betrothed of Pythias, to whom she is plighted to take the marriage vow a fortnight from to-morrow."

Damocles awoke from his nebulous condition.

"Knew you it not?" he asked, in bland and childlike manner; "all Syracuse has known. He is indeed a lucky warrior, to attain a bosom flower as fair as she. Ha! And so you thought she'd be enamored of your charms and flutter to your embrace?"

"Enough of this insensate jesting," croaked

Dionysius. "A man may view a maid without thoughts of theft or of wedding feast. She is but a pretty child. Let us proceed. The descent will not tax the breath, as did the mounting."

But in his brain the persistent taunt, "The betrothed of Pythias!" drove him to madness, till he thought aloud:

"So 'tis from him she absorbed the fire of war. It was he who filled her pretty head with battle tales. Pythias! Forsooth it will bear looking into. That Pythias should possess what Dionysius covets! It will indeed bear looking into!"

# CHAPTER V.

A SLAVE swung back the heavy folds of purple velvet that concealed the portal of the inner courtyard. From afar, the roar of voices, broken now and again by blatant trumpeting, rumbled into the silence of the dwelling of Dionysius. The slave, black ebony limbs rigid, thin arms folded stiffly, stood in silence, awaiting his master. In the polished marble floor the sheen of his flesh was reflected. From countless polished urns of brass and silver it was thrown back at him.

A sound from without caused him to shiver slightly. The next instant the purple folds behind him parted and Dionysius, followed by Damocles, strode into the room.

" Have ye not progressed? " Damocles was asking with some asperity. " We have attained the vantage ground whence your broad view may take a boundless prospect. Is it not enough to report for so short a period of labor? "

Dionysius swung upon him viciously.

" So short a period of labor! I have labored all the years that have been mine. I have labored from

50

my infancy. I shall labor to my grave. When others sleep, I plan. When others play, I dream. And my dreams merge into plans — and my plans into realities. But the striving for greater and still greater rewards in life has sapped the life blood from my arteries and dried the energies I once possessed."

"Think, when downcast, of the day when the *great* reward shall come," urged Damocles, stretching his length upon a gaudy silken couch, brave in gold trappings and fringes. "Think of the time, when borne through the city's streets, in your regal chariot, the populace shall hail you —"

Dionysius leaped forward and laid a forbidding hand over the mouth of the speaker.

"S-h-h!" he hissed, glancing from side to side and behind him, at the draped portals. "Who may not hear, when least it is expected? The word itself has never crossed my lips, nor shall it till the day when it is no more a matter of conjecture."

As he whispered the last words his glance fell upon the African slave standing motionless inside the portal. Amazed, his eyes wandered from the huge, broad-toed feet, flattened on the marble floor, to the head, bound in folds of green and crimson silks.

The expression that distorted his features was first one of nameless terror that broadened into baffled rage. With a mighty oath he strode toward the

stiffened figure and tore from its head the soft, glistening mass of silk.   As if unfurling a banner, he
whipped it against the air, till not a fold remained;
then with twitching, uncertain fingers tore it to shreds
and cast it to the floor.

The slave remained motionless.   Not a ripple of
the ebony flesh greeted this maniacal outburst.
Dionysius, feet spread, arteries on neck and temples
swelled to bursting, stood before him, choking out a
torrent of words.

" What mean you, black scum that you are, by de-
fying my commands of the manner of clothing your
body?   Have I not often said that I wish no ornamentation, no superfluous display of silken stuffs,
no —?   Bah!   Of what use to spend the energy I so
sadly need upon the crass stupidity of a slave born
without the means of thinking!   Begone!   And
bring a bowl, full, double spiced and heated through,
that Damocles and I may forget your transgres-
sions! "

As the velvet folds fell behind the retreating slave,
Dionysius sank into a cushioned seat and dropped
his head upon a trembling hand.   Twice he started
to speak, then hesitated, as if not knowing in just
what terms to couch his explanation.

Damocles, half-raised on one fat elbow, watched
him with the keenness of an obese hawk.

" Why this sudden passion vented upon an of-
fenseless slave? " he asked at length.   " Is it that

your tense control must snap, to send relief to your worried brain? "

To the half-buried sting in the words of compassion, Dionysius paid no heed. But he gave answer to the direct question.

"I ask no clemency or indulgence. I require none. When once this brain and self-control of mine shall snap, as some frail glass stem, then will the workings of my heart be still and the breath no longer ooze from my lungs. Nay! I ask no relief. But I demand obedience and it is one of my uncompromising rules that no attendant about my dwelling shall wear draperies that might act as nests of concealment."

"Nests of concealment!" echoed the amazed Damocles. "What is your meaning, Dionysius?"

An utter silence followed. Damocles with curiosity writ large upon his fat-joweled, blue-red countenance looked through, rather than at him. Dionysius' brows were shirred into a hundred creases, his lips so tightly clamped together, that they radiated blue-white lines that ate into his cheeks.

At last he spoke:

"These are the days when a man who is ambitious protects his life by warding off what *might* come, not that which is already here."

"You mean —" gasped Damocles, rising in sudden horror from the couch.

"Just that," agreed Dionysius; "but look not so

perturbed. My fears cannot jeopardize your safety, my friend."

" But here, you fear? Here, within the walls of your own dwelling, you dare not trust the hands that serve you? "

" Fear always the nearest hand, regardless of the body to which it may be fastened," warned the overlord grimly. " Remember the dagger point will find its mark, only when drawn at a close angle. Ah, the bowl! And the scent of spices touches my nostrils with a pleasing sting."

Silently the slave drew an onyx pedestal before the couch of Damocles and placed thereon a steaming tankard. From side stands of ivory and pearl, he took two goblets of beaten silver and dipped them into the hot liquid, presenting the first to Damocles, the remaining one to his master.

Dionysius placed a cupped hand on either side of the goblet and raised it, at arm's length, above his head.

" In this draught we drown all our fears and worrisome imaginings," he proposed, " and from its stimulus, shall be born the undaunted knowledge of future triumph — a future not far distant, I swear it! "

With heads erect, elbows at right angles to their bodies and hands flattened against the goblet sides, the two men drank.

But hardly had the first gulp gladdened their

throats, when sounds of an altercation, outside the portal, arose, above the distant clamor of the crowded streets. The voices of slaves and pages raised in protest were drowned by the resonant commands of one of higher culture. Nearer and nearer came the violent group, until the purple velvet hanging was swayed to and fro in answer to the physical struggle that was taking place on the other side.

With a mighty wrench the hanging was torn from its fastenings and a cluster of mauling, viciously hostile men, fell over the threshold.

From the kicking, thumping mass, one man detached himself. With a triumphant cry he headed for Dionysius, followed by the howling attendants. Breathless, scratched and bleeding, he fell at the feet of the warlord and extended a strip of parchment.

At sight of the bruised, exhausted stranger, Dionysius fell back a step or two, until he found support against the jellylike anatomy of Damocles. As the intruder remained silent and still kneeling, Dionysius flung aloft his right arm, in wrath.

"What is this?" he asked his vassals, his voice high pitched in anger. "Has this household of mine suddenly become like a thing gone mad? Are my commands not to be obeyed — nay, even are they to be ignored? Speak up, one or all, I wish to hear your miserable excuses. Then shall I say what I shall say!"

" My lord, we did protest! " one piping voice tes-
tified with all the vehemence born of a severely
bruised nose.

" Aye, protest!   And your protests, six in all, did
not quell the protest of this one stranger.   Monu-
ments of strength have I, to protect the gateways of
my home!   Who is this man? "

" A messenger from Agrigentum," gasped the
stranger.   " Spent with travel, but with news of
grave importance and requests, my lord."

Urgently he pressed the parchment into the hands
of Dionysius.   But the fingers did not open to receive it.   Instead, the kneeling figure was waived
again into the clutch of the waiting slaves.

" Take him from my presence and strip him to
his dust-bitten hide! " directed Dionysius.   " When
he has had complete change of clothing, bring him
to me.   Then will I peruse the messages from
Agrigentum."

Through a half draped doorway, to the left of
the inner courtyard, could be seen the band of slaves
ripping the armor and clothing from the body of
the exhausted messenger.   His flesh, gray-white,
where exposed, was separated in well defined sec-
tions from the purity of the sheltered stretches of
skin.   There were ridges dull scarlet and inflamed,
alternating with grooves deep cut, from the tightened
straps and trappings he had worn.

Dionysius looked on, perturbed; Damocles, as

LYING UNDER THE SHADIEST TREES WAS CALANTHE, ATTENDED
BY HER MAIDS.

IN THE DISTANCE FUNNELS OF SMOKE, ASCENDING FROM BURNING HOUSES.

though he were witnessing a performance arranged for his exclusive amusement. Dionysius broke the silence.

" All the day, yes, and for days past, have I known that summons from Agrigentum must come. A strange certainty of disaster has hovered about me, till I welcomed the night to close my eyes, if not my brain, to its insistent whisperings."

" The news may be of the best," quoth Damocles, comfortably yawning behind his pudgy, over-ringed hand. " You are unnecessarily disturbed."

" If his tidings were of the best, think you this man, lacking food, dirty, and exhausted, would break into my presence and pant out his need of haste? No, there is something needed. Here he comes, in different garb and stripped of all possible weapons! Now we shall learn the text of the messages."

" My lord, conditions are grave indeed at Agrigentum," reported the messenger. " There is immediate need of additional armies and, most urgent of all is the necessity of a master mind like yours, my lord, to diagram and strategize against the Carthaginians, who have but little of the science of warfare's finer points."

A gesture stilled the garrulous outburst. Dionysius unrolled the parchment and let it dangle from his hand. His eyes rapidly traced the scrawled characters. In the gravity of his reading, his eyes receded deeper and deeper into his skull, until the overhanging brows seemed to shelter mere cavities.

" They have need, indeed! " he exclaimed to Damocles.  " My commanders on the field have allowed early defeat to damper ardor and destroy the vision of a possible victory.  They see gray.  And I am the only one who can bring the rose gleam through the soddenness.  Yes, I must go.  Although affairs are fast approaching an important issue, I must leave my ambition to strangers and go! "

He sighed heavily.

Damocles, slow to thought, and ponderous after he achieved it, woke to the situation and struck him sharply on the shoulder.  The triumph of having solved a difficult dilemma shone from his small, sea-green eyes.  He fairly beamed upon the general.

It was this apparently foundationless satisfaction that roused Dionysius to vehement language.

" Speak! " he rasped out.  " What is the reason of this widening grin and winking eye?  Have you but now waked to the point of a comic tale told yesterday, or has the cup just quaffed touched fire to your brain? "

Impervious to these sarcastic shafts, Damocles proceeded to unfold his plan.

" Less than an hour back," he strove for oratorical inflection and effective pose, " I heard you murmur that if Pythias, the idol of Syracuse, possess that which Dionysius covet, there would have to be a sudden turn in affairs.  Can you see light now, my

Dionysius? A kind fate has made to your order the very situation you desired so fervently."

" I am rarely slow to comprehension," interrupted Dionysius irritably, " but if you wish me to grasp the import of this master stroke of yours, I fear you must speak more into my mind and less out of your own. What is it that you wish to say, Damocles? Dress it in few words and those of the plainest. One always carries low-priced cloth to a poor tailor and rich materials to the skilled one. So is it with language, my friend — simple words to the slow in thought. The brilliant-minded, only, may juggle with embroidered phrases! "

" It is this, then," Damocles explained. " Why go to Agrigentum, when Pythias is here? He has just returned from wars in the South. He is covered with glory. His name slips from the mouths of the populace as glibly as the names of their gods. Moreover he holds, in the hollow of his hand, the heart of the fair Calanthe. Once away, who knows but that your fame and that position you are about to attain will win over the maid. It is not an impossible thing."

" Send Pythias to Agrigentum? " meditated Dionysius. " If he be killed in battle, well —"

" Well —" echoed Damocles.

" It shall be done! " decided the warlord. " Know you where a messenger may find Pythias at this moment? His departure must be immediate. The

Carthaginians have chilled the blood of our bravest. Aid must go to them before that blood is too hopelessly congealed."

The messenger from Agrigentum stepped forward to hear the commands that were to follow.

" Pythias is at the home of Arria, at this moment," divulged Damocles, overinflated at the vital rôle of creator of ideas and informer of whereabouts. " Send the messenger direct and he will be here in but few moments."

Dionysius directed the messenger.

" The first house on the hill that leads down past the Academy Square. There is a grove of silver birch at the end of a flowered walk," he added, and then railed at his own stupidity.

" And now that all is settled so wisely and so well, may we not quaff in peace, and let the liquid coat our stomachs with cheer and our brains with wit? " There was a plaintive plea in Damocles' request. An unquaffed bowl was tragedy sufficient to cast down his spirits for the week.

Deaf to the entreaty, Dionysius walked out upon this balustrade and gazed aloft, where on a strip of white road, indistinct in the dusk, a single horseman urged his steed ahead. It was the messenger from Agrigentum. Dionysius strangled the chuckle that gurgled in his throat.

. . . . . . .

In an onyx-paved hall, with pillars of green mottled marble, blazed ten torches in bronze bowls. The apartment thus vividly lighted, reflected a myriad of gleams in the translucency of its flooring.

Calanthe, in brilliant yellow tunic, sat on a low-cushioned bench, her slender fingers threading the golden curls of Pythias, who was seated at her feet. Standing above them, his purple-banded toga showing dead black and white in the torchlight, was Damon. With arms folded loosely across his broad chest, his face wreathed in smiles that breathed a benediction upon the young lovers, he stood, witness to their happiness.

" A fortnight is too short a time is it not, Damon?" Calanthe pouted prettily and looked up into the fine, gentle face of her lover's friend.

" A fortnight is a lifetime, lived twice," supplemented Pythias, eagerly. " You, who have found such profound and lasting happiness in wedlock, must tell her so, Damon. The fickle maid would hold me distant many months I doubt not — if I should so allow. Ah, my sweet, know you not that life is too short a term in which to crowd the rapture of a perfect love? And Youth — that which blesses you and me at this moment, on the morrow, or the morrow after that, will take wing and never more return. A fortnight is —"

The irregular hoofbeats of a tired steed drifted in to them, through the white-and-gold draperies. Pythias jumped to his feet.

" 'Tis the sound of a horse that is goaded to hot speed," he exclaimed, running to the draped balcony that overlooked the entrance path. " He stops here! A man alights! Are you expecting messages of importance, Damon, that they seek you out here?"

" I am expecting nothing," replied the statesman. " The messages I have this day received have weighed my heart with lead — all save one. If the messenger is seeking me, it is an unexpected summons."

The curtains shrouding the entrance to the outer vestibule parted and Eunice ran to Calanthe's side.

" There is, outside, a handsome messenger. Though wan and worn of feature, yet his form is superb and like unto a —"

" Whom does he seek?" interrupted Damon, smiling indulgently upon the maid's glowing description.

Eunice's face was suffused with tender blushes.

" Had you not asked, sir, I would have neglected to say. It is Pythias he seeks. He begs admittance."

" Pythias!" Calanthe darted to her feet and ran into the protecting circle of her loved one's arm. " But why — why does he seek Pythias, at this hour?"

" Let us have him in. That is the shortest way to discern why," suggested Damon.

In an instant the messenger stood upon the threshold. His seamed face was lit by the fires of an undying patriotism. He knelt before the giant warrior.

"I have come to summon you to Dionysius, who in turn was importuned by our generals at Agrigentum. We have need of a master mind there. We have need of a steel-clad courage. Dionysius awaits you at his dwelling. I should not, perhaps, have delivered the message. I may incur his wrath that it came from other lips than his own."

"He will indeed be wrathful," interposed Damon, smiling in derision. "On a slimmer excuse than that, can our Dionysius vent his spleen. It is the training for his throne in Syracuse, eh, Pythias?"

"I know not if that be true, my Damon. Dionysius is revered on the battlefield, his —"

"Yea, he is revered when his countenance is turned to the revering ones. But let the back of his head smile upon them, and lo, the rumble of choked curses rises to wound the ears. He has lived for self alone. He has sacrificed his friends, his honor, his home, upon the altar of a boundless ambition for place and for power. He does pollute the air he breathes!"

Pythias raised a protesting palm.

"A true knight should ever wear the armor of truth and the shield of virtue; against which the shafts of vice and falsehood cannot prevail. Dionysius has ever inspired me to brave deeds — he is the model and I the — Calanthe, sweet, why do you cling to me so tremblingly? And are these tremors that shake your slender body? Speak, dear one! What has affrighted you?"

"War!" gasped the maiden. "Oh, my Pythias, you will not go — you will not! Promise me you will not go!"

"Not go, light of my heart! You have heard the command from the overlord. I am but a soldier. I obey."

"But he — he —" she faltered.

"He? What? Calanthe. Speak not in snatches, I pray you, dear. My time is short. I must accompany the messenger and receive my orders."

"No, no, a thousand times no! You shall not go, my Pythias. Would you leave me here to eat my heart out, alone and unprotected?"

"Nay," corrected her lover, smiling with deep and trusting affection into the eyes of Damon. "Not unprotected. For while Damon lives are you safe and furnished with a protector, far more capable than I. It will be but another link in the golden chain that binds us."

"But if you — if there should happen so terrible a thing that I might see you nevermore? If you should not return!"

Torn with hysterical weeping and the panic of

parting, Calanthe sank to the floor at her lover's feet. Pythias bent and drew her into his arms.

"Sweet one, you are the core of life to me. There is no thought of one save you and never shall be. This is not fitting a soldier's mate. When the call to battle comes, he must attend. He must close the tender by-ways of his heart and live only in his mind. Come, smile for me, my Calanthe."

"If you should not return!" sobbed the maid, still clinging to him in terror.

Damon walked to a low stone table on which grew a pot of myrtle. Snapping a slender sprig of it, he turned and approached Pythias.

With right arm extended, elbow straightened and fingers closed he laid the bit of green in Pythias' palm.

"See, Calanthe," he lifted the drooping head of the grief-stricken girl and pointed to the symbol. "He will return. And his eyes shall search the horizon for the sight of your lovely face and the wonder of your greeting. He will return."

Pythias released her and grasped, with both of his, the hand of his loved friend.

"You will be her protection when I am not here to see? It were absurd to ask it — so completely will you watch over her, e'en without my bidding. I have but two words more to say: '*Caution!*' and '*farewell!*'"

He gathered the sobshaken figure of Calanthe in

his arms, kissed her pale forehead, her tear-washed lids and tender mouth, then strode from the room, followed by the messenger.

Out on the moonlit balcony, a silken yellow tunic gleamed — a spot of gold in the clear whiteness of the night. And when the dark spots that were horses and their riders were swallowed by the black shadows of Syracuse a prostrate, weeping girl hid her eyes in her hands, to shut out the radiance of the moon.

# CHAPTER VI

## THE VISIONS

THE mountain slope, overlooking the sun-kissed Mediterranean, was bathed in the full glow of midday. The breeze, tossing the treetops, turned the silver undersides of the dull-green foliage to the skies. Birds, strange yellow and black striped, preened on the upper branches. As the wind veered about from time to time, zephyrs, laden with the odors of orange and olive blossoms, were borne to the sea.

Far off the blue expanse was flecked with white, and here and there moved a vessel that gave the appearance of a huge centipede pushing itself through the water — the war triremes, propelled by three banks of oarsmen.

Far up the mountain side, lying under the hugest, shadiest tree, was Calanthe, attended by her maids. On the ground was spread a cloth of blue worked in silver, and laid thereon were silver dishes, filled with fruits and sweets.

But Calanthe heeded them not. Her gaze was fastened on the line where distant waters met a still more distant sky. A trireme worked, swiftly, into her line of vision. She shuddered and again hid her head in her arms.

"What is it that has brought fresh sorrow to your eyes, dear one?" Eunice bent above her mistress and placed a protecting arm about the white shoulders. "You must not allow this utter submission to grief. It has fed upon your cheek till, even now, you look a shadow of the maid who bade her lover farewell. What is this fresh sorrow?"

"The trireme!" Calanthe jumped to her feet and clenched her trembling hands. "I hate the thing that brings the thought of war! That vessel, propelled by near two hundred men, bent on destruction of life, floats upon the calm bosom of my fair Mediterranean and blots the picture. Ah, that I should have the cruel fate of loving one whose duty it is to fly into peril at his country's command!"

"It is wondrous to be the bride of a soldier-general!" urged Eunice. "What maid but would covet the honor? And with one as beautiful and strong as your Pythias! Calanthe, you do not thank the gods sufficiently for the marvels they have bestowed."

"The gods!" the bitterness in the exclamation shocked the listening maids to silence. "I am a human and my heart cries out for its loved one. I am miserable — miserable and afraid! It is of no use to beseech the gods to send me my happiness. It was they who snatched it from me!"

" Calanthe ! " breathed Eunice, awestruck by the seeming sacrilege. " You must not speak so, or as punishment it may happen that Pythias will not return."

At thought of this terrible possibility Calanthe was again plunged into the deepest grief. Face down on the green sward, she wept her heart out, while her maids one and all tried to devise some means of solace.

" Come romp through the groves with me," beseeched Eunice, lifting the bronze-gold head to her shoulder. " We will give chase to humming birds and gather the blooms from which they've sipped. And you have tasted not one of the almond sweets that Artullo prepared for you, with such loving care, this morn."

" Ah, Eunice, my faithful companion, I care not for sweets. When the heart is hungry, there 's no hunger elsewhere. I am a sorry comrade since Pythias went away; if I were but strongly willed, I would control my sadness and refrain from darkening your existence. Love plays strange pranks. Come, dear, I'll try to do better. Moaning will not make him return earlier than he is able to. We'll stroll through the woodlands and see which of us is most apt at duplicating the call of the strange birds, which have lately flown hither from the South."

" You will be, of course," declared one of the

maidens, enthusiastically, " you are always most apt, no matter what we attempt."

" Follow me ! " called Calanthe gayly, " an extra portion of sweets to her who first lays hand on my tunic folds.   Follow ! "

Down the slope sped the fleet-footed girl.   On and on — catching at tree trunks to aid her balance in slippery places, and turning once or twice to wave a tantalizing hand at her pursuers.   At the foot of the hill where the huge, flat rocks jutted out into the sea, she waited, till they had gained her side.

With arms outspread, her face flushed from violent exercise, her background the sapphire blue of the Mediterranean, she presented an entrancing picture.

" If Pythias could see you now ! " exclaimed Eunice, bounding toward her.   " You are so beautiful that way, sweet.   Not since the day your lover left, have I seen the crimson in your cheek and the sparkle in your eyes.   Is she not beautiful ? "

Eunice turned and consulted the little band of stragglers.   One by one they knelt in mock obeisance and chanted:

" She is indeed a queen of beauty ! "

" I will not be chaffed," pouted the reigning one. " Look !   Beyond the third huge tree whose leaves are rimmed with scarlet !   What is that yawning hole — that wicked looking cavity of blackness ? "

The maids looked, with fear, from one to the other. None volunteered the answer to Calanthe's question. Struck by the sudden silence she searched the face of her companions.

"Why do you not answer?" she demanded imperiously. "What is there about that strange and unalluring place that I may not know? Is it the abode of a wicked one or —"

Eunice was the first to speak.

"We must not speak of things profane, to you, Calanthe. That is the cave of Galatea, the dwelling place of Hecati, the witch, who professes to know most things, aye, even more than the gods themselves. She is shunnned by those who live an upright life. Only the corrupt and cruel consult her ill-smelling flames and magic waters, to find out how best to thwart their foes."

"And knows she all things, as she professes to do?" inquired Calanthe with warm interest. "Can she speak of things that concern the planets and has she sight to see a hundred leagues and tell what is happening there?"

"All that and more they say she does," acknowledge Eunice reluctantly. "But it is not for you to show interest in a vile person of this sort. Come, let us away from the neighborhood of her cave. I shudder at its nearness."

"I shall enter it!" announced Calanthe.

"What!" shrieked the chorus of maidens. "Calanthe, daughter of Arria, enter the cave of Hecati?"

"You must not," was Eunice's stern command. "We, your maids, are responsible for your safe-keeping. I will not allow it."

"'Allow'! 'Tis a strange word from maid to mistress. I shall do as I have said. Let not the question of permission enter into it. Am I not staid enough to wed, when my lord returns from the wars? If so, then am I capable of entering the cave of Hecati and of coming out unharmed."

"What madness is this?" wailed Eunice in great distress. "If she were human, yes. But she is strange, misshapen and vile in tongue. You must not!"

"She is an oracle, consulted by many older and wiser than I am and for far less vital reasons. I, too, would know of things to which the vision of my young eyes is closed. I would know if —"

"You must not! See, at your feet, dear one, I plead, Calanthe! Have wisdom! Do not do this thing!"

The violet eyes looked down into the troubled black ones. The obstinate light that had glittered but a moment before faded into softness and was submerged in tears. Impulsively Calanthe dropped to her knees and placed her arms in a close embrace, about the shoulders of the suppliant girl.

THE TRIUMPHANT RETURN THROUGH AGRIGENTUM AFTER VANQUISHING THE BARBARIANS.

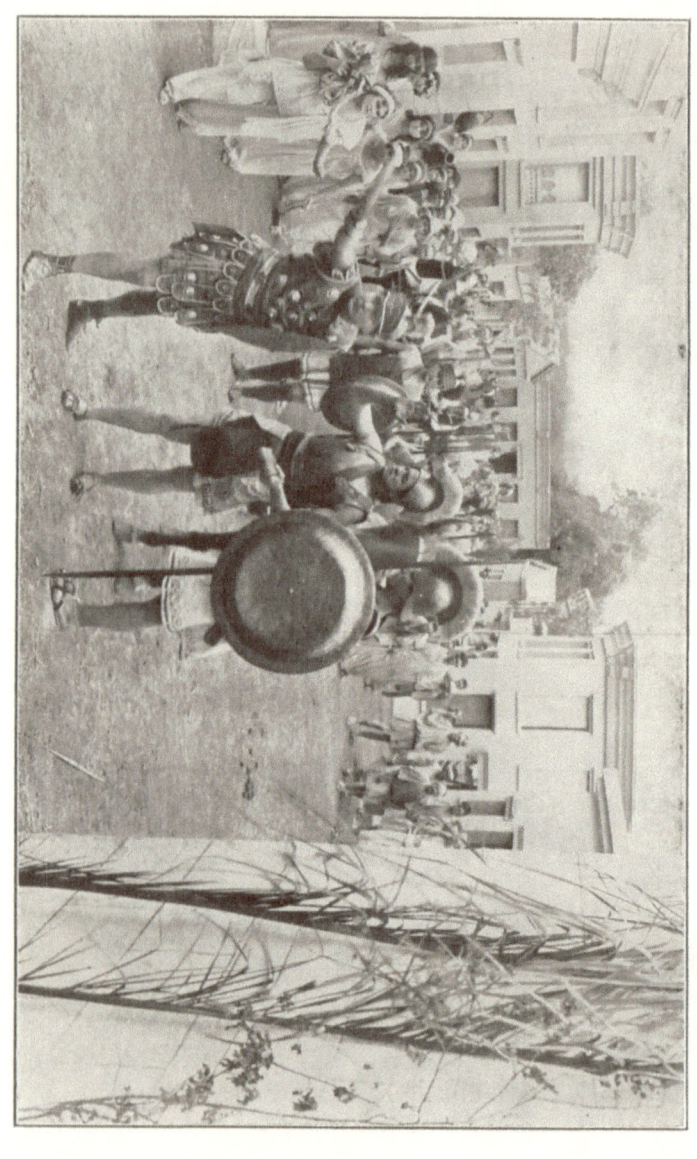

"SPARE NOT THY STEED! ON! ON TO SYRACUSE."

" List to me, Eunice," she began sadly. " A moment since when I leaped down the mountainside
and bade you follow, it was not from lightness of
heart or any desire to take up again the sports of
youth that I have so completely dropped. 'Twas
but because I knew I had made your life dreary
since my Pythias bade me farewell. The doubt of
his safety, the possibility that he may not escape the
enemy's sword, is driving me to madness! I can
bear it no longer. You would not have me torn with
torture, would you? "

" I would lay down this poor life of mine to save
you but an instant's dread," said Eunice simply. " I
serve not because it is my station, but because the
dictates of my heart make me cling to you, sweet mistress."

" I know it well. Then let me go, Eunice. And
you keep watch above the entrance, so if harm
threatens I may warn you. I go to consult sibyl's
fires and look into the depth of her charmed pools,
in hope of having visions of my loved one, my val-
iant Pythias."

" Tread softly that you rouse not her ire," cau-
tioned Eunice. " If her mood be queer she will drive
us all away."

With wary step the six young maids approached
the cave of Hecati. The mouth of the cavern was
such as must have sheltered a dragon that belched
flame and blazing cinders, in some prehistoric time.

A step inside the outer edge and all was inky blackness.

Quivering with excitement and admiration of their mistress' daring the five attendants crouched on the ground above the overhanging rock. Calanthe, alone, made the descent.

Grasping the rough edges of the jagged rocks with her slender well-kept hands, she found footing among the knotted roots that made a difficult approach. A final leap brought her to the entrance itself and for a moment she stood there, the warm rays of the sun shining on her right, the dank odors of the depths rising on her left.

Waving a courageous farewell to Eunice, whose pretty face bent over the rock edge, Calanthe stepped further into the gloom. At first there was just blackness and no sight of living thing. She seemed to be enveloped in a raw moisture that cut to her bone marrow and paralyzed her courage. Something thudded awkwardly against her sandals. In fright she darted back to the entrance and found 'twas but a cumbersome turtle trying to make room for her.

" I shall learn nothing," she told herself sternly, " if my bravery is vanquished by so small a thing. I wonder would it be best to summon her above. It is strange there are no hints of lights, if there are fires. It is strange that she herself would not come forward to —"

At the very moment a click of blunted wood, fall-

ing on the slippery surfaces of stone, smote her ears.
Taking shape from the gloom, emerged a figure,
shrouded in rags and topped by a mass of matted
hair.

The head too large for the body and elongated
by a sharpened chin, wagged uncertainly from side
to side, as if hung on wires without anchorage. The
face, of olive complexion on one cheek and smooth
as that of Eunice's own, was florid blond and choked
with warts and moles on the other.

When she stood, her back bore resemblance to
a twig that had snapped in the bending. When she
walked, the looseness of her joints gave her the
weird effect of being saved from utter disintegra-
tion by the stout branch upon which she leaned her
weight.

"Hast come to me for aid?" The stentorian
tones, heavier in caliber than those of the most powerful orator, caused Calanthe to shrink against the
slimy walls of the inner cave.

"You are Hecati?" she breathed in sudden terror.

"I am Hecati, who bringeth light when darkness
reigns, who lifteth veils and shows the scenes beyond. I am Hecati who is sought by the statesman that he may know the will of the fickle people;
by the trembling maid that she may discover the
inner thoughts of him whom she adores; by the soldier who sets forth to battle and seeks to know if

again he shall cross the threshold of his own court-yard."

"Your uncanny wisdom is the marvel of Syracuse," faltered Calanthe. "I have come to seek knowledge. Will you give me aid?"

Hecati turned, with much difficulty, and led the way. Down a flight of rough hewn steps, slippery with mold, she shuffled. At the bottom she held aloft a torch. It flared on a cave room, empty, save for a bench, a dying fire, and, in the center, a wide, shallow basin supported on iron standards.

A cold slippery something dropped from above and clung to Calanthe's shoulder buckle. She screamed wildly and strove to find the steps again.

"What fright at a harmless lizard!" scorned Hecati, removing the dreaded reptile. "My cave is filled with strange creatures that I have made my pets. Seat yourself on yonder bench and we will consult the enchanted waters."

A dark, loosely-shaped mass lumbered from a corner, advanced a short distance and settled, queerly, into a hunched ball.

"That! That thing! It moves! I must go — let me mount above! I am stifled with fear!"

"That is but an humble octopus that one day I rescued from the buffeting waves and have since sheltered in my abode. See how limply he casts his tentacles about and fuses them in his lumped body. Note how he lifts his weight to a height and then thumps forward, moving the same distance each time. That is the way he walks. Do not fear him, for, although he could fasten one of those eight arms about your slender neck, and crush the breath from your lungs, he will not do so, unless you display fear."

Calanthe sat, huddled in loathing and constant terror of a slimy attack from one or the other of these strange creatures.

" If it please you, we will consult the enchanted water on the instant, that I may again mount to the pure air and sunshine," she begged piteously.

" Tell me not of your mission," commanded Hecati. " I will tell it you, in all its detail. You are Calanthe, betrothed of Pythias, who has been sent to war by the tyrant Dionysius, who hopes that he may meet a violent death."

" I knew it! I was sure of it! " cried Calanthe. " The heaviness of my heart and the bewilderment in my brain, both spoke of death. Tell me it will not be! Tell me! " Her voice rose to an hysterical screech and echoed wildly through the hollow cave.

" Do not interrupt me! " Hecati's inflection was harsh and biting. " Dionysius himself is enamored of you. By sending Pythias to almost certain death, he strives to obtain you for his own! "

" And I have come to ask you, O Hecati, to look into the magic waters and consult the mystic flames, that you may convey to me news of my loved one's absence.  If he be safe?  When his return?  Look into the waters, O sibyl, and tell me what is there! "

Hecati seized Calanthe's wrist in a viselike grip. Step by step, murmuring strange incantations, she led her to the shallow basin in the center of the cave. With her right hand she brandished aloft a blazing torch and slowly lowered it to within a finger's length of the water's surface.

Suddenly there was born, in the depths of the pool, a sullen, red glow that spread until it had laid a vivid background.

Hecati dropped the torch.  Across the basin's width, she seized the hands of Calanthe and held them in a grip that would have tortured had the interest been less keen.

Slowly traced upon the red appeared a vision of battle.  Chariots dashed on and off the scene.  Generals standing erect, beside their charioteers, gave imperious orders and watched them carried out. Scaling-ladders of wondrous length and stoutness of construction were laid against high walls, and soldiers, brandishing shields and swords and echoing hoarse war cries, mounted them, only to be cast to earth by a well-aimed sword-thrust or huge rocks thrown with deadly skill.

In dread fascination Calanthe's eyes devoured the scene.  In vain she sought for the stalwart form of her own true knight.  As chariot after chariot

moved across the scene she eagerly scanned the faces
— always to be disappointed.

Slowly the vision started to fade.

" That is but a part of what I am able to disclose
to you," the half-intelligible words came from the
sybil's lips as she again lifted the torch. " That
was the battlefield of Agrigentum and its walled fortress, held by the Carthaginians. We will call back
the vision and search for Pythias. The third vision
will determine his ultimate fate."

The torch crackled above the basin. Breathless,
Calanthe leaned far over the dark waters and watched
for the red glow. This time it spread more rapidly. Again the steep wall with its besiegers — the
wild dashing to and fro of mounted soldiers — the
casting of javelins and the closer fighting with sword
and shield, flashed into view.

In the distance, the funnels of smoke ascending
from burning houses, the flight and capture of ter-
ror-stricken maids and the sight of bodies ground
under vicious chariot wheels, made the scene one of
utter horror and sickening reality.

With nails digging deep into her rosy palms,
Calanthe searched the war-crazed multitude for a
sight of her lover's mighty stature and blond curls.
A chariot driven with the daring of a hundred furies,
almost wholly obscured by the clouds of dust it had
raised, was forging into the foreground. One
swift glance into those fearless eyes told Calanthe

she had found her Pythias. She stretched out her
arms! — it was then the picture faded to darkness.

"It was he! I have looked upon his face! He
still lives! O Hecati, delay not an instant before
you call forth the third vision. I scarce can still the
awful thumping of my heart. It leaps and bounds
as if it would escape the confines of my breast! Call
the third vision, O marvelous sybil!"

Hecati took an unlighted torch from a corner of
the cave and approached the mystic flames. At first
contact it burst into a blaze and sent forth explosive
sounds. Chanting a strange ode, the old witch
passed the burning brand, in three unbroken circles,
around the head of Calanthe, then suspended it
above the waters. The red was more brilliant now.
For a long time the sheet of color was unbroken by
tracing of any sort. Then, slowly, a scene was born.

The first impression was that of utter destruction.
Bodies filled the grooves cut by chariot wheels;
bodies lay one slung upon the other, lifeless limbs
hopelessly mingled. Horses stark, in the death
sleep, stretched taut hoofs across the forms of their
beloved masters. Chariots, splintered to atoms,
cluttered the roads; and the gates of the impregnable
fortress lay battered from their hinges.

Suddenly a spot of light started to glow at the fortress entrance. Its brilliance sent blinding rays to
light the ghastliness of the scene. A dark spot began to assume shape in the center of the light. A

chariot drawn by four coal-black steeds galloped into view.

Its sole occupant, masterful, erect, with gold curls reflecting the radiance in the form of a halo, flung aloft a triumphant hand and led the procession of victory.

"Pythias! My Pythias! 'Tis he! Safe — safe from death — free to return to me! Say 'tis true, that which the vision discloses. It would not play me false! O Hecati, your oath that it would not play me false!"

There was no answer.

The sybil, still bent above the silent waters, was intent on the final scene. To the joyous maid's delighted eyes appeared the streets of Syracuse, athrong with people, madly rioting to obtain a view of what was happening. Down the winding road came the same chariot, driven by the same man and, amid the wild enthusiasm, he alone was calm as the heavens echoed with the cries of:

"Pythias! *Triomphe!*"

Hysterical with joy, Calanthe sought the slippery steps and mounted to the cavern's mouth.

"Eunice! Eunice!" her joyous call echoed through the cave and up the mountainside. "Eunice, I have seen —"

A dark figure blocked her path! Standing against the sunlight, his helmet a dazzling expanse of metal, stood Dionysius, a taunting smile disfiguring his lips.

Calanthe's former fear of the tyrant was destroyed. The victory in her heart gave her an exultant feeling of power. What had she to fear? Her lover, alive, victorious, coming soon to her arms! What terrors could fate now conceal?

" Never has the earth vomited forth so exquisite a bit as now! " he greeted her with exaggerated homage. " But why should Calanthe, favored of · the gods, seek knowledge from the bowels of the underground? What was't troubling her sweet imagination? "

Calanthe assumed a defiant attitude.

" Where are my maids? " she demanded. " And how came you here? "

" They were perched on yonder overhanging rock, but, at my approach, they scattered as does the frightened goose-flock at my chariot wheels. They are wandering above. I see the glimmer of their robes. And as for me — I was but riding through the woodland and came upon this fair scene."

" Then stand aside and permit me to go to where they await me! "

" Why so sudden your departure? 'Tis a pleasant place for converse. None could be better, with undisturbed view of sea and distant warships. When tempted to flight, fair Calanthe, call to mind that I am overlord; and Pythias my underling! You wish him well? Why interrupt his chances of a certain, future supremacy? "

All the pent-up anger, whipped to a frantic madness by the sudden relief from agony and suspense, burst forth in ringing recrimination.

"Speak not his name, O cruel and double-dealing tyrant! Do I not know that you sent him to almost certain death at Agrigentum? I have not mentioned word of your ill-chosen visit to my garden. If I had but breathed a word of your vile attentions to either Pythias or Damon —"

"Damon!" the name hissed from the lips of the warlord as though it were a drop of water touching a red hot surface. "What know you of him?"

"What know I of him?" Calanthe raised her brows in scorn. "He is the trusted friend and comrade of Pythias, and my protector in his absence."

The general threw back his head and gave utterance to weirdly mirthful sounds.

"Your protector? How is't that the negligent Damon is not here, at this moment, to protect you from my unwelcome attentions?"

"For the reason that when I wander in the woodlands with my maids, he does not dream that there exists a man sufficient coward, and vile-spirited, to molest me!"

"Ha! The quick retort and the vengeance of a little vixen! Your training has been in a good school since Pythias set forth to Agrigentum. 'Twill be but poor solace if it is his death-chilled body they bear back on litter or martial shield.   To whom will you turn then, little spitfire?"

"'Twill not be necessary to turn to you, e'en though your aid would be forthcoming.   I fear me not.   Aye, but the gods have other goods in store. For the second time, O Dionysius, your plans will not bear fruit.   For in a vision of enchanted waters, a source of information that never lies, have I viewed my Pythias, gloriously triumphant, hailed as king among men, drive through the streets of Syracuse, to the cheering of a populace gone mad!"

Waiting but an instant to see the effect of her words eat into his soul, Calanthe leaped from the cavern's mouth and darted up the hill, calling blithely to her maids.

While, left behind, the lean figure turned into the black, ill-smelling moistures of Hecati's cave and stumbled below to verify the vision of the enchanted waters.

# CHAPTER VII

A FORTNIGHT later, fair Syracuse had donned her holiday attire. The too-eager warmth of the sun's rays were tempered to balmy mildness by the sudden, east winds. The cloudless, vivid blue of the sky seemed but a reflection of the sea, and it, in turn, sent back the image of the sky.

Along the Sterian Way, the mansions of the rich blazed with gold-worked banners, unfurled from window ledges, and in the heart of the city's streets, the wine shops, jewelers' dwellings and tailors' establishments, ran riot with draperies of brilliant color.

Senators, in purple-or-red-banded togas, were stopped on their way to the Senate House, to be greeted ardently by those who, on ordinary occasions, would not dare to bend a head in friendly salutation.

Children, on street corners, tossed golden oranges to each other, in excited play, and were not reprimanded by their elders. The tension of suppressed anticipation surcharged the atmosphere.

Up on the hill that led from the Academy Square, in a grove of silver birch, beside a shell pink marble fountain, knelt Calanthe. Her rounded form was draped in silken folds of palest azure confined at the waist by a cestus of wrought silver. Silver sandals graced her tiny feet, and, at the moment, her maids were trying a variety of garlands in her bronze-gold locks.

" The forget-me-nots are to my taste, fair one," quoth Eunice, gazing with clasped hands, in rapt admiration. " They match so well the coloring of your tunic and set at defiance the violet of your eyes."

" Forget-me-nots are pretty," acknowledged Calanthe, bending forward to get a better view in the fountain depths, " but they are sickly sentimental. Much as I've mourned my true knight's absence and torn my soul with agony in fear of his safety, yet I could not meet him, in full gaze of the public, with forget-me-nots twined in my tresses."

" Then it must be the star-anemone," decreed Eunice, " for other bloom would but destroy the sweet coloring of your robe. Think you that from all the populace his glance will single you out for first welcome ? "

" 'Tis what I hope," breathed Calanthe rapturously. " Ne'er has the city been dressed in shades more brilliant; and the wild buzzing and bustling of the people to and fro is fair entrancing. Oh, 'tis good to be a maid who is welcoming to wedlock the victor of a hundred battles and the idol of his city!"

"Hark! I hear the sound of distant trumpeting. In what manner was Pythias to reach Syracuse? Can it be that he has touched the shore?" exclaimed Eunice, running to the pergola whence she could get unobstructed view of the sea.

"He comes in a Carthaginian trireme," Calanthe called after her. "A mighty capture, which, even before it was ta'en, he designated as the vessel on which he would make his homeward trip. At the shore he will be met by his war chariot, drawn by four dusky steeds of Arabia. From there he proceeds at the head of his conquering army through the city's streets."

"He *has* touched shore! I see the flash of armor in lines of light and restive horses held in check by pages, all in scarlet!" The high-pitched tones, fraught with restrained excitement, floated back to the lovely maid kneeling beside her fountain. She smiled at her reflection and folded soft white hands across her breast.

An excited Eunice pulled her to her feet and gave the final pat to the star-anemone garland. A sheer, white scarf, dropped carelessly upon the ground, she draped over the pretty head and shoulders.

"'Tis the command of your mother," she told Calanthe. "She thinks it not seemly for maid, upon her wedding eve, to walk in the city streets so unabashed. And besides, conceited one, the shimmer of it and the fact that it half conceals your charms, lends an added fascination to your appearance. Now let us away lest we lose our chosen location from which the view will be the best."

.    .    .    .    .    .    .

On a street corner, before the largest sweet-and-fruit shop in Syracuse, stood Damon. His arms folded closely across his chest, his head sunk in silent meditation, he was a powerful and impressive figure.

His gaze wandered to the scurrying crowds, the high-spirited horses whose steps were curbed with difficulty. From this, he raised his eyes to the Senate House, from whose portals, Philistius, accompanied by a group of his questionable satellites, was at that moment issuing.

"Ah, Syracuse!" he murmured sadly. "I am at last forced to despair of thee! Sicily, land of my birth — my country still — thou hast closed thine ears to the call of righteousness and fallen into the hands of those who would barter freedom for a great man's feast!"

A slave, drunk with the wine he had pilfered from his master's cellars, reeled against the senator and caromed into the roadway. From afar a blast of trumpets cut the air. The sodden man raised aloft an imaginary goblet and shouted to the skies:

"Pythias! Pythias! *Triomphe!*"

Damon looked down with gentle commiseration

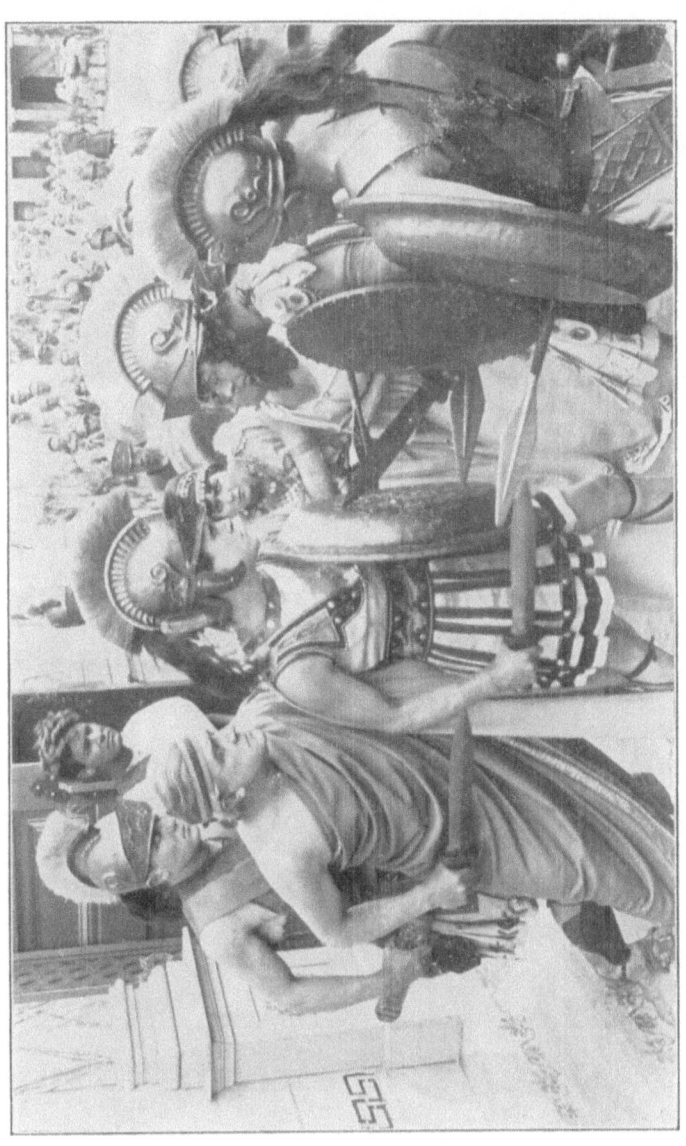

"I AM HIS SWORD, HIS SHIELD, WHEN I STAND BEFORE HIM THUS!"

"WE WILL JOURNEY HOME TO SYRACUSE IN YONDER CARTHAGINIAN
TRIREME."

and bent to lift the prostrate one, who was trying so
ineffectually to get to his feet.

"It is for the best that you find the portals of
your master's house as quickly as you can," he suggested, trying to shake him back to a half-normal
condition. "Soon the crowds will fill the streets
and byways and there is small chance for one like
you, when once they start jostling."

"Pythias! Pythias! Victor!" reiterated the
man, sullenly, and lurched from his rescuer's grasp
to stumble up the street, toward the Temple.

Now, from all sides, the populace poured in.
Esquires, warriors, senators and merchants; gay
women of the city; and mothers bearing their children aloft above the heads of the surrounding crowds.
They surged through the thoroughfares, as an impetuous stream that is dammed will gush through
the first available opening.

Damon, silent and erect, his mind busy with the
disquieting rumors that were afoot, remained where
he had taken his stand. Jostled from side to side
by the oncoming multitude, his face lost not its calm,
nor his eyes their look of deep and vital thought.

The houses bordering the street were points of
vantage for which many fought. Windows, doors,
projecting roofs and porticoes, all, were blocked with
groups of eager sightseers. From the temples issued dancing maidens bearing long garlands wound
round and round their graceful bodies. The Senate

poured forth its crowd of white togaed statesmen, and, shrilly, from the crest of the hill, sounded the blast that announced the van of the triumphal procession.

Silhouetted against the blue-gold horizon, six trumpeters on snow-white steeds led the way. Ten paces behind, a double row of youthful pages in tunics of white and gold, yellow jewels on their breasts, strewed blossoms from urns carried in their left arms.

Followed then, the line of dancing maidens, with multi-colored draperies fluttering in the breeze; gay laughter issuing from their lips, as they trod upon the flowerstrewn path.

For a second's time there was naught to follow. Then above the hill crest rose the snorting heads and arched necks of four coal-black steeds, heavy in beaten silver harness and trappings of sapphire blue. Bit by bit they mounted to the horizon line and stood, stamping their slender limbs, in impatience to proceed.

They drew a chariot of ivory and silver, that now was half-hid by floral garlands. The helmet of the man, sole occupant of the triumphal car, caught the fire of the sun's rays and dazzled the eyes of the assembled multitudes. Amid deafening cheers and hoarse roars he raised a commanding hand and extended it toward his beloved city.

The crowds, gone mad with patriotism and hero-worship, waved banners and helmets in mid air. The streets of Syracuse were rent with wild cries; and suddenly the horses, in obedience to a tug at the reins, began the descent.

Buried in the crowd, on the steps of a monument, stood Calanthe, her gauze veil folded around her head and shoulders, her tense hands crossed and gripping her own arms in an ecstasy of excitement. Her eyes, one moment darting smiles, the next bathed in tears of joy, never left the stalwart form of the returning conqueror.

It seemed as if she thought by the intensity of her gaze to draw his glance to her slim form. Until his chariot had passed her and proceeded further into the city's heart she had hoped for his radiant smile. It had fallen about her, as he greeted his welcomers; but not on her alone. Eunice, perceiving her disappointment, slipped her arm comfortingly about Calanthe's waist.

"In the great numbers he could not find your fairy form," she whispered. "Did you see how his eyes were searching? Whene'er he saw a group of maids I perceived his scrutiny of them and when he found you not, some of the laughter faded from his eyes."

"'Tis sweet of you so to concoct tales that should bring solace to my heart," murmured Calanthe, turning to leave the monument steps, "but I saw those things of which you speak, not at all. I saw, indeed, the laughter in his eyes and when they fell on strange groups of maidens, I saw that same laughter rekindle, instead of fade. Why should it not be so? Why should a man whose path is a fiery blaze of adulation, seek for one poor jasmine flower, whose fragrance can not surmount the fumes of incense?"

" Pythias worships you, the breath you draw, the ground o'er which you trod. 'Tis wrong and faithless of you to so denounce him, when in the midst of thousands, he has not the keenness of vision to discover a single maid. When but a few days back your eyes were dimmed and your cheek lily-pale, from weeping at his possible fate, you said that all the world through would you laugh, if he but came back to you in all his health and strength."

Calanthe hid her face on Eunice's shoulder in sudden contrition.

" I know I am ill-deserving of happiness, sweet," she confessed softly. " But my heart was so cast down, for I had planned and planned how it would be; that my eyes should meet his, across the sea of heads, and now —"

" See below, in front of the Senate House he has halted his chariot! There seems to be a block to his further progress. Many people are running thither, and there are loud cries and brandishing of shields. Come, let us go, Calanthe!"

.     .     .     .     .     .     .

In front of the Senate all was rioting and confusion. Damon, assaulted by Procles and his comrades, as the chariot of Pythias approached, was beating back his assailants. The surrounding crowd, not knowing the cause of the fray, stood open-mouthed and motionless.

In a flash Pythias leaped from his chariot and brandishing his sword plunged into the fighting, cursing the group surrounding Damon.

"Back on your lives!" he commanded in ringing tones. "Treacherous cowards that you are, thus to attack a man unarmed and undefended! You know this honest sword I brandish. You have seen it hew down ranks in Carthage. Would you now taste its cold steel in your quaking hearts? For now Damon has his armor on, courageous ones. *I* am his shield, his sword, his helmet! And when I thus protect him, it is but mine own heart's blood that I defend!"

Procles and his associates fell back into the surging, curious crowds. Before the sword of Pythias there was no argument.

"'Tis a lucky stroke of Fate for him, that at this instant your chariot descended the hill," muttered the henchman of Dionysius. "Here, in Syracuse, we have had enough of his long robe of peace wherein he wraps his stern philosophy. See that you teach him better manners, O conquering hero!"

With harsh laughs of derision Procles motioned to his satellites to proceed.

Thus left alone, Damon and Pythias looked deep

into each other's eyes. And with the look, went the clasp of hand so firm, so honest, so all-understanding of the spirit of true friendship.

"What was't brought this display of ruffianism?" asked Pythias, leading the way to his chariot, through the crowds of admiring citizens.

"When I was awaiting your approach, Lucullus ran up behind me and in voice trembling with excitement, broke the news that our citadel was taken. That Dionysius, heading a troop of soldiers, had, by rude force, seized the arms and treasure in it. I could not believe such base rumor and was voicing my disbelief, when lo! from the fortress wall was unfurled the standard of the tyrant and from the gateways poured his most notorious satellites, high-heaped with arms and plunder!"

"Our citadel in that fierce soldier's power!" Pythias made a move as if again to draw his sword. "Then, by the gods, is Syracuse gone mad!"

Damon laid an affectionate hand on the broad shoulders of his dearest friend.

"Do not shade the prospect of your joys with griefs of state, my Pythias. I know that on the morrow you will wed the sweetest maid in Syracuse. Your wedding day must be but sunshine and roses. Let these dark matters go."

"Nay, how can I let them go when they bring furrows to your brow and sighs to your lips? And besides, what caused Procles to draw sword against

you?   Can I be happy when your life is thus endangered?"

" In answer to my charge that his master Dionysius was a parricide and tyrant, the audacious slave
branded me liar and traitor and gave commands to
his followers to hew me down!"

" Dionysius has become a danger to our city," said
Pythias slowly.   " I have heard, on my way home
from Agrigentum, that the man has gone so far as
to wish a throne on which to rest his limbs."

" He has publicly expressed his wish," interposed
Damon indignantly, " and unless the Senate wake to
the grave menace of this man, his wish will be
granted."

" You are jesting, Damon," laughed the young
general.   " Syracuse ruled over by a king?   It is
preposterous!   Why, I would as soon think of myself as candidate, as of him.   His power in the city
is overestimated."

" If, contrary to the rules of our city, a soldier
were allowed inside the portals of our senate house,
I would take you thither, to view for yourself the
undercurrent that now runs deep in our affairs of
state.   Here lately I have so often wished that my
lot had been the blest content of private life.   This
hopeless service of the state galls me — and I grow
old."

From behind the pillars of the Academy emerged
two forms.   The one square — squat, in armor; the

other draped in purple-banded toga. Slowly, Dionysius and Damocles descended the steps.

" Look you where stand the two strange friends," observed Damocles, craftily. " The intimacy between Damon and Pythias is the marvel of Syracuse. The stern, pedantic statesman and the young soldier general. It is a strange combination for a friendship such as theirs."

" Friendship," snapped Dionysius viciously. " There is not a state of true friendship extant. Every man has the price at which to value comradeship. This pair is no different from the rest."

" This pair is the exception to the rule, Dionysius," insisted Damocles. " I have heard it said that —"

" Heard! Heard! " mimicked the other. " Do not quote from the converse of dullards. You may have heard, but you do not *know*. See the way the crowds bow at the feet of Pythias and cast glances of idolatry at his effeminate blond curls. We must do something, Damocles, to lessen this fellow's favor in the eyes of the rabble."

" Can not your brilliant mind discover some good way? "

Dionysius shot a shrewd glance at his companion, from under narrowing lids.

" It was you, Damocles, who conceived of sending Pythias to Agrigentum, in my stead. And from Agrigentum and almost certain death, he has re-

"AND FROM AGRIGENTUM AND ALMOST CERTAIN DEATH, HE HAS RETURNED TRIUMPHANT, AND RIVALS ME IN SYRACUSE."

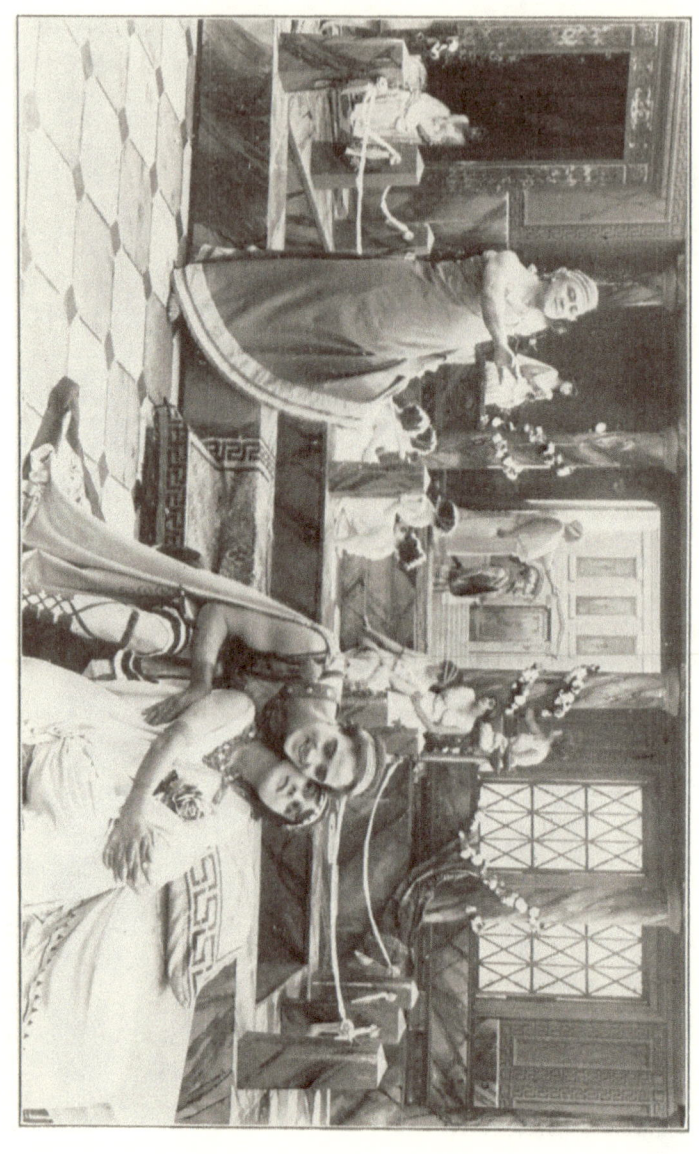

THE WOOING OF THE MAID CALANTHE BY BRAVE PYTHIAS.

turned triumphant, and rivals me in Syracuse! He
must be submerged! I will not have my toil of years
go all for naught, because a young and foppish soldier, with blond curls and a pleasing smile, has run
his sword through a small parcel of Carthaginians!"

"Think well, Dionysius, and some plan will come
to you."

"Are you speaking with sarcastic shading?"
rasped out the overlord. "I do not like the manner
of your inflection. There is no courtesy in your
tone. Ah-h-h!"

He gripped the flabby forearm of the rotund
Damocles in a sudden, vicious clutch. A shaking
forefinger designated the opposite side of the road
where Calanthe and her maids sped to the side of
Pythias.

"There is another reason why this young warrior
of ours must be humbled to the dust! I have sworn
that that maid shall find shelter in my ardent arms —
and there, too, he blocks the way!"

"Can you not send him off to the wars again?
And if there be no war, can you not, with your
wondrous ingenuity, stir up a broil that might be
called a war?"

"Do not plagiarize on your own creations!" Dionysius bade him with cold scorn. "Either cull a
novelty from your garden of thoughts or offer none
at all."

"He has magnificent steeds to draw his chariot,"

observed Damocles irrelevantly. " They appear to me of finer mettle than your own."

For an instant, Dionysius looked sharply at his friend, then slapped his palms together with a resounding whack.

" I have the plan!" he ground out between clenched teeth. " By to-morrow our bundle of conceit in yonder chariot will be prostrate in the dust, with the heels of Syracuse upon his neck! Let us hasten across and talk with our famed pair of friends. Think you they will find it wise to be civil to me?"

" Do you advance your plan, to-day?" questioned Damocles with much curiosity. " And can you not give me a slight idea of what it will involve?"

" It is sufficient for you to know, for the moment, that it was born of your witless ravings. Hurry your fat legs across the space that still intervenes. I do not choose that Pythias have too long love-sessions with this pearl whom I desire."

" The feast we did attend yesternight has filled me with complaints; and my legs refuse to hasten. Likewise, my heart thumps most uncomfortably in my breast and my head is filled with trumpet blasts, where none exist."

Dionysius raised a protesting hand.

" Add to the list that it will be very painful duty to pierce you, playfully, with my sharpest sword, so that your end from acute suffering will be swift and not an unskilled work! Forget your ailments and polish up what brain remains to you, for to-night you are to do some cunning work for me.    And then — then will dawn the morrow!"

# CHAPTER VIII

### THE PLAN IS DIVULGED

"I SHALL not pout; for 'tis not well behaved. Neither shall I weep; for 'tis unfitting a soldier's mate. Whether I shall stamp my feet and exhibit my overseasoned temper, or gracefully submit to neglect and unresponsive treatment, I have not yet decided. Yet I am sore offended."

Calanthe stood in her garden, whither Pythias had borne her, accompanied by Damon. Arria, her mother, had come from the house and approached the little group.

"Has the suspense of waiting for your return gone to our little Calanthe's head?" she interrupted, with a hint of mischief in her soft brown eyes. "For days and nights past she has been like a caged dove, whimpering for its mate; and now that he is come she deports herself in heartless manner."

Pythias rose to give courteous salutation.

"Do not reprove the child," he besought with mock gravity. "We must allow her much. For Venus, when she rose from out the sea, to smile upon our Grecian isles and fill them with everlasting verdure, was not more beautiful than she."

" Ah, you think with soft words to hide your false oblivion to me," persisted Calanthe, as a spoiled child who will not be quieted.   " From this hill that over-looks the sea, Eunice kept watch and at first sight of the Carthaginian trireme touching these shores, shouted the news to me and I did haste, with all speed, to a point of vantage on the steps of the statue of Mercury, there to watch your glorious entrance into the city — and wait for your smile.   But it came not."

" Nay, do not chide me, my soft Calanthe.   If my eyes did not single you out, my heart was bursting with thoughts of you and of our wedding on the morrow."

" You made sacrifice of your first moment here, to *friendship,* not love!   'Twas Damon you greeted with the first word, the first hand clasp! "

Pythias looked to where his friend was standing, wrapped in moody thought.   He called, to rouse him from his meditation.   Damon drew near, asking pardon for his seeming preoccupation.

" There is some malignant worry feeding upon your heart, my Damon," observed Pythias, with much concern.   " Will you not confide in me?   Come, I will make you smile.   Do you knew what this sweet maid has been pouring into my ears?   Re-proaches for the depth of our friendship.   She deems it improper to sacrifice to friendship the mo-ments that could be spent with the loved ones.   Are

you not arrogant at having caused the seeds of jealousy to spring in so fair a breast? "

Damon seized the tiny hand that hung limply at
Calanthe's side.

" Do not underrate the glory of friendship, sweet
girl.   What many deem ' friendship ' is so weak in
strength at most times, that it should not be dignified
by the solemn term.   Remember always that the
warmth of friendship, like that of love, is not
chilled by the winds that blow from the valley of
death."

Calanthe, abashed, sought shelter in her lover's
arm.

" You must not disclose all the whims which I confide to you," she whispered.   " I would not have
Damon disturbed by my silly plaints."

" Of what was Dionysius speaking when he held
you in such earnest consultation? " questioned Damon, seating himself beside his friend.   " Was't of
his ambitions and designs upon our city? "

" You are over-morose, and see but blackness in
all his deeds, I fear.   His talk to-day was of joyous
things — the games to be held on the morrow in'
honor of my return.   It has been ordered that all
toil shall cease, throughout the entire morn; that the
populace throng the Circus at an early hour; and
there will be discus throwing, wrestling, foot races
and chariot contests.   Then, in the afternoon, when
all Syracuse is feasting and pledging our happiness

in the spiced bowl, my sweet Calanthe and I will
celebrate our marriage feast."

"Are you to take part in the games and shall I be
there to gaze upon you from a box all draped in
standards?" Calanthe clapped her hands and
danced up and down in gay anticipation.

"It was for the express purpose of asking me to
compete in the chariot races that Dionysius accosted
me."

"And you consented?" questioned Damon,
hastily.

"I did. I would pit my black steeds against the
best in Syracuse, nay in all Sicily. Besides, the fever
of the race fires my blood and gives me keen enjoy-
ment."

"Against whom are you to contest? Did Dionysius name the others in the race?"

"What do the others matter? In a time of defeat the names of those vanquished sink into oblivion.
'Tis only the victor's identity that bursts from the
lips of the audience. And you well know the name
of Pythias, my Damon!"

"List to the boastful one!" mocked Calanthe.
"If it were not for the fact that I would lose the
honor of placing the wreath upon your brow, I could
find it in my heart to wish for your defeat."

"I am not boasting for myself," declared Pythias
simply. "I know the mettle of my horses, that is
all. They have drawn my chariot in times of stress.

They have never faltered, never failed me. A slave could hold the reins as well — but he will not."

" I must go to my home to rest in preparation for the sports to-morrow," Darnon laid a gentle hand on Pythias' shoulder. " These affairs of state o'er-fret me and I fear I lose my capacity to enjoy the lighter things of life. Calanthe, you must look to it that your young lord does not attempt the statesman's sorry part. 'Twill pale his face and make him find in lovely nature but one blend of dismal colorless sterility."

" I would not even if I could; I could not even if I would; so there's an end on't," smiled Pythias, tightening his clasp on his sweet burden. " But you speak of resting for the games to-morrow as if that were the day's important event. You say nothing of my wedding feast."

" And I intended, even unbidden, to be there. The wedding of a man and maid is always a joyous sight; but, when looked upon from friendship's eye, its bliss is tenfold. So, until the morn, farewell."

.    .    .    .    .    .    .

Meantime, in the dwelling of Dionysius, sat Damocles quaffing hot wines; in vain attempt to still the plaints of his mutinous stomach. A sorry figure of a senator with head-band at a distressed angle on his fast-thinning locks; and toes turned in, with no regard for grace of attitude.

" Wilt cease this sickish bellowing?" growled

Dionysius, pacing the floor in rage.   " I seek to disclose a deep-laid plan which exacts wariness and cunning from him who is to carry it out, and you sit before me with the expression of a calf gone ill! "

" I am afflicted wit'ı an inward torture that is difficult to bear," groaned Damocles, " but I will listen
with alertness and strive to execute your plans with
daring."

" With daring! "   Dionysius burst into satirical
laughter.   " From present appearance you have as
much daring about you, as a rabbit that is pursued
by a hungry fox!   Speak not of daring with a countenance gone green, for I would fain give my strength
to earnest thought instead of violent mirth."

" Proceed," moaned Damocles, too miserable to be
offended.

" I have explained the main points of the plot.
What now falls to you is the work of completing it
with prudence and sly skill.   If there should be a
shade of suspicion, the great project as well as the
lesser one of to-morrow will be frustrated and your
reputation gone."

" You lay stress on my reputation! " blurted out
Damocles, with the mournful petulance of one who is
dispirited and overruled.   " What shreds would be
left of yours, I ask, if the plot failed? "

" We are not dealing in ' ifs ' and ' buts,' " hurled
Dionysius, sending a stool, with a resounding crash,
to the polished floor.   " Get from under my feet be-

fore my temper breaks all bounds and vents itself upon your pain-ridden body! "

With lagging step and muttered phrases that he took care should not assume the definite in syllables, Damocles took his departure.

Down the steps of Dionysius' dwelling he dragged his swollen, sandaled feet and, once upon the street, heaved a sigh, whose resonance was echoed from the nearest hills.

He looked about in search of a possible spy. Not because he felt there would be one in hiding; but rather for the reason that sudden realization of his importance in a great intrigue, assailed him — and he was getting into the character.

The horizon was comparatively clear. The multitudes had departed to their homes to feast, in private, after the splendid spectacle of the day. All was silence.

With pudgy hand grasping a queer-looking bag, Damocles walked through the Via Academica as far as the public square. Then he turned sharply to his right and sought the twisted by-ways and queer, overhanging buildings that sheltered the poorer merchants of Syracuse.

As he progressed, a solitary figure in the deserted streets, bursts of laughter and the click of bowl upon bowl accosted his ears. The populace was making merry; and he, faint in spirit and disconsolate in body, was on his way to a malicious deed.

He arrived at a corner where the roofs of houses jutting out, from opposite sides, made an archway. Through this he passed.   The steps he descended a few paces on were worn smooth with shallow hollows in their centers.   His feet slipped into them as had the feet of hundreds who descended in search of wine.

As he entered the inner room a crowd of roughly clothed folk started in astonishment at sight of his senatorial toga.

The proprietor ran from his cask-room and bowed before him, uttering squeals of satisfaction, half expressions of abject subservience.

Damocles cast his weary bulk upon the hard surface of a cracked stone seat.   He rested an elbow on the stone table before him and motioned imperiously to the squawking little figure that danced before his eyes.

His order of the best in the house brought additional protestations of gratitude and humility.   The men at the adjoining table began to regard him with suspicion.   As soon as the proprietor had disappeared into the recesses of his cask room, Damocles leaned toward his nearest neighbor and designated with a lordly thumb that he wished converse with him.

The man, afright at the sudden honor, hesitated to obey; whereupon one of his companions rose to comply with the summons.   This roused the rest of the group, which, fired by wine, were anxious to be in the game, whatever it might be.

" I want but two," announced Damocles, impatiently.

The dictum caused such discord among the ruffians that for a moment it appeared as though there would be damaged countenances before the two were chosen.

The entrance of the proprietor, bearing his most vivid bowl, was the signal for quiet. He placed the most priceless treasure of his collection of pottery before the noble patron and poured the ruby-hued liquid from a queer flagon that he rested upon his hip.

Damocles ordered two bowls of the same stuff for his invited guests. At the violent protest of the owner, who was speechless at the thought of wasting such value upon so poor a pair, the senator displayed his displeasure.

" I order and you serve ! " he commanded, with grim relish in the act of treading under heel, as he had just been trodden by the overgeneral.

The two ruffians waited for him to divulge his plans. That the plans were secret and felonious in character they had no doubt. And they stood ready to comply, did the reward but fit the deed. Dionysius, with the unerring instinct of one steeped in polite crime, had sent Damocles to the right place. In the handbook of a despot there are informations that would not bear the searching light of day.

Still Damocles remained silent, his pale loose lips buried in the fragrant draught, his eyes shifting from the admiring proprietor to the group of drinkers at the other table.

The more intelligent of the two honored guests waved an expressive hand at his ignoble associates. Whether they interpreted his gesture aright could not be guessed. Certain it is they did not follow its suggestion.

Their interest was too keen to suit the visiting senator. He did not know the degree of their acuteness and he was unwilling to speculate. Also, the solicitous proprietor troubled him grievously.

It was enough to be sent on a dark mission where the body protested. To be plagued by over-attention and by too vivid curiosity when one had arrived was exasperating.

Damocles summoned closer the shrimplike owner.

" You will get rid of those men," he commanded quietly.

" You would drive away my customers? " shrilled the little man, forgetting, for the instant, the importance of his patron. Then in sudden terror, he scuttled to the adjoining table and, by a series of gesticulations and expletives, cleared the room.

Damocles put down his bowl and scanned the features of the man facing him. His glance, so penetrating and severe, had the desired effect. The two villains began to snort and shift under it. And in

their coward souls was born a fear of the mighty
one, who also dabbled in iniquity.

The proprietor, having barred the door to all customers for as long as it pleased the influential guest
to remain, hopped back into his presence and stood
with arms akimbo, displaying great interest in the
scene about to be enacted.

Damocles pointed a puffy ringed forefinger toward
the cask room and glared.   Incredulous and humili-
ated to find that he was not to be a party to the plot,
the owner shuffled from the room.

Then it was that Damocles raised to the table
edge the queer leather bag and as it hit the stone a
clink from its depths spoke of but one thing — gold!

For many minutes were the three heads in close
location; and so softly spoken were the demands and
the assents that not a syllable cut the air to where the
proprietor crouched behind his hugest vat.

Damocles rose from his bench, raised aloft a bag
of gold and dropped it once again upon the stone so
that the metal sound might fire the avarice of the
two and spur them on to perform well what he had
commanded.

" And when 'tis done and completely so, then will
another purse as large as this find its way to you,
that you may spend its contents in this place," he
said aloud, thus placating the wounded soul of the
proprietor, whom he knew would overhear.

The men cast themselves before him in servile

gratitude. Damocles clapped his hands in summons. The appeased landlord darted into sight; and muttered his appreciation when his eye fell upon the size of the gold coin dropped into his palm.

In his eagerness to unbar the door and give egress to his noble guest, he slipped upon the damp stones and in sudden precipitation met too violently the unevenness of his cellar floor. But, with a bound, he was on his feet, though sadly bruised, and withdrew the heavy oaken barrier.

Damocles went out, without a backward glance. He could now seek Dionysius and, with a certain amount of haughtiness, tell of his skill in accomplishing so soon the errand that he had set out upon. When one has no need of qualifying phrases or half-baked excuses there must always be arrogance, in some amount.

So, Damocles, retreading the way to the dwelling of the overlord found the day more bright, the poor streets more unworthy of his august presence and the malady of stomach greatly subdued.

In the square before the Senate House, he was accosted by Damon, who was about to mount the steps.

"Do you go into the Senate at such an hour?" questioned Damocles in patronizing manner. "It must be that it is indeed deserted at this time. Do you seek some one? Or are you bent on delving still more profoundly into philosophic tomes?"

"Whence come you, Damocles?" retorted Damon, making no pretense at answering the cynical query.   "'Tis a queer portion of the city from which you turned into the square.   Which seek you?   Discernment or diversion?"

"I went to aid a vassal who has fallen ill and who craved my presence.   I—"

"The publican turned priest!" ejaculated Damon; and, without further parley, mounted the steps and disappeared behind the pillars of the Senate House.

Damocles, having received so rude a jolt to his newly acquired arrogance, clenched his purple-veined fist and shook it, vindictively, at the retreating form.

Without further interruption he reached the house of Dionysius and entered its portals.   Encountering no slave in the outer courtyard, he penetrated to the inner room.

There, stretched upon a couch, gorgeous in black and gold coverings and softened with many cushions, he came upon the general.   With head thrown back and limp arms dropping to the polished floor, Dionysius presented a right ungraceful picture.   Furthermore from his open mouth there issued raucous sounds, indicative of profound slumber.

A sudden rage took possession of Damocles to find this man enjoying that which he himself so sadly needed and could not get!   He bent and rudely shook the sleeper.   Dionysius opened but one of his tightly closed eyes.

"What is it?" he questioned, drowsily.

"It is I, Damocles," announced the other, with triumph and emphasis.  "I have come to tell you that it is accomplished!  That the preparations have been perfected by my hand.  That —"

"Tell it me when I awaken," ordered the master.  "Just now my eyes are weary and I have not the will to hear you prate of your adroitness.  Conserve it for a more auspicious moment.  I wish quiet."

And once again the regular breathing told of peaceful slumber.

# CHAPTER IX

## IN THE DEAD OF NIGHT

NIGHT had fallen. In the Circus stables, the boys by the light of torches finished the rubbing down of horses that were to compete on the morrow. The restless stamping of the mettled steeds echoed through the low stone buildings, and disturbed the sluggards who had fallen to slumber, leaving the bulk of their work till early dawn.

One by one the workers ceased. Aratus, the last to cast his brushes into a corner, laid caressing hands on the glossy blackness of the four who were to pull the chariot of Pythias.

The beautiful animals, freed of their cumbersome trappings, arched graceful necks and looked with mild affectionate eyes at the boy who had been working so arduously on their shining coats.

He raised himself, on tiptoe, to whisper into the ear of Mentum, his favorite.

"You must carry your master to victory, on the morrow," he breathed, as if in conversation with a human. "Much is at stake. So light a thing it re-

quires to upset the popularity of a favorite, that if
Aristle defeat Pythias, his fame will suffer.   And
they who, to-day, shouted themselves to hoarseness,
in fervent welcome of the hero, to-morrow will forget his past glories and place upon his neck the heel
of disrepute."

The steed, with head tilted, to receive more easily
the words of warning, tossed his mane and nodded
violently.   This disturbed the others in adjoining
stalls, and they renewed their restive stamping.

Aratus quieted them with gentle words of reassurance and patted each upon the nose.   He hesitated a moment longer beside Mentum, and wound
his arm closely about the smooth neck.

" You have understanding of the words I utter,"
he said softly.   " There are those who would deride
the thought.   But I know that if it takes the last
atom of strength in your slender limbs, and that
after, you perish, you will draw your master's chariot
to victory."

Aratus pulled an armful of hay from the large
stores at the corridor-end and arranged it in a loose
mound outside the stall of his favorite.   With a
last, careful look at his four charges, he cast his lean
young body on the improvised couch and folded his
arms above his head.

Fatigued in body from his hard labors, and his
mind at rest at having so thoroughly performed
them, yet were his eyes wide in wakefulness.   Twice

he rose and looked out of the narrow, oblong windows, only to return to his twisting and tossing.

A horse in the adjoining section, watched over by Lertes, whinnied. The plaintive sound in the dead quiet that had fallen, struck his ears with a sense of warning. Then again, all was still.

With thoughts of the festive day approaching, he sank to slumber, his thin, young arms flung wide and touching the stone floor; his knees drawn up, in unconscious protection against the cool, night air which was blown through the narrow windows.

In the white moonlight without, the city of Syracuse lay shrouded in slumber. The multitude, in joyous anticipation of the sports on the morrow, had early sought their couches.

From out the shadow of a pretentious dwelling on the Via Greca, two figures crept with fear and caution in their every move. The taller of the two darted ahead and sought the shelter of the next deep shadow.

His companion, having caught up with him, the pair emerged into the full light and started to saunter up the hill.

" Mind well your gait," warned the shorter man; " 'tis not a night for errand like ours. In this brilliant moon can everything be seen."

" The city sleeps," remarked the other, looking down upon the silent roofs and deserted moonlit streets.

" Who knows? "

" After the day of feasting and reception to the warrior and in thought of the early hour at which they must rise again, the wise have long since sought their slumbers."

" And the unwise? " quoth the other, quietly. " They also have eyes to see and ears to hear. They also have tongues with which to spread alarm. Suppose the maid, Calanthe, wakeful from thoughts of the morrow, stand at her window, looking upon the beauty of the night? What if Pythias, himself, cannot content his brain to sleep and strides upon his balcony to breathe the freedom of the sky? "

" Your unquiet thoughts are the imaginings of a mind of guilt," remonstrated the companion. " Not one of the happenings of which you've spoken will transpire. So rest your soul and do your work. When your heart fails, call again to your ears the clink of the purse of gold as it fell on the stone table and recall that, on the morrow, the dose will be repeated! "

As they mounted the final steepness of the Circus hill, a low, peculiar sound smote their ears.

" What was't? " gasped the taller of the two. " Was it man or beast? Was it welcome or warning? "

They shrank into the first recess that presented its shelter. Flattened against the wall, their arms outspread and fingers clinging to the irregularity in surface, they listened, with bated breath, for a dread repetition. It came not.

Cautiously they peered without. The scene was unchanged. The dazzling white light bathed more completely the sleeping city. The shadows were blacker and more sharply defined, in contrast.

"Your wits are easily shaken!" charged one. "If but your brain could be startled into action as readily, then were the deed already completed."

"Speak not of wits shaken," countercharged the other. "'Twas your fingers that clutched my arm in terror and your feet that first sought concealment. Methinks that even now your stomach quakes with fear of an unknown spy, while I — I —"

He strode boldly into the full glare and raised his arms aloft, in brave defiance.

"Now that we have accomplished the ascent, let us approach the stables, and, looking through the windows, determine in what location these steeds are housed," he called loftily to his fainthearted companion.

"Have thought of the stable boys?" was the wary retort.

"Stable boys!" guffawed the other. "They are the last we have to fear. For first, they sleep with the profoundness of death, exhausted from their heavy labors; and second, if they should be aroused, a few drachmas would soon quell their murmurs of

dissent.    Come, be brave!    Follow in the footsteps
of your leader who knows no fear."

Inside the stable, the young Aratus stretched his
thin legs and turned to find greater comfort on his
couch of hay.    The stiffness of his wrist and elbow
joints, result of his vigorous rubbing, drove him to
sit erect, to try to ease their aching.

From outside he caught the boastful whispering
of the braggart.    At first, his mind, clogged with
unslept slumbers, strove in vain to grasp the reality
and then the import of the words.    He crawled
along the floor till he crouched directly beneath the
nearest window.

He could hear a man urging another to display of
bravery.    He did not recognize the voices, but knew
them to be none of those whose horses were sheltered
with the stable walls.    Fearing to wait too long to
learn their identity, he straightened his lithe body
and with a sudden spring, stood on tiptoe and gazed
through the opening.

He saw in the blinding glare of white light two
men whose garb proclaimed them of the sort who,
without earnest occupation of any sort, frequent the
wine cellars and are for hire when the deed is dark.

The vague feeling of danger that had clamored at
his heart throughout the early night now redoubled.
The presence of these men presaged ill.    If he were
detected by them before their plans were carried out,

it would mean his destruction. He glanced with horror at the short swords, unsheathed, that were stuck through the leathern loops of their girdles.

They turned suddenly, and, in the direct shafts of light, their features, unmasked, were plainly visible. Aratus remembered where he had seen them. That very afternoon toward dusk when the streets were still thronged with the gay crowds who were loath to seek their own roofs, he had watched them stumble from the wine cellar of Cicatrum on the Via Steres. Much the worse for wine, the one acting as standard for the other, they had proceeded to an humble dwelling on the outskirts of the town.

The boy dropped in affright to the floor and scrambled back to his couch. There, he assumed a posture of utter languor, his eyes tightly closed, his chin dropped and mouth opened to emit the deep, regular sounds of a person sunk in slumber.

A moment after, the whisperings approached the window and an ugly head, with protruding eye and bulbous nose, was thrust through. Aratus gulped in sudden dread, but did not interrupt his forced, even breathing. He was thankful that the head obscured the beam that had, a moment before, slanted through the window and cast its radiance upon his prostrate body.

The head was withdrawn and quick consultation taken. Every word, with here and there a final letter blurred, drifted in to his alert ears. He dared not open his eyes for fear that they were waiting to trap him.

As he listened, his heart chilled with the horror of the plan they proposed. His mind ordinarily not quickly roused to thought, struggled to devise a solution to the situation. The dastardly ones must be thwarted. But how?

He concluded from their talk of purses and gold and their humorous verbal caricatures, that they had been hired by Damocles, at the instigation of Dionysius. How could he, a stable boy, hope to successfully frustrate the schemes of two of the mightiest in the city?

Nevertheless he would try. For his beloved master's sake he would risk attack and even annihilation, in an attempt to prevent this vile design. Their every move, carefully planned, the two men turned to seek the gates.

On the instant, Aratus kicked the sleeping Mentum with as much force as he could summon to his fear-paralyzed limbs.

The blooded steed, which slept lightly, jumped wildly to his feet and pawed furiously at the wall that separated his stall from the next. The noise awoke the other horses. They joined in a chorus of neighs and snorts and their hoofs beat the stone until the clamor was deafening.

Aratus, in pretense of having been but suddenly awakened, called to his charges. From other sec-

tions of the stable the boys came running, stumbling
over their weary feet, their hands waving in panic at
the unlooked for agitation. Aratus jumped to the
window and saw, far down the hill, two fleeing figures. As he watched, they reached the lower streets
and disappeared amid the closely placed buildings.

He seized Lertes roughly by the shoulders.

" Keep watch! " he commanded hoarsely, " while
I speed down into the city. There is a plot afoot
that means dishonor to us all, and, if the authorities
do but hear of it, I have no doubt but that our
severed heads will stain the chopping block a sullen
crimson! "

Lertes, petrified with fear at his possible fate,
opened his lips to question; but, from the dry walls
of his frightened throat, no sound issued. Before
his moistened tongue could form a syllable, Aratus
had darted from the stables.

Down the hillside he sped. His tired legs, driven
to speed by a passionate fire of devotion, bore him
to the portal of Arria's house. His sister, Eunice,
favorite of Calanthe's handmaidens, would recognize his call and give him entrance.

Hardly had the low sound left his lips, when a
startled figure, swathed in white, appeared on the
balcony over his head.

" Aratus! " called Eunice in sudden dismay.
" What brings you at this hour? Is it a message
of alarm you bear? Is it from Pythias? Speak,

Aratus! My heart is suffocating me in its wild leaping!"

"I can not speak at this distance, Eunice," gasped the boy, clutching his parched throat. "You must open the gate to me and rouse your mistress. Come! For whate'er is done must be done quickly."

The slender form disappeared behind the heavy draperies and a moment later the ponderous door swung on its hinges and admitted the breathless messenger to the inner courtyard.

"Where is your mistress?" demanded Aratus. "It is most important that she be awakened. What I have to say is of her intimate concern. Come, Eunice, let us to her chamber and rouse her."

"No!" Eunice stayed his steps with an imperative hand. "I have but just succeeded in soothing her to slumber. All the night she has been pacing the floor, unwilling to seek her couch. To calm her restless spirit I did anoint her fair body with perfumed oils and smooth her tresses with quieting hands, until at last her lovely eyes closed in peaceful sleep. I will not wake her. Deliver me your message and speak softly lest the whole household wake and be affrighted."

"This is not a time to consider slumber. The honor of Pythias and his repute in Syracuse will be as naught on the morrow unless he is warned, on the instant, of the plot that is on foot to disgrace him."

" Disgrace him? " breathed Eunice, grasping her brother's arm in disbelief.

" List closely to my message," entreated Aratus; " do not ask me whys and wherefores.   In times like this every moment is an added stumbling block to my purpose of defeating these vile criminals.   Dionysius, who they say is enamored of your lovely mistress, Calanthe, and jealous of the glories cast at Pythias' feet this day, has got his henchman, Damocles, to hire men of low origin to perform a dastardly deed.

" To-night, when I was sleeping in the stables, I overheard the two plotting.   They were upon the point of removing the steeds of Pythias from their stables.   Their intention was to drive them many leagues in the dead quiet of the night, so that on the morrow, spent and strained, they will not be fit competitors for the fresh, highspirited chargers of Aristle.

" It has been accomplished before.   And stable boys upon awaking, have found their horses whipped to a lather, panting in the stalls.   Not knowing how they came to be in such condition, and fearful lest their masters flog them for neglect, these boys have brushed and rubbed until the sleek look has returned and none was the wiser.   But the master was defeated in the contests! "

" Why did you not assault the villains? " questioned Eunice, with great contempt.   " Would it not

have been a surer and a more manly act than to flee,
breathless, to warn a timid, defenseless woman and
break her slumbers?"

"I could not beat them single-handed. They
bristled with short swords and they had the sinews
of a Hercules. Nor could I rely upon the other
boys within the stables. For, so avaricious are they,
that their mouths begin to water at sight of ten
drachmas and they could drive their souls to murder
for a silver piece. I took the wisest course, roused
the stable, frightened the criminals away, and, without divulging my secret to any, sped here."

"Then, is't not finished? Have not the monsters
been alarmed for all time? Have they not sought
their dwellings?"

"You do not know, O sister, what a purse of gold
will do. These same men, fortified with more wine,
will again mount the hill when all has quieted. And
this time, lest they be foiled in their intentions, will
they use violence and destroy all who stand in their
path. That is why I have come. Rouse your mistress, Eunice, and allow her to say what is best to
do."

Eunice clasped her robe more closely about her
and sped into an apartment hung with folds of palest,
rose pink. In the center gleamed a square pool in
whose green-blue depths were reflected the pillars
and rails surrounding it. Beside the steps, stretched
on a couch of white, deep with silken cushions, lay

the sleeping Calanthe, her dimpled arms crossed on her rounded breasts, her sweet lips parted in a tremulous smile.

The maid stood over her sleeping mistress, loath to disturb her sweet dreams. But the pacing to and fro of Aratus, whose steps resounded on the polished floor of the inner court, and the fear that if dishonor befell Pythias, Calanthe's heart would break, compelled her to action.

She bent low, slipped a gentle arm under her mistress's shoulders and raised her to a sitting position, smoothing her brow with a quieting hand.

Calanthe thus awakened, started in bewilderment. Then, as the familiar objects of her own apartment were disclosed to her, she sought the face of her maid, in silent question.

The expression she saw there alarmed her. She darted an anxious glance about the room to see if her mother and other members of the household had been thus aroused. From without, the monotonous tread of Aratus' sandaled feet came to her ears and she jumped from her couch dragging her embroidered coverlets with her and trailing them across the floor, half-way to the portal.

Eunice seized her hands and knelt at her feet. The startled violet eyes looked with the dread of one, unknowing, into the eyes of one who knew.

" Pythias ! " she murmured at last in little choking gasps. " Harm has come to him ! I know it —

I am certain. Speak! Who is he who paces so unceasingly outside? Have you lost tongue, Eunice? Or do you torture with suspense because the truth is more horrible than the uncertainty?"

"Nothing has happened, sweet one. But unless we act quickly the honor of your young lord may be at stake. My brother Aratus, who is stable boy at the Circus, as you know, has just fled hither to inform you that he overheard a plot to tire the steeds of Pythias by driving them many miles, in the secret night, so that, on the morrow, in contest with Aristle, they must suffer defeat."

"Whose plot is this?" breathed Calanthe, her eyes aflash with sudden indignation. "Dionysius —"

Eunice nodded assent.

"'Twas he who conceived of it and his gold went for the purchase price. Men do these things and lay the burden of their crimes at love's door, hoping to receive absolution from Eros, at whose shrine they worship. Come, let me clothe you in your softest robes and you and I, attended by my brother, will speed to Pythias and warn him of his danger."

With swift hands Eunice fastened the silver shoulder buckles and put in place the broidered cestus. The rosy feet were slipped into soft padded sandals and the bronze-gold head swathed in gauze scarves.

"So that your disguise may be complete," urged Eunice, "throw this mauve mantle, that is your mother's, about you and hold the thick folds well over your mouth and chin, for the night air is treacherous and the dew, though naught but drops of opal moisture, chilling to your tender feet."

" My mother! " panted Calanthe, shivering in vague dread of the weirdness of her errand. " Should I not rouse her and bid her accompany us? She will think it strange if —"

" She will not know — you will not tell her of it?" implored Eunice on her knees. " Because if the information become too-widely known, those in authority will search for the informer and my brother will be put to death, in secret, by the followers of Dionysius. Do not wake your mother, sweet."

Calanthe raised the pleading maid and folded her in her soft arms.

" Do you think that I would knowingly bring harm to one who has risked so much to save my Pythias from dishonor? Think you I do not know that if your brother did but submit to bribery, he could have made a goodly sum and no one would have been the wiser? I would have ta'en my mother with me as protection."

" Aratus will be our protection," answered Eunice, wrapping her mistress closely in her mantle. " He would kill one who'd dare to interfere with our progress. For, as you know, his worship of your sweet self is as profound as mine own."

"THEN DID THE PEOPLE STAND UPON THE BENCHES AND THE CLAMOR DEEPENED."

KNOWING DAMON IS AT THE WEDDING OF PYTHIAS, DIONYSIUS ARRANGES TO BE CROWNED IN THE SENATE.

Silently, with cautious step, the two maidens sought the inner courtyard.   At their approach Aratus ran to the heavy portal and swung it wide.

" Be careful lest it clang," warned Eunice, bracing her slim, young body against the oaken panels, to decrease its impetus.   " Now that we are safely out, we must do naught to arouse suspicion."

" We must not go by the road," announced Calanthe as she caught sight of the dazzling white stretch that led to the dwelling of Pythias.   " Let us through the garden, then along the wooded path that follows the brook in whose purling waters we bathed our ankles that day, so many months ago, when first my Pythias saw me."

" It is a longer way," objected Aratus, who lived in dread lest the knaves return and bribe his associates while he was absent.

" It is a safer way," reproved Calanthe.   " And it is wise to sacrifice time to safety, when we are surrounded by plotters all intent upon our downfall. Lead the way, Eunice."

The three figures, now hid in the complete obscurity of dense, overhanging foliage, now distinct, where the silver rays penetrated to small cleared spaces, moved silently on their way.

Strange wood-calls that sounded ghostly on the silent night, made the maidens shrink more closely into their all-enveloping mantles.   Obsessed by the weirdness of the night and the unearthly radiance of the moon, Calanthe thought of Hecati and wondered if she were wandering at large.

She uttered a wild, little cry and clutched at Eunice's arm.

"We have reached the outer hedge," the maid reassured her. "Just a step inside and we are safe. Aratus, quicken your steps and rouse Pythias' slave. He sleeps outside his master's chamber. Tell him to give message that Calanthe awaits him, in the garden. Haste, for the cold night has chilled her hands and tremors shake her form."

In the black shade of an arbor of evergreens, Calanthe clung to Eunice and watched, with suspense-sharpened eyes for first sight of her lover. The minutes seemed an eternity. She felt her knees lose their strength. Her brain reeled in bewilderment. What was the delay? Had he sickened? Had he been slain on his couch? Had Dionysius —?

Suddenly, in the white light reflected from the marble steps, she saw the form of her knight. As he advanced the moon caught the glitter of his helmet and made it a dazzling crown for his handsome face.

Calanthe, not recovered from the shock of her rude awakening, exhausted from her hurried journey through the woodland and torn with the agony of suspense, watched his approach. But the sight of him in all his strength and beauty, safe, and eager for her greeting swept over her in a great engulfing wave and as he reached her side, she swooned in his protecting arms.

# CHAPTER X

## THE PLOT FRUSTRATED

AT the stables Lertes held sway and threatened, with instant punishment, him who first showed signs of flight — or great fear.
" I know no more of this sudden riot and dark mystery than do you. Harm threatened, of that I'm sure. Did not Aratus warn me that unless he should flee and carry warning, on the instant, our heads would stain to sullen crimson the murderous ax of the executioner? "

" And does belief of all you hear penetrate so sharply to your brain that you must needs follow every edict and not stop to call your soul your own? " derisively questioned one of the boys, who tended the horses of Aristle.

Lertes frowned darkly on the speaker and shook a defiant fist under his broad and flattened nostrils.

" Give not tongue to your ignorance! " he menaced shrilly. " Your closed lips might vaguely suggest that pearls of wisdom fell from their shelter. But when you separate their closeness and sounds do issue from between, then are all thoughts of wisdom but a merry jest — and you the jester! "

" What waked the steeds when they had but just fallen to slumber? " questioned another, rubbing his heavy, red-rimmed eyes and showing his huge teeth in an all-enveloping yawn.

" That I know not," acknowledged Lertes, " nor does anyone of us save Aratus. And he fled with such suddenness that not a word of information was forthcoming. He will tell us all when he returns."

" But will he return? " asked a third, stretching his limbs so tautly that his joints cracked in rebellion. " I trust him not. He is too learned, too given to dreams and too full of devotion to his masters. Will he return? "

" What advantage to him not to? " argued Lertes, not finding logical denial to launch against this latest skeptic. " Voice no more of your doubts and misgivings for should he return laden with rewards to bestow on us for having done our duty, I will see to it that he who was most distrustful goes forth with empty palms to seek position elsewhere."

The Arabian steeds of Pythias, unused to strange voices and chafing at the absence of Aratus and his caressing pats, pulled at their ropes and shook their manes from side to side, until the evenly combed hairs were all atangle.

Lertes entered the stall of Mentum and sought to quiet his exhibitions of ugly temper. He reached up and strove to smooth the arched neck, as he had seen Aratus do. The thankless animal, as reward,

swooped down and caught his tunic between his
strong, even teeth.    Then with his struggling, kicking burden he tossed his head and struck first one
wall, then the other with the helpless Lertes, while
the boy's comrades looked on aghast and motionless.

"Kick him!   Lash him!   Help me!" gurgled
the powerless one as his shins came in sharp contact
with the stone-edge.

But rather than risk their sound limbs and cow-
ardly hides to the viciousness of the exasperated
steed, they watched their companion receive bruise
after bruise, and lifted not a finger to aid him in his
peril.

Suddenly there was a sound of scurrying feet and
Aratus and Pythias dashed into the stables and made
for the spot where the craven group watched the
antics of the enraged Mentum.

"Down!" shouted Aratus in ringing tones.
"What means this display of temper, O wicked one?
The whip shall greet your hide for this!"

Mentum, at the first familiar syllable, pricked up
his narrow pointed ears and dropped his victim in
a sudden heap.   As Lertes scrambled to his feet and
dashed from the stall to guard against a possible
repetition, the horse hung his head and looked sadly,
but with a tinge of drollery, from the corner of his
large, soft eyes.

His dilated nostrils quivered sensitively and he

sought to condone his sudden aggression by laying his head softly on the shoulder of the stern Aratus, who was about to administer punishment.

"Do not lash him," interposed Pythias, placing a protecting hand on his well-loved favorite. "He was disturbed at the clamor and missed your touch to quiet him."

Aratus, only too glad of an excuse to pet the animal, dropped the leathern thong to the floor of the stall, whence as if in gentle rebuke, Mentum lifted it between his teeth and laid it carefully in Aratus' palm.

"I will make it right with the boy who suffered through his playfulness," said Pythias, looking to the corner where Lertes, nursing his cuts and bruises, glowered, while they made much of the animal who had just treated him so harshly.

"We have no time to lose," warned Aratus, as Pythias, his cheek pressed closely to that of the culprit, whispered words of consolation into his listening ear.

"Yes, we must act quickly," he agreed, stepping outside the stall and advancing to where the boys stood, their mouths wide with curiosity, their eyes dulled from disturbed slumbers. "I will explain the case in few words. Do you all pay strict attention, grasp well my instructions and in the end will you all profit! A silver piece to each who does well what he is bidden."

The situation having assumed a definite monetary value, the interest shown became vital. They crowded close about the young general, fearful of losing a word that might aid them in the performance of his demands. Even Lertes, whose soul was wounded far more deeply than his flesh, pressed close and forgot his animosity of a moment since.

" You all were on the streets of Syracuse this day and saw the people welcome me from my Carthaginian triumphs," said Pythias, with not a vestige of the braggart in his words. " My reception has not pleased one who is most powerful in the city and he has plotted to cause my defeat in to-morrow's contest in the arena.

" My horses are to be driven and purposely tired, while Syracuse sleeps; so that after the first dash of the race, the steeds of Aristle, fresh from their stables, will far outstrip me. Thus has Dionysius planned for my downfall. Two ruffians will visit the stables, perform the deed and receive as payment a bag of gold.

" I have come to defeat their plans and I desire your aid. If you had assisted them in their foul purpose they would have bestowed, as bribe money, not more than five drachmas apiece; while I will give, for faithful service and a quiet tongue, a silver piece to all alike."

Aratus walked to the stalls of his charges, untied the ropes that held two captive and led them to the

center of the stable floor.   Pythias seized the halters and waited till Aratus had released the two remaining.   He then led the way to another section
of the stables and halted before the stalls where the
horses of Aristle were confined.

"Loose their halters!" he commanded Aratus,
"and lead them to the other section."

At first comprehension of the plan on foot, the
swarthy stable boy in the service of Aristle, the fore-
most charioteer of Sicily, darted under the arm of
Pythias and made for the open door.

"Pursue him!"   Aratus raised the cry.   "A
double reward for him who makes the capture!"

In but a moment they dragged him back, protesting
all in vain, his clothing caked with mud where they
had thrown him to the ground.

"Thought you to warn your master?" queried
Pythias.   "'Twas a loyal attempt and so shall I tell
him when the race is o'er and I have won.   For
the present you shall be bound and gagged so that
when the scoundrels come again, your lamentations
will be choked to silence.   Bind him securely, you
others, and cast him where the eyes of the intruders
will find him not."

A gag of hay forced between the complaining lips
prevented all sound from escaping.   The squirming
arms and kicking legs were bound securely at wrist
and ankle with slender leathern thongs that bit deep.

Thus, securely guarded against future outbreaks,

the helpless form was borne to an inner room where
were stored the worn trappings and harnesses of
other years.

"The time draws near for a second attempt."
Pythias walked to the window and surveyed the scene
before him. At the base of the hill, he thought he
discerned two black specks creeping from shadow to
shadow. He rubbed his eyes and looked more
closely. Just then they reached a space that was
without shadow. He saw one man leap with great
bounds across the moonlit spot. In sudden anger
he turned from the window.

"Even now they mount the hill!" he shouted to
the boys who eagerly awaited the signal to take part
in this exciting comedy. "Remember well my warning. Cast yourselves about the floor and assume at-
titudes of deep slumber. When they enter, do not
stir. If they should trip over your prostrate bodies,
make no sign. I would enjoin you to be most careful, for if they detect that you are but acting,— inflamed with wine, as they are, they might do violence and turn this jest of ours to tragedy. As for
myself, I will seek concealment in the stores of hay.
From that shelter I can watch the proceedings, unseen and unheard. Haste! For I hear their heavy
feet crunch into the gravel of the roadway."

The scene that met the eyes of the two hirelings
was one of utter peace and quiet. Here and there
the sleeping form of a stable boy was lighted by the

moonbeams that penetrated to the main corridor. The horses in their stalls, quieted but not yet asleep, nodded drowsily.

The taller of the two grasped the arm of his companion and pointed a finger of scorn at the sleepers.

"Did I not tell you that they would be our last fear?" he questioned boastfully, and with strange mouthings, due to recent draughts of wine. "Mighty guardians of blooded steeds are they! See their deathlike stupor. One could blow a trumpet blast and succeed only in ruffling their dreams! They are but poor beasts, who are driven to work, that they have food to place between their lips. While we, just for a night's pastime such as this, are presented with a double purse of gold and are enabled to feast for weeks to come. 'Tis well to be born with skill."

Pythias, secreted in the hay, began to suffer from the intense heat. If they would but hasten to their deed and give him freedom! He stretched forth his hand and pulled loose a small clump that choked his breathing. As the cool air greeted his nostrils he breathed deeply.

The shorter rascal, who was bent on untying the first horse, rushed from the stall and clutched frantically at his accomplice's arm.

"What was't?" he gasped, his swollen eyes blinking in terror, his unsteady knees clicking in comic manner.

"What was what?" blandly inquired the other,

throwing off his uncomfortably tight grip. "Ne'er shall I take you again on such errand. You would shatter the calm of the surest of men, with your wild gibberings and your hearing of sounds that never were born. When next I am commissioned to carry out a difficult problem you shall remain at home. And when I return victorious, you, white-livered craven, shall sit the other side of the table and try to stem the tides that rise from your watering lips, as I quaff bowl after bowl and offer you none."

Thus threatened with an arid future, the timorous one took courage and led two of the horses from their stalls.

"See," he mocked in newly-acquired bravado, "I can kick the hounds and rouse them not!"

He applied his broad knobby toes to the back of the feigning Aratus. The slim body lifted slightly from the floor, in obedience to the kick, and, when it was withdrawn, sank, as supine as before.

This caused great mirth between the two. And if it had not happened that the wiser one, through his soddenness, awoke to the realization that dawn was not far distant, the foolish member would have spent the hours that were to come in lavishly distributing all kicks that he was capable of administering.

Carefully they piloted the four steeds to the open doorway. Each, after many unsuccessful attempts, mounted one and led the other by shortened halter.

Down the hillside, in a direction opposite to the city, they galloped.  As the echoing hoof beats grew fainter and fainter, Pythias crawled from his lair, wellnigh spent with the humid heat, and roused his conspirators.

Unfastening a leathern pouch from his wide belt he presented a silver piece to each.  Unrestrained joy reigned.  Not only was the pay munificent, but the complete deception delighted their souls.  For, in the frail mind of each of us lurks the fond thought that he shelters the genius of an actor.

While the happy ones joined hands and jumped about in high glee, Pythias entered the room of old harnesses and trappings.  Squirming on the floor, in a dark, cobwebbed corner, lay the gagged and bound stable boy of Aristle, bitter hatred and revolt shining from his flashing eyes.

Pythias bent, loosened the clenched fingers of one bound hand and placed in the hot, wet palm, *six* coins of silver.

# CHAPTER XI

## THE RACE

DAWN broke, mauve and silver, from the horizon of the sea. It coated the still waters with a frostlike sheen, that warmed gradually to color. It deepened from mauve to dull rose, from rose to pink, from pink to scarlet and gold; until the vaulted skies reflected its radiance and the feathery clouds curled soft corners and dyed themselves in its shades.

The hush over the city of Syracuse lifted, first with low, indistinct rumbling as of preparation far distant, that shook the surface of the earth. Later, the monotony of sound was punctuated here and there by a shrill call, a crash of metal gates and the excited conversation of gathering crowds.

Looking down from the Circus Hill, the narrow streets and by-ways assumed the appearance of an uncovered beehive. Streams of humanity moving, yet having no definite objective point, wound in and out the gayly decorated houses.

In the richer neighborhoods, the gates remained closed. But in the gardens, slaves ran excitedly to and fro. Handmaidens gathered sheafs of rich blooms for their mistresses' litters. Stable boys

groomed stamping horses and guardians of the wine
cellars filled huge flagons with gold and ruby liquids.

In the apartment of Calanthe, Eunice, wan from
insufficient sleep, took from its wardrobe the tunic
of silver cloth embroidered with coral beads that
her mistress was to wear to the games. Calanthe,
in her bath, sang softly a simple melody taught her
by an old nurse.

"Do you not feel the thrill that throbs through
the very air?" she demanded eagerly. "'Tis a
wondrous day! Think you that ever before had
maiden so much happiness crowded into a single
block of hours? First the games and the chariot
race in which her lover will be victor! Then —"

"Hush!" Eunice bade her in sudden apprehension. "When you are so sure of victory it is but
tempting the gods to thwart your assurance. Since
our troublous night I have had strange misgivings.
If the subterfuge were discovered! If Dionysius —"

A handmaiden folded a fleecy robe about the glistening, wet body of her young mistress. Calanthe
stepped from the pool and threw herself at length
upon a couch.

"If it were not imperative that I be robed so
early to proceed to the Circus, I would love it well
to slumber but a little while longer. My broken
rest and our strange errand, in the dead of night,
have weighted my eyelids. But was it not an unusual
adventure?" she finished, enthusiastically.

Her maidens, with soft cloths, dipped into jars of porcelain and gently rubbed her rosy flesh with perfumes and nourishing oils. She lay looking up with dreamy eyes at the star-flecked ceiling of her chamber.

"No one but Eunice may arrange my tresses on this day," she said, glancing with deep affection at her favorite maid. "And it must be so marvelously done that when my Pythias gazes upon me, from his chariot, in the arena, his heart will bound with pride in his possession!"

"Has his heart not bounded thus, always, since the first moment your sweet lips agreed to be betrothed to him?" questioned Eunice, indulgent in her adoration. "I fear you wish to attract the glances of others that they may whisper, 'All his luck lies not in the games. Look what a pearl beyond price he takes to his bosom to-day!' Is that not so, spoiled one?"

"No, it is not so!" was the indignant denial, as Calanthe sat erect to add vehemence to her words. "And yet," she mused naïvely, "it will be well for the criminal and ill-featured Dionysius to see that which he has so completely lost."

"Rid your mind of such worldly thoughts!" Eunice exclaimed in mock-reproof. "On the wedding day of maid must no thought of other than her lover dwell, even for an instant, in her pretty head. If Pythias but knew your designs in making your appearance so wonderfully alluring, then would he shroud your features in a thick veil and drape your rounded form with mantles not transparent."

Calanthe raised her glowing arms and sighed happily.

" That will come soon enough," she pouted. " For from this night forth, it will be expected of me that I consider all the earth populated by just one man — and that my husband."

She ran to the edge of the pool and gazed long upon her reflection there.

" Am I beautiful enough for him? " she asked at length, a shadow of doubt creeping into her voice. " In this new tunic I have not the youthful look that I have been accustomed to gaze upon. A sedateness rests upon my shoulders that makes me fear to look too close, lest I see age creep on with stealthy step."

" Foolish girl! " Eunice shook her playfully and pulled loose a curl or two that they might rest lovingly upon the damask cheek. " The breaking dawn envies your fresh beauty. 'Tis the fault of the tunic. The rich material and the stiffness of its folds conceals the youthful grace of your figure."

" Then will I wear one I have worn before. Bring me one of azure and bind my hair with silver fillets. Oh, Eunice, I desire much to don my wedding robes and catch but a tiny glance of my reflection in their chaste beauty. But my mother says that the wear-

ing of a bridal robe before the bridal hour presages
ill.  Think you the tale is true? "

" I think whate'er your mother speaks is truth,"
replied Eunice, shocked at the thought of doubting
her elders.  " Come, hasten, Calanthe!  Slip your
feet into the silver sandals that I may adjust the
straps.  There is still much to do and our appearance at the Circus must not be delayed."

" I would not give thought to starting for a full
hour, or still longer," objected Calanthe.  " None
but the rabble enters the gates of the Circus at this
hour.  The noble and very rich, with seats procured,
make their entrance but just before the start."

From the streets arose a very hubbub of cheers;
and voices, some dissenting, some with hearty words
of greeting, intermingling with shrill accusation,
floated in through the heavy draperies.  Snatching
up a veil Calanthe wound it round her head and
shoulders and drew Eunice out on the balcony beside
her.

" Oh, is't not wonderful? " she breathed in hushed
tones.  " Ne'er before, in this short memory of
mine, has the scene been so amazing."

Calanthe threw her arms about her maid and held
her tightly, in a sudden rush of ecstasy.  Thus,
clasped closely, they surveyed the bustle of the scene
before them.

In Syracuse, on a day of this sort, the games were
free; therefore, at the first hour of dawn, the rabble,

fearful lest there be not room for all, despite the huge capacity of the Circus, wound their way from the city's streets to camp about the entrance gates.

This struggling stream of humanity was now in progress. It wound, snakewise, from the Senate Square, up to the portals, where it seemed to flatten and spread. Only the Circus attendants knew what scenes of violent contention would take place when first the blast sounded as signal for the swinging in of the huge, bronze-bound gates.

And once admitted, would they feast and doze upon the benches, whence naught but an upheaval of the earth or a menacing group of short swords could drive them forth.

"What is it they bear in their arms?" questioned Calanthe, looking upon the queer bundles of all sizes and shapes.

"Food, wine, robes to protect against the elements, if the elements do protest," Eunice told her. "They go prepared for comfort for the day. These great times come but seldom in the poorer man's existence, and when they do, he gets from them all the gayety they contain."

"Oh, let us haste to the scene, ourselves!" urged Calanthe. "I would be seated to view this strange assemblage burst into the Circus and find their places. Would it not be sport, Eunice, to see it all, aye, from the very beginning?"

"Your mother would not allow it. Neither would

Pythias countenance your presence there before the proper time. Besides, the garlands for your litter will have to be exchanged. I had given orders that they were to be of coral-colored blooms to match the coral beading of your tunic. And now, since you have changed to azure, must white be substituted? Wilt change your mind in love, as easily as in costume?" she asked playfully.

.     .     .     .     .     .     .

Outside the entrance gates of the Circus all was confusion. The first arrivals, in fear of being displaced from their position, flattened themselves against the massive, oaken panels, so that when the signal sounded and the gates swung in, they would be the first to enter.

They did not stop to calculate that, in the fearful pressure, the impetus with which the crowd behind pressed upon them would result in their being cast to the ground, where over their prostrate bodies the others would rush in and there seek choice position.

Grasping their bundles closely, with faces strained and eyes darting from side to side, they waited for the signal.

Suddenly the air was rent with a shrill blast. Three times it sounded. Dead silence followed. Then there fell upon the ear the harsh brazen clang of a huge metal gong, struck with iron hammers.

As the last stroke died upon the dawn, the massive

bolts of the Circus portals were shot back and slowly they yawned on their hinges.

Into the emptiness shot the mob as if projected from a catapult. Those in the van were overwhelmed as they had been many times before. And while they struggled, prostrate, to maintain their hold upon their treasures, they shouted hoarse curses at their oppressors.

In an incredibly short time the unreserved spaces were filled, with no chance of any future arrival finding room. It now remained for the nobles and the very rich to make their entrance. This, as much as the games that followed, delighted the soul of the proletariat. For, on this day, was all the splendor of wealth and position flaunted in extravagant glare. The classes came to be admired, the masses to envy and give homage — as it has been and always will be, world without end.

When the first sharp rays of the morning sun slanted up from the horizon line and struck the edges of the roof-tops, the procession of wealth began.

Warriors, resplendent in full regalia, their breastplates dazzling mirrors for the rising sun, strode in on foot, followed by their vassals laden with various aids to their comfort.

Statesmen, with white togas edged in scarlet and purple; rich merchants whose robes were overladen with trimmings of great cost, so that they might impress more deeply the success they had made in trade.

Beautiful women in shimmering draperies, lounged upon silken cushions, in their covered litters, and were borne to their private boxes by ebony-skinned slaves. Children in short, full tunics and bare dimpled knees, drank enthusiasm from their elders and waved gay banners in the crowd.

Preceded by six attendants bearing bowls and covered dishes, from which there were wafted savory odors that assailed the nostrils of the hungry, Dionysius, seated in a huge chair of gilded woods, cushioned in purple, made his entrance.

He had discarded his armor. Upon his brow his fast-thinning locks were bound by a golden band. His frame was folded in a black mantle, broidered with a design of golden laurel leaves.

The rabble, realizing that this was an entrance of the first magnitude, got to its feet, and cheered madly. The chair was borne around the arena, skirting close to the lowest tier, so that all might see the Great One. Dionysius lifted a bored hand in greeting, as the people of Syracuse shouted their enthusiasm. It was the cause of comments, as he meant it should be.

But, in his sunken breast, the triumph in his heart was pounding thickly and his brain conceived the thought:

" A step nearer. There are not many left for me to travel. I have the people with me."

Some one called his name. It was taken up on all sides and soon all the Circus rang with shrill cries of " Dion-ysius-s-s ! "

His four stout servants bore him up an aisle and rested his chair in the exact center of his box. Immediately was he followed there by Damocles and Philistius.

" We have done well to rouse enthusiasm of such power," commented Damocles, with a chuckle of smug satisfaction.

" We ? " Dionysius' brows arched themselves in derision. " And what have *you* done, O noble sir, to further the enthusiasm? Did the crowd perceive your Apollo-like physique in my wake? Or did you cast coins to the rabble and thus move them to this great display of spirit? "

" I did neither," was the irate retort. " That show of patriotic fire was not a case of spontaneity. It is the result of hard and honest labors on the part of Philistius and myself. We are the ones who have educated the citizens of Syracuse up to your standards. Where would be your prospects of a throne if it were not for us? Is not Philistius president of the Senate? Can he not say yea or nay? Is it not to him you'll look upon the great day, to take your hand and lead you to the crown? "

Dionysius leaned forward in his chair, his chin sunk in the palm of his hand, his brows meeting, in rounded protuberances over his nose. His eyes, baleful from the depths of their bony sockets, scored the plump anatomy of the prince of sycophants before him.

"Philistius, as it happens, will be the lucky man upon whose arm I'll lean to ease my progress to the throne. You will be there to tread behind. You will bear my mantle and my reproaches. And if you chafe my amiable nature, you will be there just so long — and not a moment longer. All that you've said is true. But you have not laid stress upon the fact that, lacking both Philistius and yourself, Dionysius would have gained the position that he sought. And so shall it be, when centuries after your repute has vanished from the page of history, will the fame of Dionysius blaze from tongue to tongue, as though his life were but just lived."

A litter, brilliant with spangled hangings, was conveyed past the box. As if by magic, the mask of malicious sarcasm on Dionysius' face dissolved into a veneer of suave benignity. He smiled. The fair occupant fell back, panting, on her pillows. The mighty one had shown his favor! The little by-play was not lost upon the two men. This was but another mild proof of the hold that the warrior general exerted over all who came under his hypnotic sway.

Damocles spoke, his tones honeyed with submissiveness.

"My hasty speech was born of that same physical

upset of which I did complain yesterday. My stomach is so —"

" Truths that would not otherwise fall upon the outside air, find utterance from an afflicted stomach. When a man is bent with suffering, it matters not, at the moment, whether the future hold for him opulence or oblivion. And so his words come ungarnished from the depths."

Damocles searched for phrases to smooth the ire of his lord — and found them not. No one, but himself, knew how he had lost slumber, performed distasteful errands and risked the disfavor of his associates in the Senate, to find patronage in this man's eyes. And now, in a careless-uttered accusation, had he destroyed what advancement he had achieved! The pity of it overwhelmed him. He huddled into his billows of fat and pondered on his desolateness.

At the gates appeared another procession. It comprised a group of slaves, two litters (one mauve, one azure), with occupants veiled, and a band of graceful handmaids, from whose slim shoulders hung a continuous rope of blossoms, that hedged their mistress in.

Dionysius sat erect, his eyes strained, his nostrils quivering in sudden perturbation.

" It is Calanthe and her retinue, is it not?" he questioned Damocles, sharply.

" None other but that haughty maid!" exclaimed

the wily sycophant, his heart aglow at being again restored to the position of informer. " See how erect she holds her disdainful head and her lips are curved in scorn as if she knew your eyes were upon her ! "

" They are ? " Dionysius, whose eyesight, at a distance, was none too good, laid compelling fingers on the arm of his sycophant. " Look well. See if her glance travels to this box. Her own is on the opposite side of the arena, and perhaps they will bear her litter only halfway 'round."

" That is their intention," announced Damocles, as the gay little cavalcade turned sharply to the left. " Methinks that in a few hours' time the haughty maid, cast down at the utter defeat of her Pythias, will be glad to smile upon your advances. When others scorn him instead of casting garlands at his feet, then will *her* scorn become assured. A maid of wondrous beauty, accustomed as she is to adulation, does not continue to worship where others deride. That much have I culled from my study of human nature, Dionysius."

" We shall see," muttered the other. " And, in the seeing, hope that this profound observation of yours have more weight than other gems of your over-fat philosophy."

At the other side of the arena, Calanthe's maids arranged her chair. Her eyes sought the gayly decorated box where Dionysius and his satellites were seated. She would have rejoiced could she have leaned far over the rail and shaken a small, vindictive fist at the base plotter. Instead, she clenched her tiny palms, when her thoughts fell on the manner in which his design had been frustrated.

At last every available space was filled. The gates were closed to those unlucky enough to have delayed too long; and a flourish of trumpets called for silence.

Instantly the gaze of all those thousands seated in the fifty tiers of the Circus structure was directed towards the tribunal, reared on a stone platform, jutting out over the arena, opposite the main entrance.

There, under purple awnings that later in the day, when the sun was high, would cast a grateful shade, sat the ædile. The multitude, sunk to silence and motionless in the grim intensity of their interest, waited, breathless, for the first announcement.

A low, broad entrance, under the tribunal, threw back its doors and slowly there issued the great procession. First, the editor and civic authorities of the city, givers of the games. They were resplendent in vari-colored robes of superb quality and heavy ornamentation, and their chariots were a riot of gay blossoms.

Followed, then, the contestants of the day, each in the costume in which he would wrestle, box or run. When this part of the procession had covered a quarter of the arena course, to the wild cheering of the people, all eyes were again turned to the entrance.

With a sullen rumbling, faint at first, then growing more distinct, the two chariots dashed into view; then did the people stand upon the benches and the clamor deepened. Hardly a man in that vast assembly but had laid a wager, no matter how small, upon the outcome of the race — hence the doubled enthusiasm.

The splendid chariots, the one inlaid with ivory and silver, the other rich in mother-of-pearl and thin, gold lines, were drawn slowly around the entire course. The high-spirited fours, their coats the glossy black of polished jet, lifted their slender limbs in haughty consciousness of being the admired of the throng.

As the chariot of Pythias reached Calanthe's box, a figure of noble proportion and massive head, wrapped in white-and-red folds of a senator's toga, rose from concealment behind her chair and waved a triumphant greeting.

On the other side of the arena, Dionysius darted forward in his chair.

" It is Damon! " he exclaimed excitedly. " I had not seen him enter. Where came he? By what portal? And why secretly? Neither is his wife Hermion nor his boy Xextus with him. Yet, at sight of him, is Pythias' faith in his own infallibility redoubled."

" So wonderful is their friendship ! " supplemented Damocles.

" I still maintain that each would have his price. Would there might be test of my assertion ! Look ! Here they come. Note the fire of Aristle's steeds. E'en before the start, do they show their superiority. The plot so well accomplished as it was, was worth full double the purchase price."

Calanthe's gaze was fixed upon the face of Dionysius as her lover's chariot approached his box.

" See ! " she bade Damon look, with sudden intensity. " He consults Damocles and curls his mouth corners in scorn. They are discussing their vile plan. Ah ! What a change will come over those two hard countenances when once the race is run ! "

The chariots disappeared whither they had come. Now the crowd settled well forward in their seats. The aedile rose. Few could hear his words, but the introductory remarks were always much the same. Two heralds, one stationed at each projecting corner of the tribunal platform, sounded blasts on their trumpets.

The gates flew open and a group of discus throwers ran to the center of the arena. The contest was close. At the ending, the victor was borne around the course, astride the shoulders of the defeated athletes.

Then followed foot races, jumping, tests of endurance and wrestling matches. Between each two events, the voices of the crowds rose to a babel of sound.  There were controversies, good-natured and otherwise.  Twice did the guardians of peace interfere where, on the commoners' benchs, men grew too free with their blows and too careless of their epithets.

At midday, the programme, with the exception of the chariot race, was concluded.  The editor announced the period of recess.

At once all those who had coin to buy with, made hurried exit to the outside portico, where the food vendors had set up quarters.

Those remaining in their seats opened the various bundles they had carried since dawn and started to feast.  There was much competition in display of what each had brought.  And upon the quality of the bundles' contents was the caste of its owner rated.

At a table, in a place of prominence, reclined Dionysius, flanked on either side by Damocles and Philistius.  They ate little, but their purchases of rich wines soothed the chief vendor, who wished all there assembled to see his distinguished patrons and judge his service accordingly.

Nearby, Calanthe and her mother were seated with Damon and Pythias.  In answer to Damon's pleading with him to quaff a bowl, to add strength to his wrists, Pythias raised a protesting hand.

"What need have I of artificial strength, born of

the treacherous grape?" he scoffed. "I leave such bolstering to my rival."

He glanced significantly to where Aristle, having paused beside the table of Dionysius, had raised a flagon to his lips. Dionysius caught the look and, in defiance, refilled, himself, the empty tankard that Aristle set upon the board.

Pythias leaned close to Damon.

"If he will fill it a few times more, then will it not be necessary to run the race at all! What folly to befog his brain, even though they think his victory assured!"

Dionysius, misinterpreting Pythias' expression for one of empty bragging, and slightly the worse for wine, himself, decided that the time had come to perform his well-planned maneuver that was to deflect any suspicion from him.

He clapped his hands. A slave standing near, whose eyes had wellnigh fallen from their sockets, watching the rare wines disappear into the gullets of his master's friends, woke from his trance and fell on affrighted knee before Dionysius' couch. In answer to the curtly delivered command, he darted back into the Circus.

When he returned, he bore on his left arm a robe of state. Dionysius lifted the folds of this garment, extracted what was hidden underneath and strode to the table where Calanthe and her party were feasting.

He bent low in exaggerated humility and drew
from under his mantle a wreath of laurel leaves
knotted with the colors of Syracuse.

" I have brought to you," he murmured in appro-
priate tones of gentle felicitation, " the victor's
crown.   E'en before the race is run, I place it in your
care, with confidence.   For the victor," he indicated
Pythias with a wide-swung flourish, " I am sure,
would not care to have it placed upon his brow by
any but your fair hands."

He extended the tribute of honor in both bony
palms.   Calanthe, startled, half rose, but made no
response.   Damon, with a mighty effort of will, con-
trolled his clenched fist, in its upward flight.   Pythias,
alone, remained calm and with the same expression
of pleased pride upon his features, took the slender
green wreath from the grasp of the warlord and
placed it gently in Calanthe's hands.

" We will try, with all our strength," he made
answer, " not to betray your fond hopes in our superiority.   And in pledge of it, will you not drain a
bowl with us ? "

" I think it were wiser not," Dionysius, non-
plussed for a moment, spoke more of the truth than
he intended.   " I have partaken freely, and, the heat
of the day upon us, my senses may not be keen
enough to appreciate to the full the joys of your triumph."

With an over-low reverence, he left their board

and found his way, a bit uncertainly, to his own circle.

From within came three shrill trumpet blasts, the signals for the end of feasting. Many, leaving their pages to pay the accounting, hastened back to their seats, loath to lose a moment of the exciting contest that would end only too soon.

Pythias stood erect, extended both hands to his loved one, and besought her to set the seal of success upon his brow. With love and sincerity and not a hint of abashment at the scurrying crowds, Calanthe took his handsome face between her rosy palms and pressed her red lips to his forehead. Pythias extended his right hand to Damon.

The grip of the two whitened the knuckles and strained the veins to prominence. Then released, their palms slid gently past each other, till only the finger tips remained touching.

Back in the Circus, enthusiasm, fortified with much food and wine, had risen to fever heat. Wild shouts and snatches of stirring song were heard. Men waved banners and besought all to become seated as quickly as possible, so that the great event of the day, upon which their silver would be won or lost, might take place.

At last, confusion silenced, all listened with alert ears to the announcement of the editor.

The course was two *parasangs* long.  The starting and finishing point was the granite pillar directly
opposite the tribunal.  The contestants were Aristle,
first charioteer of all Sicily, and Pythias, hero of
Carthage.

All this the crowd already knew.  But they listened with as much intensity as if they were re-
ceiving, for the first time, information that meant
life or death.

The editor resumed his seat.  The trumpets
sounded short and sharp.  The starters, one for
each of the contestants, leaped from the sides of
the arena to give aid, should any be needed in starting the excited fours.

Once more the trumpet blasts crashed upon the
air.  Instantaneously the gatekeeper threw open the
stalls.  From each rushed a chariot, with the thun-
derous velocity of a fast-approaching storm.

The vast assemblage rose, irrepressible and elec-
trified.  They leaped upon the benches and rent
the air with screams and hoarse yells.  This was
what they had been waiting for!  The pent-up enthusiasm, mingling with the fever of hero worship,
whipped them to a frenzy.

The chalked line was stretched across the course.
It was a difficult feat to force the two fours to nose
it evenly.  The midday sun beat down upon the
fine white sand of the arena and cast a dazzling
glare into the eyes of the competitors.

Not for an instant did they remove their gaze from the heads of their chafing steeds. The clamor of the multitude struck their ears and turned to fire the blood that coursed through their tense bodies. At moments like this, the souls of men, in the frenzy of triumph, can laugh at death, or regard it with an utter calm.

Aristle dark, lithe, his sleek, black head with snowhite forehead-band thrown back, held his taut reins with a skill that brought delight to those who had laid their wagers on his previous record. His tunic was orange, striped in gold. His bared legs, glistening from the brisk rubbing he had just received, showed swarthy against the white high-laced boots.

Pythias, blond and statuesque, a monument of strength, was clad in crimson, striped with white. His gold locks, escaping from the broad crimson band that bound them tightly, were lifted by soft breezes that had just risen from the sea. The crowd that had cast garlands at his feet on his return the day before cheered him madly.

Above in her chair, soothed by the firm confidence of Damon in his friend, Calanthe bent forward with tightly clasped hands. The laurel wreath, on a stand before her eyes, seemed but an omen of defeat. She understood full well Dionysius' method in presenting it.

At the finish, if Aristle won, he would send a delegation of pages to her box and have them bear back, across the arena, in full view of the multitude, the victor's crown.   This would so strongly emphasize the defeat of Pythias that there would follow hisses and other signs of violent disapproval.   Also would it put Dionysius, himself, in the fair light of having desired that his general, who rivaled him in warfare, be the victor.   This would be proof sufficient, to the rabble, that the noble heart of the overlord sheltered no jealousy.

The trumpeters, at a given signal from the editor, blew a vigorous blast.   The judges dropped the rope.   An attendant leaped to position behind each charioteer.   The two contestants flung wide their long leathern lashes and cracked them fiercely. With vicious snorts, their nostrils blood red, their eyes, with crimson-flecked whites, rolling madly, the fours dashed forward!

Thousands held their breath.   Up where the ædile sat, merchants of high station redoubled their wagers.   The race was on!   The souls of two men waged battle.   And a multitude, with strained eyes and throats parched with excitement, bent over the course and urged them to victory or defeat!

The first round was half accomplished.   Aristle a full length ahead, leaned over his horses' backs and slashed their sleek coats.   Pythias, still erect, used his long whip not at all.

Voices shouted directions at him.   His admirers

urged him to the lash. But he heeded nothing save the judgment of his own calm brain.

The first round completed, Aristle had gained in the lead. The speed with which his wheels ground into the white sand cast glistening sprays of the tiny particles. They struck the nostrils of the steeds behind and drove them to frenzy.

With feet spread and tunic snapping sharply in the breeze, Aristle plied his whip. Wider and wider grew the space that separated the two chariots!

Calanthe jumped from her chair and bent her slender body over the box edge. Her shrill cries were drowned in the wild roars about her. Damon seized her arm and drew her gently to her seat. In wild despair she hid her face in her trembling hands and wept.

Opposite, Dionysius, with mouth drawn at one corner and lids half shut, looked upon her grief and smiled.

The third round accomplished, the multitude drew breath. It was resolving itself into a one-sided affair. With a lead as great as his, even a poorer charioteer than Aristle could not help but conquer. The stake holders began to figure up their gains or losses.

At the beginning of the fourth round it was noticed that the sides of Aristles' four were flecked with creamy lather, while the others were but glistening wet.  A few feet further on their mouths dripped foam and their jaws sagged at the sawing bit.

Then did Pythias raise his arm.  Stretched taut, with muscles like rippling steel, he unfurled his lash and brought it down with a demon's fury on the satin hide of Mentum.  The animal, accustomed as he was to caresses and words of deep affection, reared on his slender hoofs and then dashed forward, as if from death itself.

With heads down and bodies flattened to the ground so that they had the appearance of actually skimming the surface of the course, Pythias' four devoured the space intervening.  On and on they dashed!  Each revolution of the wheels diminished the lead of the chariot ahead.

With feet braced against the *quadriga* sides and reins held loosely in his iron grip, Pythias smote the air in a continuous cracking of his whip.  Not once again did the sting eat into the coats of his horses.  But the dire sound and the mad fear of a repetition of their punishment crazed them till their hoofs shot from under their steaming bodies with redoubled speed.

On and on!  Their noses came abreast of the tail end of Aristle's chariot.  The body of Aristle lunged forward over the chariot edge as if suspended from above.  His curses rent the air.  His whip curled and flattened, cracked and cut.  The lines

where it had burned into the flesh, spurted red.  The
foaming lather was dyed crimson with the drops
that oozed so slowly.

On and on!  The eight black steeds, nose and
nose, spun round the curve of the fifth lap.  At its
completion would the victor be proclaimed.

Inch by inch, urged by words of impetuous pleading that sank into their ears despite the deafening
cheers, the horses of Pythias gained upon their competitors in the race.

Leading by a head, then by a neck, further on by
a half body-length they flew over the ground.
Within a half a round of the goal they left the
others in their wake.  Faster!  Faster!  Into the
home stretch they galloped!  Drunk with triumph,
Pythias flung his whip from him, and, with a final
plunge, whirled across the goal line — *victor!*

Halfway down the side, the chariot of Aristle
came to a dead half.  The outside horse, his hide
cut to ribbons, dropped in his tracks; and over the
chariot edge hung the limp body of the best charioteer in all Sicily; his whip frayed and broken, dan-
gling from his unconscious hand.

# CHAPTER XII

**D**IONYSIUS paced the floor of his inner courtyard. His threatening brow, under his disordered locks, grew sterner and more creased. His bony hands now clasped behind him, now clenched aloft in menacing gesture, brought terror to the heart of Damocles, who, muddled with much wine and an afternoon devoid of slumber, sat as one drugged, or foolish.

In the background, silent, and shrouded in deep thought, stood Philistius, full of wise suggestions, but fearing to offer one. Twice he put foot forward as if to interrupt the ceaseless pacing of the over-general and twice did he withdraw it in imminent fear of the burst of wrath he might bring down upon his whitening head.

" Didst see the frenzy, the utter madness of the crowds?" hissed Dionysius between his tightly clenched teeth. " Didst note how men of prominence leaped into the arena, and throwing themselves upon his chariot, did permit their bodies to be dragged through the burning sands, as proof of their insane worship? Didst behold the women

PYTHIAS DEFEATS ARISTLE, THE BEST CH/

TEER OF SICILY, AND CLAIMS THE PRIZE.

cast garlands, aye, even their jewels, at his horses' feet and clasp their hands in rapture as the animals trod upon the tokens and destroyed their beauty and their value?"

There was no answer. Both had seen. But reply, in the affirmative, would have been but oil upon the flames of Dionysius' mighty wrath. The wise man would allow him to continue his soliloquy without comment or interruption.

A slave bearing a message bidding his master to a huge feast at the dwelling of one of his generals, was seized by the neck and thrown with violence to the marble floor; where his poor thick skull struck with a resounding whack.

Damocles' nerves, in such a tender condition before the incident, were wellnigh shattered at the sight. It would have taken but little more to reduce him to maudlin grief. Philistius, perceiving his sad plight, administered a telling thump between his shoulderblades and warned him, silently, against succumbing.

"There is no time to lose!" thundered Dionysius, halting in his angry pacing to shake a violent finger in the face of his plump satellite. "This afternoon, while Damon attends the festival of Calanthe and his companion, Pythias, is the auspicious moment for them to proclaim me king in the Senate. Mark well, 'tis the first time the word itself has passed my lips. Nor would it now, but my ire is raised to boiling and I am bound to conquer this pair who would submerge me, no matter how rash the deed that accomplishes it! Haste to the Senate, Philistius, and propose the plan. Damocles shall follow and, when I am declared a monarch, will he speed to my side to summon me thither. I shall await, with impatience!"

Philistius sought to question, but on second thought, and second sight of the midnight brow, resolved that deeds without questions were what was desired. He turned and left the chamber.

Damocles, awake to the realization that he was the only remaining target for the venomous shafts of the irate warrior, rose, with bland, ingratiating smile and observed that if he were to follow 'twere well the following be immediate.

"Seat yourself!" commanded his chief, without once turning to ascertain if he had risen. "Would you amble to the Senate and muddle, in your bovine way, a situation as momentous as this? 'Tis best you store your carcass here until it has been decided. Then can you act as messenger."

"What think you will be said, when the great plan is propounded?"

The platitudinous query acted as bellows upon the smoldering embers of Dionysius' wrath. He strove for speech drastic enough to penetrate the elephantine hide before him. He choked, sputtered, purpled in the face, and, lest he commit bodily harm, strode from the room.

A half hour later, a messenger, fleet of foot, ran down the steps of the Senate and darted off in the direction of the outskirts of the city. If one had followed, it would have been ascertained that he sought the home of Damon, where, spent and panting, he arrived, to find that the Senator was at the house of Arria, waiting to be present at the wedding feast of Calanthe and Pythias.

Lucullus, faithful slave of Damon, took the grim message and without a moment's delay leapt astride a saddled steed and sped, with all haste, to deliver it to his master.

In the dwelling of Arria, all was rejoicing. In her private apartment, Eunice and the other handmaids robed their tremulous young mistress in her wedding garments. They carried on a steady stream of gay chattering so that her mind would not have time to dwell upon the parting from her mother whom she adored.

There was laughter closely mixed with tears and ready blushes displaced too soon by lilylike pallor. When she rested her slim fingers on Eunice's arm, in gentle caress, the chill of Calanthe's flesh struck terror to the heart of her handmaid.

"What is it, sweet?" she asked at last. "Why have your hands the chill of death? The hour ar-

rives when you are to be joined in wedlock to the
one whom you worship. Your mind is secure in the
fact that he adores you above all else — and only
to-day was he made the idol of all Syracuse and
victor in the great chariot race. You have all things
to make you delirious with joy; and underneath it all
I know there lurks a dread. Of what, I cannot
fathom. Will you not confide in me, dear one?
If there is aught that I can do, no matter at what
sacrifice, you know it shall be done."

Calanthe clung to her in sudden fright and sank
sobbing to her knees.

"Oh Eunice, there has been an unknown fear in
my heart the livelong day. I cannot fix it to any
cause, nor can I rid myself of it. It clutches at my
soul when I am gayest and shrivels the laughter on
my lips. It dances before my eyes, when my sight
is rosy, and draws a pall of black that shuts out the
sunshine."

Eunice caressed the bent head and shaking shoulders.

"It is the effect of your long period of anxiety,
while Pythias was at the wars. That, followed by
the great joy and excitement of his glorious homecoming and the later agitation of the games, has
played havoc with your health, dear. Cease weeping, foolish child! Would you hurry to your husband with orbs red-rimmed and swollen? It cannot
be at all pleasing for a man to take a weeping bride

to his arms. Look, Calanthe! There in the garden he awaits you. See how strong his body and how handsome his features. There is not a maid in Syracuse but envies you this day. What would they think if they could see you weep?"

"I do not want to weep," whispered Calanthe piteously. "I love him so, Eunice! With all the ardor of my heart I adore and worship him! I know that life can hold no greater joy than to belong to him for always — and yet, there is a something that grips my brain and warns me of approaching disaster."

"Walk to your bath and gaze upon your beauteous reflection," suggested Eunice slyly. "What you will see there would drive the tears from any eye. And when you have looked, stroll into the garden where they await you; and when you see the light of admiration and the pride of possession gleam from his dear eyes then will your sadness take wing. Oh, Calanthe, never has your beauty dazzled as it does this hour, as you stand there in your spotless wedding robes, white as the breast of a tender dove!"

"I will gaze at my reflection in his dear eyes. From this time forth will they be my twin mirrors. But I fear me they will flatter. I go. Oh, Eunice, I could weep with happiness — but I will not."

She trailed her glistening robes over the smooth, green sward. Under a huge tree her mother held

gay converse with Damon and Pythias. In spite
of charitable intentions she found it in her heart
to resent this devoted friendship. Nay, one could
not call it friendship, according to the common
definition. This was something vital, of the sublim-
ity of deathless love. And was there room in the
life of one man for two such loves?

Damon turned and caught sight of her dazzling
white robes through the green foliage. He laid a
gentle hand on Pythias' shoulder and revolved him,
slowly, till his eye, too, caught the lovely picture.

With arms extended, and eyes earnestly fixed on
his, Calanthe advanced and did not halt until, her
head on his broad breast and his arms clasping her,
she murmured against his cheek:

"I love you, my own true Knight. Never must
you leave me. For I will flourish only on your
breast. And if it be withdrawn from my support,
will I fade and die. Hold me to you closely for
all time and I will ask from the gods no other favor
all my life long."

Damon looked upon the two, so beautiful in their
young love dream and smiled with a great joy.

"Ne'er before have you known the completeness
of life, my Pythias," he said softly. "With this
sweet flower in your heart, will you be able to achieve
even greater things than formerly. A love like
yours and hers makes all things possible. Oh, cherish her well; for her heart is pure — and all yours,

alone. See, on yonder dial the sun proclaims that 'tis but a short hour to the festival. My heart is light within my breast to think that I am able to see my dearest friend accomplish his greatest wish."

The hoof beats of a horse driven to its topmost speed, echoed loudly, through the trees. A tall, spare figure, dark of skin, bounded swiftly over the path and dropped to one knee before Damon.

"Lucullus!" the stately Senator spoke his disapproval. "What brings you? Have I not told you times without number that when I am on friendly visits, you must not follow or summon me on foolish pretext?"

"Oh, my lord!" gasped the slave, "this is no foolish pretext. But a moment since a messenger from the Senate galloped up to your house to bid you hasten there immediately. The members of your faction implore your speed, for Dionysius has been declared a king!"

Damon bent and dragged Lucullus to his feet.

"Has *been* declared, you say?" he questioned, unbelieving. "Is there not a slip in your way of joining the words? Do you not mean he *desires* to be named a king? Think well, Lucullus!"

"Nay, my lord," declared the slave vehemently, "' *has been* ' is the message as I received it. Oh, please, my lord, hasten to where thy presence is sore needed."

Pythias stepped forward and twined his arm

through that of his friend. His face, so lately
steeped in smiles, had shadowed.

"He is sore needed here," he rebuked Lucullus.
"Would have him leave me at the hour of my wedding feast, to fight for a thankless city?"

"Have you not fought for that same city?"

"But in warrior's fashion, my Damon, which
is —"

"Which is no different in principle than that of
statesman. Only in method are they unlike — and
yours the greater peril. A king! Think on't,
Pythias! Now are we and our wretched city un-
done. But, by the gods, will I oppose him, e'en
though Aetna vomit fire on his behalf!"

"Go you to the Senate, now, before the hour
for our festivities?" Pythias, doubting his ears,
searched his friend's face for answer.

"Assuredly I go," was the amazed retort. "Do
you suppose that I could remain away and let the
coward Senate sanction this dastardly deed, without
my words of — Ah! I have forgot my sword. As
guest at thy banquet, my Pythias, I came unarmed
— give me your weapon."

Pythias' hand closed on the sword's hilt and
pushed to one side Damon's eager fingers.

"What use will you make of it, should I give it
to your keeping?"

"No matter!" Damon reached impatiently for
the steel.

"DIONYSIUS, KING? BY ALL THE GODS, I WILL OPPOSE HIM!"

Universal Film Manufacturing Co.

"DO NOT DELAY ME, SWEET," HE IMPLORED.

Calanthe threw herself upon her lover's breast, her white arms tight about his neck.

"Stay his mad passion, dear one!" she pleaded wildly; "by my love do I beseech you."

"You go to the Senate? Then go I with you," said Pythias quietly.

Calanthe tightened her grasp convulsively.

"Nay, you must not! You shall not!" she screamed, in shrill terror.

"He shall not," exclaimed Damon decisively. "Give me your sword, Pythias. I promise on the faith of an old friendship that I will do naught in passion. Come, Calanthe, sweet, assume thy right and take him deeper into the garden where he may learn the names of all of your favorite flowers. Soon the hour for the sweet rite will come and then —" he sighed deeply and clasped his feverish brow with a trembling hand.

"Nay, Damon, Calanthe knows not what is at stake. I must —"

"You must remain here, at her side. And may the gods pour over your dear heads their choicest blessings. Farewell, my well beloved friend. If I am not here in person, yet will my heart be beside you at the banquet hall, when your feast is merriest. And, who knows, it may be possible that I return to see you united. Farewell, sweet maid — and you, stanchest of friends."

"Damon!" called Pythias, making an effort to

break from the soft arms that bound him fast. "Damon! I —"

Calanthe pressed her soft cheek against his and clung to him in wondrous sweetness.

"On your wedding day, my knight, think you 'tis proper that you call 'O Damon!' in great distress, when here, upon your breast, there lives a maid whose heart hungers for your lips to breathe 'O Calanthe, *dearest!*'"

The powerful warrior enclosed his sweet burden in all-protecting arms and inclined his head till his full, red lips brushed just the edge of her rosy ear.

"O Calanthe, *dearest,* best beloved!" he breathed, with fervent passion.

# CHAPTER XIII

## A FRIEND'S STRONG ARM

"YOU do not scorn my deep friendship for Damon, do you, dearest?" Pythias searched the face of his loved one with anxious eagerness. "I cannot well expect a maid to understand the profoundness of it. 'Tis not like the love of man and woman that can be severed when assaulted by an unkind word, or deed — and be ne'er thought of again. 'Tis not the love that is slain through pride or pique. Nay, no matter what my Damon's words or deeds, always will the deep walls of my heart be open to him and likewise will my strong, right arm do battle for his cause!"

Calanthe, murmuring in petulant fashion, unclasped her dimpled arms from about her lover's neck and wandered a little way from him. In her childish pettishness, she crushed, under her tiny, white sandals, a clump of purple violets.

Arria, her mother, spoke her disapproval.

"If in her obstinacy she will not understand, then would I not waste both patience and breath in trying to explain. In her willful heart she knows full well

that a friendship such as yours for Damon is unusual in this world of deceit and conspiracy among
men. Yet she will not grant its beauty, because her
jealousy is roused and she fears your love for her
will be diminished by this other drain. 'Twere well
to punish such perverseness! "

Pythias took hold of one little, trusting hand and
drew his sweet one back to the shelter of his arms.
She hid a scarlet cheek in the folds of his tunic.

" I shall have to spend all the idle hours of my
life in trying to persuade her that naught but deep
love for her sweet self fills this worthless heart of
mine," he murmured indulgently. " But also must
she learn that whate'er I'd do in friendship's name,
for Damon, that would he do for me — and more."

" It would render your cup of happiness complete
if he could escape the Senate in time to reach here
for the sweet feast that is to join you," observed
Arria, with gentle understanding. " Think you he
will find it possible? "

Suddenly there arose from without the garden
gates the sounds of violent controversy.

Pythias leaned forward to ascertain, if possible,
what the trouble was. He heard a rough, deep
voice shout insolent taunts. These were always followed by a chorus of derisive epithets.

Arria, in great distress, begged him to discover
who had chosen the quiet spot before her home for
challenges and the measuring of swords.

But before he had chance to step outside the gate, Lucullus, panting and disheveled, appeared before him.

"My master craves your indulgence for his persistent intrusion upon your happy hours, but in trying to leave this dwelling, on his way to the Senate he found that Dionysius had forestalled him by placing outside the walls, as guard, a band of ruffians headed by Procles. With drawn swords and shields brandishing in air, do they seek to prevent my master from reaching the Senate in time to offer protest to this crowning. So he bade me hasten to you and tell you of his plight."

"Where is he, Lucullus?" demanded Pythias, driving his helmet far down upon his brow.

"Hark! From here can you hear the impertinent threats of the hired minions of Dionysius. Right outside yonder gates is he detained at the sword's point."

With a muttered oath that boded ill for the hirelings, Pythias seized from an attendant the latter's sword and started down the pathway. Midway in his flight he was pursued by Calanthe who besought him earnestly to beware the violence of the men in the employ of his bitterest enemy.

"Do not delay me, sweet," he implored and shook loose her clinging arms. "Each moment that is lost diminishes Damon's chances of reaching the Senate in time."

"I will accompany you, then," she declared obstinately. "I cannot stay this side the wall to listen to menacing sounds, not knowing how you fare."

Pythias dashed ahead and sought the main entrance of the dwelling. Once outside he ran to where he saw the band of ruffians threatening his friend. With sword raised in defiance he bore down upon them.

"Hold, ye cowards!" he shouted in ringing scorn and plunged into their midst like some fury sent by the gods. "Why, Procles, what game is this you play? Are you not ashamed to rush upon a single man, in coward numbers? Bah, I have seen you do good work in battle time and so I took you for a soldier. Fie upon you!"

"They are orders to be obeyed," was the sullen answer. "It has been decreed that this man be kept from the Senate for the day — and we have kept him."

"Nay, be not so calm in your assurance," warned Pythias grimly. "Not yet have you kept my friend, a Senator, from his rightful seat in the Senate house, nor will you. You know well I am not given to empty threats. You also know the strength of my right arm and the clean cut it makes when my lifted sword descends. And, by the gods, I swear that unless you and your band of scoundrels stand back, and give Damon free passage, will I hew down as many as I may, before I am overwhelmed!"

The group broke into sullen mutterings and half-affrighted, half abashed, fell back a few paces to wait the decision of their leader.

" I know the meagre sum that Dionysius promised you, when the errand was arranged for," ventured Pythias cautiously, as he saw them confer among themselves. " He does not pay well in proportion to the dastardliness of his missions. So look for an increase in your pockets if you fall back without another attempt to prevent Damon's anxious haste."

" Because you are a warrior like ourselves, will we observe your wishes," growled Procles, wondering what his fate would be when Dionysius found out his treachery.

" Amend your statement, my friend," said Pythias with smiling sarcasm. " Because I am a warrior who can plate your fingers with gold, instead of silver, is what you meant to say. Well, here it is."

He cast a small, soft leathern pouch upon the ground at the feet of Procles and turned to speed Damon on his way. The older man grasped his hand in fervent grip, while tears suffused his eyes.

" Thanks to you, my gallant soldier and fast friend, I am safe and free to proceed in my poor attempt to halt this monster ere he complete the ruination of our beloved city, our fickle Syracuse! Now go you again to your sweet maid's side."

Calanthe ran forward, and, in deep remorse,

thrust her little hands into the sincere grasp of Pythias' friend. His noble face was lined with the cares that were being thrust, so unceasingly, upon him. In her heart a great pity stirred. Pythias, delighted to see her capitulate so completely, drew her again to his side.

"Now must Damon hasten to the Senate, dear one; may the gods watch over his path, and grant that he may quell the tyrant who sought so basely to humiliate me and now seeks to make us all slaves, under his iron hand."

Together they watched him descend the hill. At last, a mere moving speck, they saw him disappear between the huge pillars of the senate house.

Philistius sprang from his bench as the irate Senator, his locks disarranged, his breath coming in quick, short gasps, dashed into the senate room and raised an enraged, protesting arm.

"Who is't breaks in so rudely to disturb our grave deliberations?" he thundered.

Damon halted before the president's seat and looked upon him with scorn.

"Who is it?" he echoed. "Why, a Senator, my good Philistius. None but a Senator. But one who has so many biting questions with which to ply you that methinks, before your tongue has answered them all, must it call for water to ease its parched surfaces!"

"Seat yourself and wait until the important business of the day be finished," commanded Philistius angrily.

"That I will not!" exclaimed Damon, moving still a step nearer. "What strange times have we fallen upon that, in the open streets, nay at the very doors of a friend's dwelling, have I encountered soldiers and satellites with brandished swords, attempting to obstruct my way hither? Whose mouth in this assembly here gave privilege to a ruffian soldier, that he dare hold a pointed weapon to my throat and threaten boldly to bathe it in my blood, should I protest? Answer me that, O Philistius, and we will have done with the first question."

Disregarding Damon's burning rage and his dramatic interrogation, Philistius apologetically addressed the Senate.

"Let not this rash man, with his unbridled tongue, disturb the grave consideration with which we were discussing the —"

With a savage gesture, Damon wheeled upon his fellow-Senators.

"Aye, that is what he will do! It is for that that he has fled from the wedding festivities of his dearest friend and been accosted by a band of hired scoundrels, upon the public streets. It is for that, that he will talk until the breath that fills his lungs shall be exhausted."

From a corner of the third bench, a ponderous figure, but lately arrived, rose and walked to the front of the senate chamber. He was greeted with much acclaim. Assuming a still more central position, he coolly pushed to one side the imposing figure of the protesting Senator, and opened his mouth to speak.

"I do but require to know from you," he began in oily accents, "what now would be our likely fate had we not had to guide us a hand and head as marvelously skillful as that of our Dionysius?"

A moment's pause. Waiting for the applause that he so thoroughly expected, Damocles blinked his small eyes and smiled encouragement with his fat lips. Damon took advantage of the silence.

"What fate, you ask, O unctuous pessimist? Well, here's your answer. The fate of freemen, in the full exercise of all a freeman's rights. Free to walk unmolested in the streets. Free to speak and act in our councils. Free to cast to earth a man who dares declare himself a —"

Philistius stepped down from the president's chair and raised his arms in supplication.

"I do entreat you, Senators," he petitioned, trying to drown the excited tones of the speaker, "to protect me from this scolding damagogue."

Damon whirled upon him in mighty wrath. His right arm raised, with clenched fist, seemed about to descend upon his maligning chief.

"Demagogue!" he cried hoarsely. "Who was the demagogue, who, at my challenge, was denounced

and silenced by this same Senate? When you have
once begun the list of accusations, follow it to its
end — and rest assured that you, and not myself,
will suffer most before 'tis done."

Damocles, in half-drowsy protest, stepped between.

"Silence, Damon, silence!" he reprimanded.
"Let the council use its privilege."

At sound of the whining voice that strove so hard
to be sonorous, Damon bent low, in mock humility.

"Who bids me silence?" he questioned with cutting sarcasm. "Ah! 'Tis none other than Damocles! The pliant willow — Damocles! The pro-
ficient parasite — Damocles! The fawning fool —
Damocles! What is it that you dare propose?
That I be silent and listen to your words of wisdom?
Very well, that much will I grant you. I shall be
silent as the tomb — for a limited time. Proceed."

Damon took his seat. His right arm rested
lightly upon his knee. His left, concealed beneath
the folds of his crimson-bordered white toga,
guarded carefully its burden.

# CHAPTER XIV

## FROM GLADNESS INTO GLOOM

" AND these are impertinent and strangely fashioned pansies. Upon each velvety bloom there is concealed a saucy face — that is if you look with the eye of understanding. And these are violets, brought first from Parina, which is the city of their origin. And these — lilies which do contain in their tiny bells a perfume that delights the nostrils, and these —"

Pythias gazed over his shoulder toward the city. His eyes were troubled, his lips compressed in dread suspense.

" You do not listen," objected Calanthe with petulance. " Did not Damon bid me tell you of all my favorite plants and flowers? And when I do, you reward me with an unseeing gaze and a mind that wanders."

" Ah, dear one, if you could know how I fear for Damon's safety. Those men who are plotting so vilely against our fair city, with no thought save for their secret gain, will stop at nothing to achieve their ambitions. Damon will oppose them — and he took my sword! "

Calanthe felt him tremble under her loving clasp. She leaned her head against his shoulder and sought to comfort him.

"I was amazed that you saw fit to give it to him," she said gently. "Why did you not remain firm in your refusal?"

"He promised me that he would do naught in passion — and his promise is more binding than the solemn oaths of ten men!"

He clapped his hands suddenly. A slave standing in a grove nearby obeyed the summons.

"Haste you to the senate house as fast as feet can fly and bring me word of Damon. It is now a full ten minutes since I dispatched a messenger and he has not returned. Bring news! Whether it be bad or ill. I must have news!"

The man did not wait for the final words. His body was already a brownish blur upon the roadway.

"Will you hear more of flowers?" pleaded Calanthe, desolate in her failure to amuse him.

"I will hear of one flower, dear. Never will I close my ears to news of you, my own true flower. What is't that you resemble, sweet? A moss rosebud, or a dainty bluebell? In my eyes shall you always be a very garland of blossoms, with every beauty of each and the perfume of them all. Ah, I fear 'tis a sorry bridal day for you, my loved one. It is an unkind fate that —"

A messenger, whose brow dripped sweat as he pushed back his matted locks, ran through the trees and knelt before the pair. Pythias shook him impatiently.

"What is the delay? Speak, fool! What is your message?"

"I have none," panted the slave. "When I approached the senate house those on guard recognized that I belonged to you, O master, and drove me hence at the point of daggers drawn from their wide belts!"

"And you heard?"

"I heard naught but a hum of conversation within the walls. Only once a shout arose — and it was quickly stifled."

"A shout?" Pythias questioned him in an agony of doubt. "Was it Damon's voice that shouted?"

"I do not know, my lord. It would require a closer knowledge of his voice, to say if it were his or no."

"What did you see?"

"I saw nothing. Not one has entered or left the Senate since I arrived. But on every step does a soldier stand and guard, as if in expectation of trouble."

"And naught else that your eye rested on, struck you as peculiar? Neither on the way there, nor on the homeward trip?"

"O my master, I had almost forgot in my disappointment at returning empty-handed. As I was driven from the senate steps, the hangings concealing the wide portal of a dwelling opposite, were pulled aside and I did witness, sitting at a table surrounded by his friends, Dionysius, splendid in robes of state. He was smiling broadly at the sallies of his satellites and —"

"Ah!" Pythias breathed more freely. "Then Dionysius is not within the senate house? That is good news, even if you have brought no other."

The slave rose and fell back to await further summons. Arria came from the house and moved toward them, her face betraying her unhappiness.

"The hour has arrived. The maids are waiting with arms piled high with blossoms plucked to strew upon your path. The solemn wedding feast is awaiting you and the guests are assembled and eagerly demand your coming. Come, my daughter. Once more before you leave your mother's house let her enfold you in her arms and kiss your brow, as was her wont when she held you, a rosy infant, to her breast."

Calanthe left her lover's side and twined her arms lovingly about her adored parent.

"Do not speak as if I were to leave you and go to a far distant place, my mother. Always will a great portion of my heart be yours. In years to come, if I have children of my own, I will but wish

that they may love me with one half the tenderness
I feel for you."

Arria folded her closely to her breast and pressed
a long, solemn kiss upon the snowy brow.

"Now we will proceed to the feast," she announced. "See, Calanthe? Here come your
maids. Are they not beautiful, garbed in their shining bridal robes and with their fair young arms so
choked with perfumed blossoms? Art prepared to
start?"

"Yea," murmured the little bride, extending a
timid hand to her lord.

"Attend a moment," he requested, a hint of
apology in the words. "I am sore distressed. If
we can wait but a moment more, the second messenger will be here with word of Damon. Then
will I go to the feast with lighter heart. If it were
possible, I would postpone the feast an hour longer
so that he could be present."

"We cannot delay even for a moment," declared
Calanthe, racked with a return of jealousy.
"Would you have the freshly culled flowers wither,
so that our pathway will be strewn with dead petals?
An ill omen e'en before the festival. Come, join
your hand to mine, my Pythias. The maids approach."

"I cannot!"

"Cannot?" Calanthe flared under the finality in
his voice. "When your bride bids you to the feast,

you lag behind with eyes fastened on the dusty city and languish for word of a friend?"

"Be patient but a moment longer, sweet. The messenger must return at any instant. You would not have me plight my troth with mind upset and aching heart? Do not be harsh, my beloved. Just a moment longer!"

"Speak to him, mother," implored the girl, trying her best to choke back angry tears. "Tell him that I will not be flaunted before my friends. Why, even my maids will smile me to scorn if I am made sit back to welcome a slave who will tell if Damon is without, or within, or vanished from the scene!"

"I can understand his state of mind," remonstrated her mother. "He fears a dastardly deed from which he could protect his friend were he there beside him."

"But he is not beside him, nor could he be." Calanthe's tones rose shrill and hysterical. "Has he not told me, often, that a soldier may not lift his helmet in the senate house. What good will be accomplished by his fixed watching from a hill?"

"I think it would be wiser to proceed and have the festival over," acknowledged Arria, reluctantly. "It is of such short duration. Then can he go to procure news himself."

Standing where he could obtain the best view of the winding road, Pythias, with anxious brow, kept a strained watch upon the approach.

Calanthe, with crimson cheeks and flashing eyes, ran to his side and tapped him sharply on the arm. He started, suddenly, from his troubled revery. And when he saw her white robed figure close beside him stretched out a tender arm and sought to draw her to him.

" Well? " she questioned with strange feverishness.

" A moment longer," he begged.

She threw back her head and laughed. A laugh that was not good to hear and illsuited to her dainty beauty.

" Come now — or not at all ! " she challenged resolutely, her eyes alight with a harsh brilliancy.

Pythias stared as if unhearing. He seized her elbows and looked deep into her hostile eyes.

" Why, Calanthe, dearest," he murmured, hurt and broken.    " You did not mean to —"

" I have not uttered a word that I did not mean from the depths of my heart," she interrupted defiantly.    " Do not waste breath upon a useless repetition of my name, or in a string of endearing terms. I have lost interest in words.    If you would give me proof of your love, do as I request.    I would have laughed in derision had anyone suggested to me, ever, that I, Calanthe, would so far lose her maidenly reserve as to beseech a man to drag her to her nuptial feast."

Pythias faced her sternly.

"In a moment of possible tragedy," he accused coldly, "you speak of your lightly wounded pride and give me choice of flying to the feast, sick at heart — or not at all. Cannot your mind grasp the horror of this thing? Think you that, I, who, I am sure, have proved my adoration of you a hundredfold, will consent to give such sinful added proof? For 'twould be but sinful to face the festive rites, when my dear friend, surrounded by his enemies and unprotected by my presence, may perish? You ask that which I cannot do."

Calanthe's scarlet cheeks faded to a ghastly pallor. Her lips parted as if to question, but no sound came. Her rounded arms that had been clasped so proudly to her breast, dropped, lifeless, at her sides, spilling their burden of waxen lilies. She bent her head and looked upon their spotlessness.

"I remember once I said that lilies were beauteous blooms for shrine or for tomb — but not for love. Not for love," she repeated in vague soliloquy.

# CHAPTER XV.

## A FREEMAN'S LEGACY

A SINGLE ray of the bright, afternoon sun shrank along the marble floor of the senate house, now splashing into a brilliant pool of gold, now wavering and fading, governed by a blowing clump of foliage directly outside the window by which it entered.

The cool breeze penetrated to the inner room where excited statesmen welcomed it, and breathed with renewed delight.

Philistius bent forward in his chair, kept a sharp eye on the figure of Damon, silent and forbidding in his corner of the bench. He noted the convulsive opening and closing of his hand, the fire that darted from his eye as words in praise of Dionysius fell from Damocles' lips.

"And so do we prove that 'twas he who governed our fair city, though we have feigned the governing, ourselves," declaimed the speaker, trembling lest he should forget the words his master has thrust in his mouth.

"This being so," interrupted Philistius sternly, "who is so fit as he, in this extremity, to be the

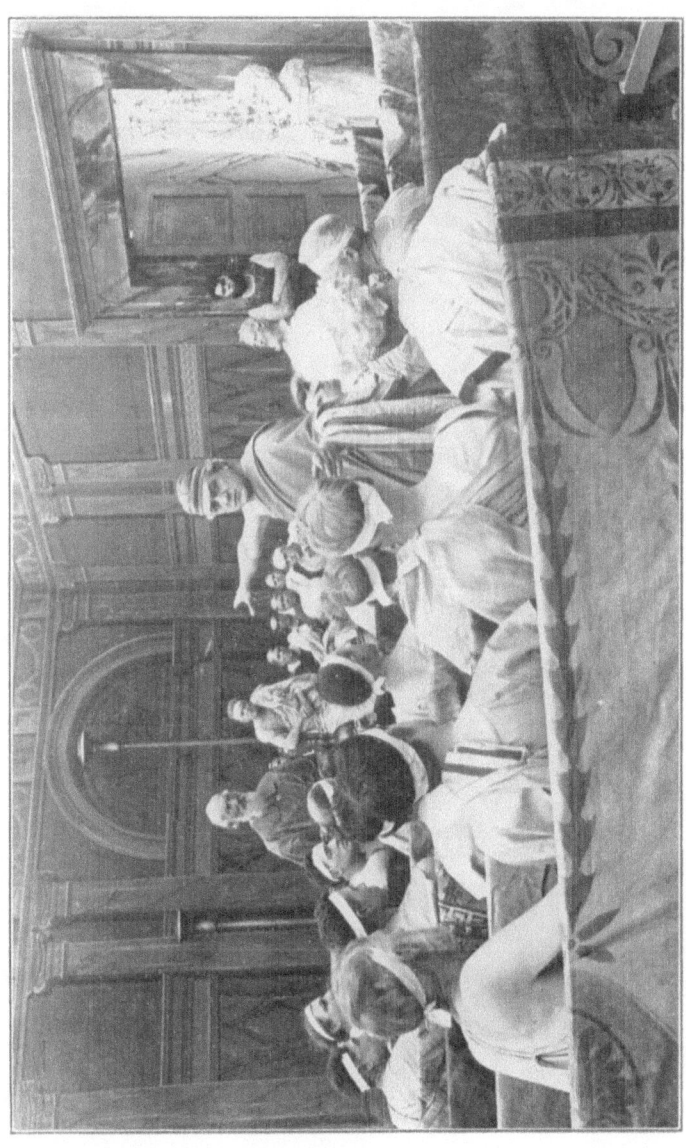

DAMON BOUNDED FROM THE BENCH. "A KING! A KING! KNOW YOU WHAT THAT MEANS?"

LOYAL TO THE CAUSE OF FREEDOM, THE SENATORS URGE DAMON'S RESISTANCE.

single pillar on whose strength all power should rest? What need has the state of our crowded and contentious councils? And therefore, Senators — countrymen from henceforth — I do submit that we dissolve. That for the purpose of a better and a wiser government and for the general welfare of our great city we choose as king — Dionysius — our natural ruler."

Damon bounded from the bench, his face flaming to purple, the arteries swelling to ropelike prominence on his temples.

"A king! A *king!*" he shouted. "Are your ears sealed, O fathers, that you hear not? Or do you hear and suffer your lips to be dumb? A king! Know you what it means?"

From various points of the room came voices raised in approbation.

"I do approve," said one.

"And I."

"And so do I," declared a third.

Damocles turned to the amazed Damon wearing a look of smug gratification that seemed designed for his rippling jowls, so well he wore it.

"All are content," he remarked.

Damon strode indignantly to the steps that led to the president's chair.

"All? All are content? A nation's right betrayed and none dares open his mouth to shout, 'Nay, I am not content!' Content? Mark well my form, for here am I, a Senator, and from the depths of my being do I cry to the echo of the vaulted heavens: 'Slaves! Parricides! Assassins, all!' I blush to look around and think that once I called you men. What are your thoughts that with your own free, willing hands you tie a stone each to his brother's neck and drown like dogs, in the tide of this disgrace! What strange hellborn power, working for evil, in your minds, has persuaded you to dig your own dark graves and creep into them to die, while common cutthroats stand above and moisten the earth that covers you with the blood of your children and their children?"

"I have not sanctioned it," a voice, afraid of its own sound upon the air, drifted to the fore.

"Nor I!"

"Nor have I!" the refrain gained slightly in the power of repetition.

Damon stretched out his hand in gratitude.

"For these few voices, thanks. But, alas, they sound too lonely. Oh, open up your hearts, my brothers! *Think! Think!* There you sit, inanimate as if you, yourselves, were of one material with the benches on which you crouch! See! I will not chide nor rail, nor curse you. With blinded eyes and weak words, with heart shattered by this fell blow, do I *implore* you. If I were gifted with a flow of words that could paint pictures for your eyes to gaze upon, would I speak of our fathers' sacred

images; of old men, our grandsires; of affrighted
mothers, holding forth, in shaking hands, the squirming bodies of their innocent infants, whom you would
make slaves. But I am not blessed with eloquence.
My tongue makes but a poor attempt to put in
gilded dress the agonies of my heart. So do I
but entreat you to think once again."

Philistius rose from his chair and descended the
steps. His lips broadened into a grin of ridicule.
With stately step he found his way to the main entrance of the senate house. There he raised an
arm, in signal, to one who was standing without.

The eyes of all the Senators were fastened on him,
as he remained there, motionless. Curiosity ran
riot. A subtle whispering rustled on the air.
Damon, on the steps, bent forward in tense concen-
tration, held the folds of his toga more closely to
his body. His eyes burned into those of his hostile
brothers.

Suddenly, there was a ringing shout of triumph
from the guards outside. Philistius extended his
hand, grasped one stretched out to meet it, and
turning, led Dionysius to the center of the senate
chamber! Dionysius, whose gorgeous robes of
state, donned to lend regal atmosphere, trailed over
the marble blocks and weighted his squat shoulders.

Left, unsupported, the cynosure of eyes both
friendly and inimical, he raised a deprecatory hand
in answer to the cheering.

" Is this indeed the vote? " his first words, soft, with unbelief well-feigned, inflamed Damon to frenzy!

" There is no vote! " he exclaimed violently. " Philistius, keep your seat! Keep in your places, Senators! "

Seemingly oblivious to the interruption, Dionysius spoke again.

" I ask, is this the vote? "

" Oh, gracious liege and sovereign, it is indeed the vote, echoed from every throat here, in reverential acknowledgment of your dominion." Philistius voiced the lie with glib serenity.

Damon forced his way through the group of admiring satellites. He stood glaring fiercely into the sunken eyes of the newly proclaimed king.

" I say it is not the vote! " he ground out through his tightly clamped teeth. " Think you that by criminal process you can build a throne in this, our senate house? "

" In my capacity as head and organ of the city council I do asseverate it is the vote. All hail, then, Dionysius, King of Syracuse, all hail! "

Philistius dropped in servile worship. With one accord the senators, save those few whose faint dissenting voices had been submerged, and Damon, bent the knee.

Dionysius, with superbly simulated self-abasement, mounted the steps of the chair of state, his

kingly mantle of royal purple splashed with gold,
flowing over the steps, from the topmost one to
the base. Having attained the summit, he leaned
his weight upon the president's table and raised a
hand in benediction.

Damon, aghast at the triumph of the conspiracy,
stared, wild-eyed and raving.

"My country! Oh, my ruined, pillaged country."

Dionysius addressed his subjects:

"That we may have fitting quiet and solemnity
in which to assume, with dignity, our garb of power,
we do now take our first right; and order from this,
that was the senate house, the rash and tumultuous
men who would still tamper with the city's peace.,
We have no objection to rivalry that has weight,
but this, the vain contentious variety, is preposterous
and vexing!"

With a low, wild cry, Damon bounded up the
steps. He thrust his rage-distorted face so close to
the cold cynical eyes, that his hot breath seared the
paleness of Dionysius' cheek.

"There is no rivalry between us!" he hissed,
pressing still closer. "Only one move is left by
which to still forever your base ambitions. Know
you what it is?"

Cowed by the nearness of the man, Dionysius
sought support lest he fall backwards to the platform floor.

"Know you what it is?" reiterated Damon, following, inch by inch, as the other retreated.

"Away!   Out of the Senate!" commanded the king, his voice breaking with hysterical terror.

Damon's lips shrank back from his teeth in a widening, ghastly smile.   From his throat issued a weirdly guttural chuckle.

"Know you what it is?" he repeated with maddened persistency.

But now, his body, pressed against the shrinking man, in calm, tenacious obstinacy, had forced him to the extreme side of the platform where he clung to the wall to save himself from the sheer drop to the floor.

As if congealed where they stood, the Senators looked upon the drama that was enacted.   Not a man but felt that his very breathing was a disturbing element in the dead silence.

Damon, his forehead-band pushed from his head and hanging by one whitening lock, his face purple — blotched, with insane rage,— his eyes narrowed to two fiery slits, in his head, thrust his feet forward and pressed his knee against the thigh of his shrinking enemy.

Dionysius suffocated by his nearness, his soul quaking with guilty dread, threw his arms across his face and cowered in his corner.   They made two striking, tragic spots — the crimson and the royal purple splashed with gold — against the marble walls.

"*Know you what it is?*"

Maddened by the dogged repetition and the blood-curdling fate that it suggested, Dionysius screamed a command:

"My guards! My guards! Here! I —"

"Know you what it is?" the phrase drilled the craven brain. The new king swayed upon his numbed feet.

"My guards!" he shrieked helplessly.

A chorus of hoarse shouts and the trampling of many feet sounded from without.

The bronze doors of the senate house were swung back until they struck the granite pillars with a harsh and deafening clang. Procles and his soldiers rushed over the threshold.

Blinking in the half-light, they stood without comprehending the situation.

"I proclaim him a traitor! Seize him!" yelled Dionysius, with shrill impatience.

"Traitor, say you? Traitor! Well, then, before they seize this traitor, receive, O King, a freeman's legacy!"

With a mighty wrench Damon tore loose his left arm from its confining folds. The force of his gesture ripped his toga from his shoulder. It dropped to his hip, exposing his splendid chest and massive arm.   In his clenched fist the glitter of a short sword rent the gloom.

As the weapon was about to descend, Procles bounded forward, and, with a flying leap, seized the upraised wrist and bore it backward, wrenching the arm in the socket and almost tearing the ligaments from their fastenings.

In the first agonizing pain, Damon whitened and swayed as if to swoon.   The voice of Dionysius brought him back to consciousness.

" Behold this proud, assassinating demagogue! " he exclaimed; his bravery returned at seeing his assailant in the grip of two strong men.   " He whets his dagger in philosophy, this pupil of the cutthroat school!  His last deed is done, however.   For here we do condemn him to a public death; and from his blood will we mix a rare cement to our monarchy! "

His white lips compressed in agonizing pain, his face ashen, Damon flung back his retort:

" To one who never yet has wished to survive his country, death is indeed a royal gift.   Lead me to the scaffold, sever my head from my suffering body, yet will my dead lips move once again and, gushing blood, form the word ' Traitor! ' "

# CHAPTER XVI

## A LIFE FOR A LIFE!

THE wail of strange stringed instruments was wafted from the interior of the house. The maids laid upon the stone steps their floral burdens, and gazed sadly to where Pythias strove to bring back to reason their angered mistress.

"How extravagant are his promises, now that she is deaf to them!" thought Eunice, and curled her lips in unconscious sarcasm. "Methinks it is the habit of men to appreciate that which they have only when it has slipped so far from their possession that it requires mighty effort to bring it back. Yea, that is the mold of men,— mayhap of women, too," she added, reluctant to credit the latter statement's truth, however.

"I will attend her to her chamber," she announced, her angry eyes scorning the figure of Pythias.

"It is not necessary," he rebuked sternly. "I will bear her hither in my arms if she desires to go. Do you wish me to place you on your couch, sweet?" He bent and attempted to look into the eyes that were turned from his.

"Can you not see that she is in no mood or condition for questions?" exclaimed Eunice, appealing to Arria for corroboration. "If you will let me soothe her for a short time, then will she recover her normal state and come into the garden, her rosy, happy self once more."

"Calanthe, turn not your dear eyes from mine," pleaded Pythias, piteously. "Am I grown so distasteful to your heart that you cannot bear to look upon my features? See, I make promise to do all that you desire. And on my knees, I'll beg forgiveness for my obstinate refusals of a moment since."

The white, forbidding face held no sign of yielding. Arria touched her daughter's hand and smoothed her soft cheek.

"There must be forgiveness granted when forgiveness is sought," she advised gently. "Always in the lives of man and woman do occasions arise when the mantle of humility must envelop one or the other. Remember that if its folds fall upon your beloved to-day, and you refuse him absolution, so will he turn a deaf ear, when on the morrow the cloak enshroud you. Forgive and be forgiven, child. Well learned, this formula will do much to bring you everlasting happiness."

Eunice not daring to add to, or detract from, the counsel given, looked on, filled with pity for her sweet Calanthe, who had in one short day learned so completely that e'en the brightest sunshine and the bluest sky can be darkened by ungracious acts and harsh words.

Pythias tightened his hold upon her in dread lest she disregard her mother's admonition and dart from his arms in anger. Her body, weak from mental struggling and many tears, her mind cleared and receptive, Calanthe lifted her white arms and brought her lover's mouth down to her soft lips. In a long, solemn kiss were all hard thoughts brushed away, and smiles reigned where frowns and deep lines had been.

"Will you proceed to the feast now?" asked Pythias, anxious to prove on the instant how firm was his purpose to please.

"First must I seek my chamber and repair the ravages that this long waiting has put upon me." Calanthe smiled as she made answer: "Now will I keep you chafing with impatience, outside my door, while I call out to you, 'Be not impatient, Pythias, 'tis but with a moment longer.' Come, Eunice, you must smooth with perfumed cream the tracks that frowns have left behind them; and bathe to their accustomed brilliance my reddened eyes. I would be as fair a bride as e'er trod bridal dance. Come make me so, my Eunice."

Pythias watched her disappear through her draped balcony. Then only did the dread thoughts return. As if waking to the realization that he had been unfaithful to a solemn vow, he bounded to the spot from which he could obtain a full view of the road. Then, on the dusty whiteness, a dark spot that flew over the ground drew nearer and nearer.

Pythias pressed tense fingers to his throbbing temples. He could feel the terror in that bounding figure. Before he knew the message that it brought, his soul was plunged into an agony of despair, firm in the knowledge that the worst had happened.

Nearer and nearer flew the dark spot. The short brown tunic and swarthy legs could now be distinguished. Dreading the moment when the actual words would fall upon his apprehensive ears, Pythias stood as if turned to stone, his eyes straining in their sockets, his lips dry and burning, parted by short, gasping breaths.

A moment longer! The man who had been the spot dashed through the trees and fell flat, his arms and legs outspread, before the young general. It was Lucullus! His black face blotched where dust had caked in the sweat that poured from his brow. His eyeballs bloodshot, his beady eyes rolling in an agony of terror, he sought to deliver his message. The lips moved, the tongue shot out from between the parched lips, but all that was audible were rasping sounds that rattled drily and then ceased.

" Damon? Your master? What — what —"

Lucullus rolled laboriously to his side. He at-

DIONYSIUS, WITH SUPERBLY SIMULATED SELF-ABASEMENT, MOUNTED THE STEPS OF THE CHAIR OF STATE.

"GO I MUST! MY FRIEND IS IN DANGER."

tempted to prop his aching body on one elbow and
thus rise, but strength had deserted his limbs.
Pythias slipped his hands under the slave's armpits
and lifted him, allowing him to rest his weight
against his own body.

"Now speak! Every moment wasted may mean
much to him. Tell me briefly. Tell me what —"

"O my lord," panted Lucullus, "I have brought
news that will rend your heart in two. And when
I have delivered it, then do I wish for naught but
to die. My master, my worshiped master, is — is
condemned to public death. But an hour they have
given him before he mounts the scaffolding and
bends his noble head to the murderous ax."

"Death! Public death! Condemned to
death!" Pythias muttered the words unintelligi-
bly. Then suddenly becoming lucid, "For what?
By whom?"

"For assaulting Dionysius when he had just been
declared king. He had a sword. He rarely carries one. And this was not his own. With the
weapon he sought to assassinate the sovereign, but
before he could accomplish it, was his sword-arm
half torn from its socket and he was taken prisoner.
O my lord, my master's dearest friend, can you not
do something to prevent this awful thing?"

The slave sank again to the ground, his black
body torn with sobs. He kissed the feet of Pythias
and besought him to hasten to the city. Then, half

dead from lack of food and over-straining, staggered to his feet and pointed a shaking hand toward the rooftops, glistening in the sun.

Pythias passed his dry palms over his burning forehead and following the pointed finger, could discern a slow procession moving from the senate house. It was headed by soldiers bearing spears, whose sharpened points caught the rays of the sun and glistened, at that great distance, like diamonds rolling in the sand.

In the center of these dazzling spear ends, he could detect a spot of white and crimson, and shining above it a whitened head. A dry sob shook his huge frame. He stretched his arms in piteous supplication toward the city, and, without a backward glance, rushed from the grove, Lucullus following at his heels.

All was quiet in Calanthe's garden. A mocking bird's taunting call quivered through the trees. A sudden breeze borne upward from the sapphire waters of the Mediterranean stirred the flower beds and filled the air with an intoxicating riot of perfume. From the temple the wailing of the stringed instruments was wafted to the gardens. The light laughter of maidens who pelted each other with roses, rang out with gay insistence.

Calanthe, radiant in her freshened robes, crept slyly from the portal. It was her intention to steal upon her lover, unsuspecting, and throw herself into his eager arms. She glanced about, cautiously. His form was nowhere visible. Oh! he was in hiding from her! 'Twas too bad he had forestalled her.

She darted lightly from corner to corner, peering behind huge tree trunks, stooping to part the spreading branches of flowering bushes. Not a vestige of his tunic or bright armor was to be seen.

Petulant at his success in eluding her, she called his name:

" Pythias! Come from your place of hiding. I am weary of searching. Pythias! Dear one! Disclose yourself."

The mocking bird's jeering call floated again on the breeze — then all was stillness.

In abrupt, petrifying fear, Calanthe turned her eyes toward the city. Far down the road, fleeing as if from death, instead of toward it, were two figures — and one was blond of curls, with stalwart form clad in polished armor.

# CHAPTER XVII

## LOST!

**D**OWN in the public square, the crowds that had assembled in the Circus at dawn of that same day, now satiated with games and the feasting and drinking that followed, again surged into the streets. Their dulled senses, anxious for sleep but a moment before, had been whipped to a new, keen excitement.

The news spread as will a tongue of flame upon a sea of oil. Those who had buried themselves behind barred doors and shuttered windows were roused by considerate neighbors, who knew how acute would be their disappointment were they to miss this marvelous event.

Along the streets, each by-way tributary adding its small stream to the flood of humanity in the main squares, poured the frenzied mob, now solemnly silent, now rumbling low, whether in protest or approbation, no one could determine.

In the center of the hollow square of soldiers, who carried their spears in readiness to defend, walked Damon. From his fine shoulders his toga hung in tatters. His flesh so fair in contrast to the sunbaked skins of warriors, showed milkwhite against the crimson of his torn mantle. His head well up and eyes defiant, though not bold, conveyed to the excited crowd that here was no craven — no trembling coward was about to find his fate. The spirit of a brave man mixed with the gravity of a philosopher and the keen intelligence of a statesman was to be sacrificed on the block.

As the people grew accustomed to the thought, there arose muffled threats and violent denunciations. These were quickly snuffed out, however, by an impressive spear point, or a well-aimed kick from a soldier's metal-tipped sandal.

When the procession had advanced halfway, a group of men issued from the main portal of the senate house and, posed upon the steps, presented a strange, gorgeous note on the background of this grim tragedy.

Dionysius, attended by his satellites, his crown upon his brow, gratified to think that his first act of royal authority was so spectacular in character, looked upon the scene in search of his servants to bear him, in his chair, to the spot of execution.

Damocles was sent to summon the negligent slaves. As his flat feet descended, ponderously, upon each successive step, he mused upon the happenings of the day.

He had played a tedious, uncomplaining part in

each event that had brought Dionysius a step nearer to the throne. In the crowning moment to-day, in the senate house, had he not acted as target for the violence of this same Damon, upon having proposed the kingly candidate? It was by the mercy of the gods that that audacious dagger had not been drawn at his plump throat. Yes, he had been a victim of insult and insinuation, but now his assailant was on his way to the headsman's block. *He* had met his fate. There was some satisfaction in that. Damocles' step was lighter at the thought, but only a few paces further on, it again grew weighty. Another thought had come. What, after all this service, was going to be his share? When he had made plaintive request for reward, before this, the answer had always been " Wait until 'tis accomplished."

Well, it had been accomplished. And yet here was he doing errands in the same manner, not one bit elevated from his former position of super-page. Damocles halted in his path and glanced back over his shoulder. His small eyes, blazing with sudden resentment, sought the royal purple spot that betrayed the arch-conspirator.

There came to him, in all its significance, the certain knowledge, that never, promises or no, would he get reward of any sort. His labors had been obtained, under false pretense and spurious promises. Angry humiliation overwhelmed him, and, in deep-dyed revenge upon his betrayer, Damocles went to his dwelling and did not seek for the chair-bearers of the king!

Before it turned into the adjoining square, the procession halted again to give the soldiers a chance to clear the choked thoroughfares.

Damon's eyes, unseeing, scanned the horizon. First he gazed toward Lutania, where he pictured his beautiful summer home nestling in its verdant setting. He could imagine, so easily, his wife and child, under the blossoming orange trees. His wife! His child!

Tears, unbidden, sprang to his eyes. He bent his head in shame. A man he was. And men, with right graven upon their hearts, go to their deaths uncomplaining. His vision cleared, he gazed aloft, to the nearest hill. There in the white marble temple, heavy with the scent of blossoms, was Pythias, his beloved friend, joined in wedlock to his sweet Calanthe. There would he have been, a happy spectator, if —

A wild shout rang out upon the air. The crowd parted as if cloven by a mighty sword. Coming toward him, with arms outstretched, was Pythias! And directly behind shone the dark face of Lucullus. His friend and his adoring slave — both come to comfort his last hour.

Pythias attempted to rush into his eager arms. On the instant, the two first soldiers crossed their long spears and formed a barrier to his progress.

"MY MASTER IS CONDEMNED TO PUBLIC DEATH."

"OH, HE WILL NEVER COME BACK!"

# CHAPTER XVIII

## THE VOW

"I MUST speak to him! I *will* speak to him."

The attendant guard was adamant.

"O Damon! My Damon! Dearly beloved friend, doom and death in one short hour! They cannot butcher you before we have talked together. Even a criminal is allowed to tell his dying wish to a friend. Stand aside! Here, Procles! Bid these men allow me to embrace my friend. Ah!"

The barrier removed, Pythias dashed into the hollow square and folded Damon in his strong young arms.

"What can be done? Speak quickly, that I may do all that lies in my poor power. Will Dionysius —?"

"With Dionysius naught is of avail," said Damon bitterly. "He has denied me but a few hours' respite that my wife and child may journey from our country home and bid me farewell!"

"He has forbidden that?"

"Yea, 'twas the only request I made, and as quickly as 'twas asked, so quickly was't denied."

217

" And you would see them to bid them farewell? "
asked Pythias earnestly. " It is the most important
of your last desires? "

Damon gripped his friend's hand in the clasp of
steel. His eyes, for the first time, brimmed over
and tears rained down his livid cheeks.

" If my life were measured by destiny, into a
thousand years of happiness, yet would I give every
minute of that thousand years for just one moment,
now, in which I could press my wife and son to my
heart! Just to have kissed them — my sweet wife
and my adored son."

Pythias gave him an earnest glance. It held out
promise, promise of hope.

" Lead me to Dionysius, Procles. I mean unto
the king since that is now his name. Lead me unto
the king; I have a request to make. Ah! Here he
comes, borne in his chair, flanked by his satellites —
all save Damocles. Halt him on his way! "

In the center of the densely crowded roadway,
where the people were torn between their desire to
view the new king and their curiosity about the
'doomed Senator, Pythias threw himself upon his
knees.

" Behold me, Dionysius, at your feet," he cried
in great distress. " Hear me! I have won many
battles for you, I shall win many more before my
day of usefulness is over. Also, I do not wish for
glory. If there is any, I will bestow it gladly on

your shoulders. This is my one prayer: Grant
that Damon journey to his summer home to take
leave of his sweet wife and child.

"Nay!" as he saw the hand raised in cold denial. "Dost think that I would ask it if I were not
prepared to give security for his return? I *am* prepared. Permit that he do this and put me in chains,
in his stead. Plunge me into his dungeon, a pledge
for his return. If you do this, may the gods build
up your greatness as high as their own heavens!"

Dionysius smiled in amused contempt.

"What is the cause of all this agitation and talk
of sacrifice and such? Is he your brother, this Damon?"

Dionysius motioned to have Damon brought to
him. The doomed man, expecting nothing save the
harsh treatment he had already been accorded,
looked with deep hatred upon the seated king.

"If I should grant this, your friend's request,"
Dionysius questioned him, "are you quite sure that
you would come and ransom him at sunset?"

A radiance overspread the features of Damon.
He advanced his left foot, placed his left hand upon
his left breast and raised his closed right hand as if
about to strike a downward blow.

"I do solemnly swear I will return at the appointed hour," he recited slowly and with imposing
gravity.

"Then 'tis granted," announced Dionysius,

"Away, at once, and haste! Conduct that man to prison." He indicated Pythias.

The two friends' hands remained locked in a close embrace, for the duration of a minute's time. Then Damon, his face lighted by a divine happiness, broke through the crowd. As he disappeared from view, Pythias, with hands clasped behind him, took his place in the hollow square and marched with buoyant step to his cell.

# CHAPTER XIX

A GRAY-BEARDED man, whose tangled white hair cascaded out from his hood and over his forehead, loitered near the city gate.

Few gave a second glance to the somewhat bent old form in its sober woolen garb of a freedman. Such few as chanced to notice him turned away in pity or in disgust. For his lean and wrinkled face was blotched and twisted as by the blood-fire sickness, and one of his eyes was wholly closed as by the same malady's ravages. He was not a sight to inspire interest or liking.

Through the dusty gateway plodded the noon-day throngs: the water-vendor, his wares in dripping pigskins athwart the back of his mangy donkey; — the camel-train, the ugly beasts' padded feet stirring up puffs of hot white dust at every step: — the half-naked slaves of some rich man bearing along their master in a curtained litter; sweating as they moved under the avalanche of coppery sunlight; — these and hundreds of others filled the space on either side of the wide-flung gates.

To all, the old man granted but scant attention. His single eye was piercing the throng for something he sought; his ears seemed strained for some special sound, through the babel of traffic.

And, as he stood there humbly, unnoticed, in the glare of dust, it seemed that he saw at last what he sought.

Out through the crowd that debouched from a nearby street thundered a mighty gray horse, on whose back rode a spare, stern faced man, his senatorial toga blowing loose behind him in the wind. At his side, clutching his stirrup leather, ran a swart-faced slave.

At sight of the plunging horse, a buzz of exclamations arose. No swaggering bully nor overhurried shopman but made room for those rearing forelegs and flashing hoofs. A lane was cleared for the rider's passage. The way to the open gates was free.

On dashed the horse, spurred by his senatorial rider; the slave at the stirrup being jerked from the ground at each bound. Then, all at once, in the very gateway, the horseman pulled back his steed with a suddenness that wellnigh threw the nettled gray brute on its haunches.

There, in the very center of the broad gateway, heedless of the peril of death beneath the thundering hoofs, stood a girl; — Calanthe! In her bridal

white, she stood there, her face upraised and pale,
unprotected beneath the blazing sky.

"Hold, sir!" she cried, throwing forward one
smooth arm to check the rider. "Damon! One
moment, wait!"

Damon, irked at the halt, none the less bent courte-
ously toward her. From his impassive face, the
girl could not have guessed how bitterly he grudged
these moments he must waste in speech with her instead of adding them to the hoarded minutes he
wished to spend at the side of his adored Hermion.

"Damon!" cried Calanthe, "I must speak with
you. I hurried here. I feared I would be too
late."

"There was delay," said Damon. "Lucullus,
my slave, here, lost his road in fetching my horse
from the stables. I must —"

"Stay, Damon!" she implored. "Is what they
tell me true?"

"I would gladly stay at any time but this," he
broke in. "A brother's betrothed is sacred to me,
and her wishes are as his own. But I entreat you
not to shorten the mere hand's breadth of time given
to my heart. I —"

"Is it true?" she insisted. "Is it true that you
have pledged my husband's life for your safe return?"

"It is better that I should say to my wife, 'Her-

mion, I must die!' than that others should say to
her to-morrow: 'Hermion, he is dead!'"

"No!" blazed the girl. "On the morrow you
will say to her, 'Pythias has died for me!' To-
morrow, safe from Syracuse, you will —"

"Calanthe!" he cried, aghast. "You believe
that? You believe I would betray him? My
friend, my brother? You believe —?"

"I hear folk around me whisper: 'Damon goes
free! Pythias pays the price. Damon will not return. No mortal would twice thrust his head into
the lion's jaws.' I heard —"

"You heard, Calanthe? When the breath of
scandal touches the garments of a fellow-being, many
are ready to condemn! I'll not swear to you that
I shall come back. For when men lift their hands
in oath to the gods, it is to give assurance to a
doubt. To swear that I will return to my friend
would profane the sanctity of friendship. Good-by.
On the sixth hour I come back."

"No, no!" she shrieked, seizing his bridle in an
ecstasy of terror. "You shall not go. You shall
*not!* I am a woman. I know what women's
hearts lead them to do. Even as now I grasp the
bridle rein, so will Hermion grasp your soul and
your will-power. Her arms around your neck; her
tears on your face, her sobbed entreaties in your
ears — you cannot withstand her. You *cannot!*
Mortal man cannot. I know! *know!*"

"DIONYSIUS IS RESOLVED ON DAMON'S DEATH."

PYTHIAS COMMANDS MERCY FOR THE GALLEY SLAVE.

Lucullus darted forward, waiting for no word of command from his master. Tenderly, yet with irresistible wiry strength, he loosed the anguished girl's grip from the rein, lifted her from the ground and set her to one side of the roadway.

"Damon!" she screamed. "Mercy! Have mercy!"

"May the gods help and comfort you, maiden!" groaned Damon, striking spur again into his horse's flanks. Lucullus, at a bound, was once more at the stirrup. And, out through the gateway, shot the great gray horse.

"Oh, he will never come back!" wept Calanthe, heedless of the ring of staring, sympathetic faces around her. "He will never come back. His wife — his child — they will not let him return. His heart will bind him to them with ropes of steel. Pythias! The friend who must die for his craven friend!"

A light touch on her arm made her turn. Through a mist of tears she saw the old one-eyed freedman beside her.

"You are Calanthe?" asked the old man, his voice very gentle. "You are Calanthe, the bride of Pythias?"

"His bride?" echoed the desolated girl. "I *was* to be his bride. But — oh, Damon will not return! I know he will not."

"He will not," assented the old man, his voice

as solemn, as hopeless, as the toll of the passing bell.

"What are you saying?" she faltered, trembling at his words and tone. ".What do you know of him?"

"I know," sadly repeated the old man, "that Damon will never come back. Not at the allotted sixth hour or at any later day."

"What do you mean? Who are you?"

"Who am I? My name will mean little enough to you. I am Creugas, a freedman. I am a servant in the house of Dionysius, the tyrant."

"Of Dionysius!" she shuddered.

"On whom be the black curse of Pluton!" he added. "Yet, now you must believe I know whereof I speak. Damon will not return."

"Will not return?" she repeated, womanlike defending where late she had accused. "What can the tyrant or any of his household know of such devotion as binds these two friends together? They —"

"We can know nothing of it," sighed Creugas. "Friendship and loyalty are strangers to our house. But we who serve him can know something of the tyrant's mind. It is from that knowledge I say Damon will not return."

"You mean that he —"

"I mean that my master has sent ahead a half score of his mounted guard, to intercept Damon ere he can mount the hillside to his home. They will be awaiting him in the patch of woodland at the mountain-foot. Damon will not emerge alive from that strip of forest. Think you it was by mistake his slave was kept so long at saddling his horse and bringing the steed to him? The guards must need gain the start they needed."

"No! No!"

"That is why I say Damon will not return — and that Pythias is doomed to die!"

"The monster! To give Damon the six-hour reprieve, as a cat might let a mouse think to escape! Oh, Pythias!"

"It is not the way of Dionysius," said Creugas, grimly, "to give aught in foolish generosity. As well might both Pythias and Damon have known, had they but paused to think. He is resolved on Damon's death —"

"But Pythias?"

"Pythias won the chariot race. Pythias overthrew the foes of Syracuse. The mob and the soldiery shout overloud when Pythias appears in the streets. Dionysius is glad to rid himself of so popular a man. A man who might well threaten the throne itself. He dared not lay hands openly on Pythias; for the people love the blond giant. But none dare censure him for taking the life Pythias has willingly placed in pawn."

"Oh, gods!" she moaned in mortal terror. "Is there no way to save him? No way? Sir, you voice

is kind.   From a kind heart you have come to warn
me.   Help me now!   Help me to save my beloved!   You can help Pythias escape?   Oh, you can
do it?   You will?"

"Yes," said the old man, simply.   "And so shall
I pay two debts:   A debt of hate to the tyrant, my
master; a debt of love to Pythias, who once saved
the life of my only son in battle."

"May the gods, in their mercy, bless you!"

"I am blessed by your gratitude.   I ask no more."

"How can you save him?"

"By helping him to fly with you from Syracuse."

"Can you release him first from the serpent's
coils?   From the power of Dionysius?"

"Yes.   If you both will obey my directions."

"Oh, we shall obey you, sir.   Do not fear for
that.   And to our death-day we shall pray the gods
to shower rich blessings on the head of Creugas, our
rescuer, our hero, our preserver."

"Then come with me at once to Pythias."

"But he is in prison.   How can we —?"

The old man thrust from his cloak a skinny hand,
clothed and distorted.   On one of its fingers blazed
a strangely carved ring.

"The tyrant's," he explained briefly.   "His
signet ring.   Before it, all doors must open.   He
laid it aside as he entered the baths but now.   I was
in attendance on him.   Come."

Side by side they girdled the gateway square and

passed down a tortuous and ill-smelling alley. At the alley's farther end they came out upon the agora, or market place, the vast area at whose farthest corner loomed the dirty brownish mass of stone that was the city prison.

Midway of the agora,— still crowded on this day, despite the heat of the hour — they were confronted by a dazzlingly clad young officer of the newly arrived regiment encamped upon the Epipolae to the north. The officer, seeing a gloriously beautiful girl accompanied only by an old man shabbily attired, made his way forward through the press and stood smiling down on Calanthe.

" Will Venus not pause to brighten the day for Mars? " he begged, laying his hand caressingly on the shrinking girl's shoulder. " The sky is aflame from the sun's kisses, and my heart too is ablaze. Does love find no place in your dear eyes? "

As he spoke he uncermoniously thrust aside the old freedman.

" Oh, let us pass, sir! " begged the terrified Calanthe. " We —"

" Your old scarecrow of an escort may pass, by all means, to the gutter where he belongs," laughed the officer. " But you will pause, I know to —"

" Friend," quietly interposed Creugas, " you seem to have traveled far. Have you? "

" Yes," said the officer, with marked change of manner, as he glanced at the old man.

"*In the East?*" asked Creugas, with an imperceptible gesture.

The officer, saluting stiffly, stood aside for the freedman and Calanthe to pass.

# CHAPTER XX

## THE PRISONER

THE grilled steel portcullis leading from the roadway into the prison yard next halted the two. With his open hand, Creugas smote on the portal. A drowsy turnkey hobbled into sight.

Beholding merely an ill-dressed old man and a veiled woman (for Calanthe, warned by her meeting with the officer, had drawn her veil across her face), he was turning away again with a growl of disgust at having been disturbed at his nap, when Creugas sharply hailed him.

Creugas had thrust his lean arm through the grill. A bar of sunlight fell athwart the monarch's signet ring he wore.

The turnkey hobbled nearer, blinked owlishly at the ring, then scuttled off, returning presently with the captain of the guard. At a word from the captain, the portcullis was raised, and Creugas and Calanthe entered under the gloomy stone arch.

Creugas stepped to one side with the captain. For a moment, the two men conferred in low tones. Then Creugas rejoined the waiting girl.

" Come," he said.

Following the captain, they made their way across the courtyard, through a narrow and low-vaulted corridor through an iron door out into a stone terrace. The door clanged shut behind them.

The terrace was wide and was worn by the tramping of many feet. On its farther side it was bounded by an eighteen-inch stone wall; a walk which overlooked a sheer drop of two hundred feet to the rocky seashore below.

On the other side of the terrace was a line of barred cell doors. Toward one of these doors the officer pointed, handing Creugas a huge key. He himself withdrew through the corridor opening, closing its door behind him.

"Sit yonder," Creugas bade Calanthe, pointing to a stone seat against the prison wall. "Sit yonder. And when I beckon, come."

From the moment the officer had indicated one of the barred doors to Creugas, Calanthe had been unable to keep her eyes off that one oblong of rusty iron.

Creugas, seemingly reading her thoughts, had held her back by turning his skinny fingers in a fold of her robe. Now, as he released her and indicated the stone seat, she half turned toward the cell door instead.

"Remember," he warned her, as tenderly as a fond father might chide a willful babe, "remember your promise to obey me, maiden."

With a quivering sigh she bowed her head and walked obediently to the stone seat.

Here, such prisoners as by special favor were allowed a few minutes of daily exercise on the terrace, were wont to sit and rest, when the brief pacing to and fro on the stone flagging had proven too much for their wasted strength.

Here, seated on the bench of stone, they could look across the dazzling blue sea to the happy Sicilian hills that laughed with their wealth of vine and corn and olive. Here they could gaze wistfully at the free clouds racing across the blue sky overhead; here watch the sea birds at play, the fisher children shouting gleefully to each other from boat to boat; here, lost to freedom, see all that was most free.

Calanthe's great pansy eyes welled with tears at the thoughts, as she sank down on the greasy stone seat; perhaps the saddest-hearted mortal of all the sad-hearted who had sat there. For the others were captive of body but free of heart; while she, free of body, felt her heart loaded with carking fetters that crushed it beneath their weight.

Old Creugas, key in hand, meatime, had gone to the door of the cell indicated by the captain.

"My lord! Pythias!" he called through the bars.

"Damon is returned at last?" came the voice of Pythias from the darkness of the cell. "I thought the six hours were long since passed. I have waited an eternity! And yet — I would he had not come."

"The six hours have not yet sped. Nor all of one hour of them, Pythias," replied Creugas. "I wonder not you were deceived as to time's flight. I, too, have been a prisoner. And I know that to him who lies in a cell every hour is as a whole day whose hours are long. But come! Time is precious."

As he spoke he was fitting the huge key in the lock.

"Who are you," demanded Pythias, "that bids me before my time? Has the tyrant relented and —?"

"Dionysius does not relent. It is not his way. Stand forth!"

Creugas, as he spoke, threw wide the creaking iron door. Pythias reeling a little, moved forward across the threshold, shielding his eyes from the unaccustomed glare by means of his upraised arm."

"Where are you leading me?" he queried, dazedly. "Since Damon is not returned and since Dionysius does not relent. Why do you —?"

"I am come to lead you to liberty."

"Who are you?" queried Pythias, wonderingly surveying the ugly old man in his shabby woolen clothes. "Who are you that can set me free?"

"A servant of Dionysius. I dwell beneath the tyrant's roof. By chance, a half hour since, I learned the secret of his plan."

"His plan? To hold me as hostage for my friend? 'Twas not his plan but mine."

"No. His plan against your life."

"My life?"

"Your life."

"You croak like a raven!" declared Pythias impatiently. "He dare not plan against my life. He has publicly sworn to free me on Damon's return. A hostage may not be slain, unless the pledge be broken, whereon he is held. When Damon comes I shall be free. Dionysius is a warrior. He will not break warfare's rules that govern the treatment of a hostage."

"He will not break them," agreed Creugas. "You are right. Even Dionysius dare not break such a law. 'Twould wreck him with the army."

"Yet you say he plots my life."

"It is so."

"But how? When Damon shall return —"

"Damon will not return."

"You lie! Lucky it is that age and disease have scarred your face and form and that you are of plebeian rank. Else bare-handed I would cram the vile lie down your throat."

"Damon," repeated Creugas, flinching not before the advance of the indignant warrior, "will not return."

"By Castor! You presume upon your age and weakness! I —"

"Damon will not return, because a dozen of the tyrant's men even now lie in wait to slay him."

"Almighty gods of high Olympus! What are you saying?"

"You have known Dionysius. You have known him long and well. Does this deed of his seem so strange to you, Pythias?"

"I had not thought that mortal man could —"

"Pythias, you are a warrior, not a thinker. I wonder not that this surprises you. Yet Damon might have thought, had not his brain been so filled with —"

"Quick!" ordered Pythias. "The way out! I must go!"

"Go? Many a prisoner has hoped that. But whither?"

"To mount my fleetest horse! To ride after Damon. To warn him of his peril or to share it with him! To die, if need be, sword in hand, at his side."

"But —"

"He is my friend!"

"He is leagues away by now and riding fast. A bird could not overtake him. Moreover, how would you go? Yonder lies the sea, two hundred feet below. On the other side is the prison wall."

"Oh, my friend! My friend!" groaned Pythias. "And in his hour of mortal peril I stand helpless. I who would blithely die for him. I see it all,—

too late! Dionysius hates us both. By this foul trick he rids himself of us."

"No," contradicted Creugas. "Not of both of you. Of Damon alone."

"What does life hold for me when my friend lies slain?"

"It holds what all men seek and what you have won: Love!"

"Calanthe!"

"I come to save you. To give you freedom — and your bride."

"Is this a trick, too?"

"I blame you not," said Creugas, sorrowfully, "that in your black hour you would smite aside even the hand stretched out to save you."

"Speak out! I —"

"I owe you much. I hate the usurper king. I wish to serve you. I wish to thwart him. So I am here. Here to set you free. Calanthe shall share your flight. Your aged father —"

"My father!"

"He shall join you. I have arranged it all. In Syracuse harbor lies a ship that will set sail at word from me; at the captain's first glimpse of the ring I wear."

"I —"

"You doubt me? Turn and look! There is my proof."

As Creugas spoke, he beckoned. Pythias, half

suspecting a new ruse of the tyrant's, turned sharply about. Down the wind-swept terrace toward him, shining like a goddess in the sunlight, Calanthe was advancing.

" Calanthe! " gasped Pythias. " Jove above! Calanthe! "

# CHAPTER XXI

## TEMPTATION

HE sprang to meet her. But as he reached her the girl stepped back. A fugitive memory had come to her of their last meeting.

"Pythias," she said brokenly. "You shrank from me as though I were unworthy. Only this very day you spurned me for a mere friend's sake. You forswore love and me for Damon and friendship. How can I trust such love as yours?"

"How can you trust it?" he cried eagerly. "As you can trust the high gods, as you can trust the golden sun and the tides. I love you! With the heart, the soul, the body I have kept clean for your sake, I love you. Above all life and heaven I love you. Above all — save honor. And for honor's sake I gave myself as pledge for my friend. My love for you shall not be less, Beloved, because my love for honor was greater."

"Let us forget everything, then, except this wondrous love of ours, my Pythias. Love waits for us. Love and — Freedom!"

Pythias caught her in his arms; crushing her close

against his broad breast; showering kisses on her lips, her eyes, her fragrant hair.

Then, as though parting from all that life held dear, he put her from him. Long and earnestly he looked upon the glory of sea and land and sky. And again his eyes rested adoringly on Calanthe. But there was no hope in their worshiping gaze; there was naught save the light of a great renunciation.

"It has been good," he said simply. "It has been good to hold you once more in my arms. It will make death sweeter."

"Death!" echoed the girl, wonderingly. "Why, dear one, there is no talk of death. You are free."

"No."

"But, Pythias, surely Creugas explained to you —"

"That Damon will not return. Thus my pledge is forfeit. I must die, as I agreed, in his place."

"You are a madman!" exclaimed Creugas.

"Perhaps. Dionysius spared the life of Damon for six hours on the security that I would remain imprisoned in his place until his return, and that if he should not return, I should die. I gave the pledge. It is forfeit, and my life with it."

"But Dionysius has broken faith with you!" protested Creugas.

"Then would you have me sink to his level by breaking faith with him?"

"Think of me, Pythias," besought Calanthe. "Think of me! Is my love nothing?"

"It is earth and heaven!"

"And is it nothing that my heart must break for you?"

"It is the bitterest drop in my death cup. I would eagerly die ten thousand times if I might save you grief."

"Pythias, this monster, Dionysius, has broken faith with you. You owe him nothing."

"I owe my honor everything."

"He has cheated you!"

"So this man says. It may be true. It may not. A thousand things may prove true or false. But my honor must stand true. Suppose this man lies? Suppose, at the appointed hour, Damon should return — as return he will, if one breath of life be left in his body — suppose he return to keep his pledge? Return and find me faithless? Of his own wish he will come back to save me from death. He would come back to learn that of my own wish I had proven faithless and fled; that I had chosen happiness instead of honor."

"If for one fleeting moment you think to impress Dionysius by such fortitude as yours," suggested Creugas, "then once and forever dismiss that hope. He will laugh at you as a fool who might have won freedom and who lacked the wit to outwit those who have maltreated him. A strange man, this king of ours.   Deaf to honor, deaf to mercy, yet with a strange vein of philosophy in his head.   A vein of philosophy stolen, perhaps, from the Athenian sages he loves to quote."

Pythias was not listening.   Again he was gazing deep into Calanthe's eyes as though to carry the memory of their loveliness with him into the next world.   Creugas maundered on:

"Why, but last night when oily Damocles supped with him and fell to praising his greatness, what does Dionysius do, of a sudden, but point upward — so! And Damocles looks up to see hanging above his head his own keen edged sword, suspended by a hair! My faith! he rolls from his banqueting couch and scrambles across the room as though all hell were in pursuit.   'See!' prates Dionysius, after the fashion of Athenian philosophers.   'See how all greatness and safety and life itself hang on a single hair. When next you would fawn upon human greatness, remember the Sword of Damocles!'"

"Pythias!"   Calanthe was whispering.   "Once more, for my sake, fly!   The opportunity may not come again."

"Here I abide," firmly responded Pythias, "and when Damon returns — if return he may —"

"He will not return!" interposed Creugas.   "By now the assassins are at his throat.   There is nothing left for you to await here.   Look!" he broke off, pointing seaward.

Across the harbor a galley had moved from the farther shore. Now she came to anchor barely a furlong away from the terrace.

Her colored sails were half raised. Men crouched ready to run them up the polished mast at a single word of command. The slaves bent over the long, burnished oars, holding them above water, ready to catch water at the same word.

Like a beautiful bird, ready and poised for flight, lay the galley on the glittering summer sea, a sight to thrill a traveler's soul.

From the vessel's side a small boat was putting forth, propelled by half-nude blacks, toward the watching group on the terrace.

"Look!" repeated Creugas. "Yonder lies the ship that waits to bear you and your dear ones to freedom. Her boat is even now coming hither to fetch you away from this place of living death. At my orders, backed by this signet ring, all these things have been done. All these and more. A rope ladder hangs from the coping of the wall behind you. Come —"

"Pythias!" cried the girl. "Come with us! Come! It is Liberty! Liberty and love!"

"It is dishonor," Pythias made reply, white to the lips with the battle against his heart.

"It is Happiness!"

"No! It is disgrace!"

"Pythias," urged Creugas, "your father is old

and weak. He will die of grief at tidings of your death."

"He would die of shame at tidings of my shame."

"The boat!" sobbed Calanthe. "See, it is drawing near. So near! Would you break my heart?"

"You will remember me as the lover who loved you too well to ruin his honor for your sake."

"Pythias," again broke in Creugas, his old voice vibrant with tenseness; the sweat pouring down his disfigured face. "Pythias, I have risked my life to save you. If we three do not make our escape, and make it with all speed, I am a dead man. Dionysius knows horribly well how to punish. I have risked all for you."

"If all the world risked everything to lure me from honor my answer would be the same. Go, if you are in peril, man. Though by your own showing, you have merited death by betraying your master who trusts you and deems you his friend. The seeming friend of to-day may be the enemy of to-morrow. Go or stay. I have given you my answer."

"Pythias," pleaded Calanthe. "Hark! Do you hear the oars? They are below us, just below. Their plash is a song of freedom, of joy, of love, of a golden future for us both."

"Of a black future built on blacker dishonor. No! Oh, Calanthe, my own, why make me taste

the bitterness of death before my hour? I cannot
go, I will not go!"

"Pythias —" began Creugas.

"Enough!"

"No. One word more. A word that must be
spoken," insisted Creugas. "Yet a word I would
fain have left unsaid. Dionysius has looked over-
closely at Calanthe. You know how a fair face at-
tracts him and to what lengths he will go to win
what he desires. The tyrant's eyes have followed
your love. The tyrant's longing has compassed
her about."

"Peace!"

"When you are no longer alive to protect her —
when by your mad folly you leave her defenseless in
his hands —"

"Pythias," shuddered the girl. "He speaks
truth. It is not alone yourself you will be saving.
It will be I as well. Save me!"

The face of Pythias was ghastly. His lips were
invisible from fierce pressure, his mouth was a hard-
set line, his eyes were ablaze.

His mighty body trembled as with an ague. His
nails bit deep into the palms of his clenched hands,
bit so deep that trickles of blood oozed out and
flecked his whitened finger joints. He was in mortal
anguish, in a travail of soul that shook him like an
aspen.

Creugas stood aside. His work was done. He had played his last and strongest card.

Calanthe threw her soft white arms about her lover's muscular throat and buried her face in his breast.

"You must save me!" she wailed. "You can-not leave me to such a fate! Come! If not for your own sake, then for the sake of the woman you would vow to protect and to cherish. My sweet-heart, save me!"

A groan that seemed to tear spirit and body asun-der burst from the white lips of Pythias.

"May all the gods protect you, my loved one!" he panted. "If the vile tyrant lay so much as one finger on your dear head, I swear I shall rend my grave clothes and the earth that covers me, and come back from the tomb to destroy him."

"No, no! It is in life you must succor me! Come! The boat lies waiting!"

"No! Here honor and I are waiting. For the end!"

"Pythias!" she wept. "My lover, Pythias!"

He broke from the sweet prison of her detaining arms and rushed back to his cell, clanging its iron door shut behind him. Calanthe took a wavering step toward the cell, then sank in a deathlike swoon at the feet of Creugas.

# CHAPTER XXII

## " CAUTION! "

**D**AMON, meantime, did not slacken rein until he had left the city far behind him and had breasted the slope of the hills whereon stood his white villa.

Through the plain and through the strip of woodland at the mountain-foot he galloped, Lucullus still running at his stirrup leather, the slave's tireless wiry strength easily holding out in spite of the fearful pace.

So had the Scythian foot soldiers for centuries been wont to run at the side of the cavalry; unwearying, no matter what the pace or how long the journey; and helped along by their grip on the stirrup.

The blazing noonday heat poured down on Damon's unsheltered head, his prematurely grizzled hair shining like soft silver in the pitiless glare. He heeded not the fierce heat, nor his sweating horse's gallant efforts.

His eyes were fixed on the far-off hillside villa, the villa to which each stride of his horse brought him nearer; the villa that held all he loved most on earth; the wife of his heart, the child of his hopes.

By set of sun he would have passed forever from them. And he yearned unspeakably for the brief hour he might yet spend in the sunshine of their love.

The moment's delay he had suffered through Calanthe he had grudged as a man dying of thirst might grudge a spilled portion of his last cup of water.

He was doing all in his power to atone for that delay by riding his horse with unsparing speed. And nobly did the splendid gray respond to the urging of spur and of voice. He seemed, by instinct, to know his master's gnawing desire; and with every atom of his peerless strength he sought to grant that desire.

Through the woodland road at the hill-foot raced the gallant gray. Scare did he slacken speed as he breasted the steep rise of the hill. His nostrils were red and his eyes suffused. Yet he held to his task.

The slave, by this time, was beginning to pant from fatigue and to stagger in his run. Damon alone of that speeding trio was unaware of the wild pace at which they were traveling. To him, the gray flying feet crawled at a snail's pace, so far did his own yearning outstrip the matchless horse's flight.

At last, after what Damon fancied were centuries of wasted time, the plateau on the hillside was reached. And, presently — foam flecked, bathed in sweat, his mottled sides heaving — the grand horse

dropped from a run to a walk and stood at his master's door.

Damon sprang to earth, shouted a direction to the
wearied slave to care for the horse and to have him
ready at the courtyard door in an hour's time, then
dashed through the marble gateway.

Xextus was playing in the sunken garden below
the house; his tiny helmet and sword girded on, he
was vehemently marshaling an army of scarlet pop-
pies to an advance against some unseen invader.

Hermion was nowhere in sight.   A question to a
passing maidservant brought news that the mistress
of the house was in the forest beyond the lawns,
gathering myrtle for votive wreaths.   Damon sent
the maid running to fetch Hermion with all speed.
Then he descended into the sunken garden.

Xextus, turning at sound of his father's step, caught
sight of the approaching figure and with a shout of
delight, ran to meet him.

" Father !   Father ! " he hailed, flinging his sturdy
little arms about his sire's knees.   " You are at home
again !   We did not look for you.   Oh, you have
come back to play with me !   See, you shall help me
mass my army.   You — you shall be general," he
added in a burst of generosity, " and I will be your
*angelos* or else your second-in-command ! "

Damon, his throat contracting, picked up the martial boy and crushed the tiny fellow to his heart with

such convulsive force that had not Xextus been a stoic warrior he would have cried out with pain.

"Oh, my little boy!" murmured Damon, brokenly, "my little, *little* boy!"

Xextus looked up in sudden concern into the haggard, drawn face so close to his own.

"Why, father!" he exclaimed, "you are sick. Or are you wounded? Tell me!"

"No," denied Damon, regaining Spartan control of himself by mighty effort. "No! But my time is short. I have but an hour here with you two who are so dear to me. Then I must go back."

"To work?"

"No. To rest."

"But only one hour? It is not fair. Mother will be unhappy again."

"Then her boy must comfort her. She will need all your comfort, my little Xextus. Remember that. And remember I leave her to your love and your care. As you grow up, think always of that; no matter what may happen. Your place is at her side; to be her soldier, her comforter. You will remember?"

"Yes. Why, yes. But you will be here, too."

"If I am not, you must still remember. If she had only you —"

"But you must be here, my father! You must. There would be no fun without you."

"My soldier-boy, the day has come when other

things than fun must claim you. You must be the staff and consoler of your mother when I am gone."

"Gone? Where? Oh,— I — I — am afraid!"

"A soldier must slay fear. You will slay it? And selfishness, too? And all thoughts save those of your mother, my Xextus?"

"I — I will try, sir. But how strangely you talk! And how pale you are! Where are you going and why must you go?"

"I am going on a long journey, little son of mine. A long journey. I am come here to say good-by to you and to your mother."

"But why?" asked Xextus. "Why do you go? Why do you want to leave us?"

"I do not want to. I would give my all to stay."

"Then why do you go? Who sends you on this journey?"

"The high gods."

"The gods?" repeated the child in reverence. "Then — then, I suppose you must go. Mother says we must always obey the gods. She has gone to weave a myrtle garland to lay at our shrine for your safe home coming. But — but why can't the gods send some one else? Some one who hasn't a little son to miss him. Couldn't they? If I prayed very, very hard to them?"

Damon's thoughts flashed back unbidden to a dungeon opening on a prison terrace, where even now awaited "some one" whom the gods stood ready to send on the journey in his place. And his keen eyes grew misty at the vision.

The light sound of a woman's running feet and the swish of a woman's drapery came to the ears of both; breaking in on the strange scene.

" Go," he said gently. " Go back to your play, my lad. Your mother is returning and she and I have much to say. The time grows short."

# CHAPTER XXIII

## HUSBAND AND WIFE

**H**ERMION appeared at the head of the white stairway that led from the house down to the sunken garden.

"Damon!" she called in glad wecome.

Ere she could descend to him, her husband ran lightly up the steps to where she stood and caught her in his arms. The boy stood hesitating where his father had left him.

"Damon!" cried Hermion, an almost hysterical rapture in her sweet voice. "Oh, my husband, what a joyous surprise! I could scarce believe the news that you had returned. Hour after hour I have strained my eyes following every moving speck that journeys hitherward from the city; each time praying the gods it might be you. And when at last you came I was not on the housetop watching for you. The world is worth living in again now that you are back."

"Are you so unhappy, then, when I am absent?" he faltered.

"Unhappy? I do not live. I only *wait*. Oh, my own husband, if I should tell you how I fear and

253

how desolate and sad I am when you are down in that distant city, away from me,— oh, if I could make you understand all your presence means to me and how your every absence blots out my sun, you would never again have the heart to leave me."

"To leave you!" murmured Damon under his breath. "Pitying gods, give me strength!"

Hermion did not note his sudden agitation. Her eyes had fallen on Xextus, still standing at the foot of the steps.

"Go and weave a garland for your father!" she called to him gayly. "The fairest garland that ever you wove — to welcome him home to us again."

The boy turned and went upon his mission. Hermion noted the unwonted lagging of Xextus' feet and the sorrowful droop of his head; and she wondered at his lack of wild spirits over his adored father's return.

Hoping that Damon had not observed and been hurt by the child's dearth of eagerness in the homecoming, she glanced from the departing Xextus to her husband. So suddenly did her eyes meet Damon's that he had not time to mask the hopeless misery in his gaze.

"What is it?" she asked in quick alarm. "Are you ill? The sun, the long ride —"

"Hermion," he interposed, his voice wondrous gentle, yet his words such as never before the calmly self-contained man had spoken to her. "Hermion, my wife, have I, in our married life, ever willingly made you suffer? Have ever I wounded you with hasty word or angry glance?"

"You?" she cried. "Never in all my life! How strangely you speak! What put such thoughts in your mind?"

"Have my thoughts strayed from you? Have I, save for urgent business of state, ever remained an hour from your side? Have I put aught before your happiness?"

"No. No! You know you have not. My true, gentle husband, you have been all the world to me! You have made my life an endless joy. You have —"

"Be that my epitaph! It is good to have heard such words from you, my glorious wife. They will be graven on my heart forevermore."

"What are you hiding from me?" she demanded, womanly intuition warning her even more sharply than did his words. "Why speak you of 'epitaphs' and —?"

"When I am dead you will remember with comfort the praise you have just lavished on me."

"When you are dead? Oh, I cannot understand you, Damon! It is not like you to speak so. Why do you talk of death? You are ghastly pale and your eyes are dark with pain. Are you ill? Or does something cause you secret grief? Some new sorrow, it must be.  For in all your brooding over the ill-fate of Syracuse you were never like this. Speak!  Tell me!  Oh, how politics and the wars and the city's corruption have wrecked our home peace!  Tell me, I implore you!  I am your wife; the partner of your grief.  Not your plaything, to share naught but your idle joys.  I must know.  I must help.  A wife can always help!"

"Hermion," he said haltingly, "suppose I were to tell you the heaviest news your mind could imagine,— could you bear it?"

"Bear it?  I could laugh right blithely at it if it did not touch your life or our love.  Those two are all that can matter to me.  They are my world: — your life and the love the high gods have given to us twain.  What are your black tidings, dear heart?  Dionysius has undermined your hopes and risen to power?"

"Yes.  And to the throne.  But that is not my news."

"The Carthaginians march on the city again?"

"No.  For the moment they crouch in their kennels and lick their sore wounds."

"I can think of but one other tragedy that could move you so.  Your friend,— Pythias,— something is amiss with him?  He is not — dead?"

"No!  Praise the gods!  Not *dead!*"

"Then the tidings are of yourself!  I knew it.

Some misfortune has befallen you! Some danger threatens you. Tell me."

" A hundred times, my Hermion, I have told myself that you are the bravest woman I have known. I have told myself that whatever might befall, you would bear it gallantly; for my sake; for our boy's sake. That if death should be my portion —"

" Death? Death?"

" Here is my will," he said, handing her a scroll. " Let that break the news to you. I cannot tell you. I thought I could. I cannot."

" Death!" she repeated dully. " Death threatens you? From what evil source?"

" From the law's hands."

" The law? You who are the law's stanchest upholder in these troublous days! It is not possible! For what offense?"

" Dionysius has doomed me to death."

" Dionysius?" she babbled, dazedly. " To death?"

Then her dooping figure straightened and a sudden light of joy burned the tear mists from her eyes.

" But you are here!" she exulted, "you have escaped! Escaped to your own home; unguarded, uncaptured. We have only to fly — to Greece — to Italy — to Egypt — anywhere! We shall be safe beyond the tyrant's reach. You must fly at once, to —"

"To Syracuse," finished Damon; and his voice was dead.

"Into the very jaws of the death from whence you have escaped? Are you mad?"

"I must go back to Syracuse," he insisted in the same lifeless voice. "Even now I would be lying dead there but that my friend —"

"No! No!"

"But that my friend, Pythias, put on my fetters and gave himself up as hostage for my return. In this way alone was the tyrant persuaded to grant me these six hours of grace to ride hither and say farewell to you and to our boy."

Hermion sank heavily to the marble steps at his feet. She gripped the cold stone to save herself from fainting; to cling to her senses that swam so dizzily.

"You are allowed —"

"To come here to bid you farewell and to place my testament in your hands. It was a strange freak of Dionysius' ever-strange mind. When Pythias volunteered to go to prison in my stead, and to the scaffold itself were I not to return at the appointed hour —"

"Return at the appointed hour?" gasped Hermion, rising to her knees and enwrapping him in her arms. "You shall not return. By all the gods of Olympus and of hell, *you shall not.*"

"Not return?" Damon repeated. "Hermion!

Not return? Not go back and free my friend from
the fetters hung on him for my sake? Is this my
loyal, honorable wife who gives me such vile counsel?"

"It is your *sane* wife — the wife who loves you
too dearly to let you throw away your life in a fit
of madness! Here you are safe until we can flee.
And here you shall stay."

"And sacrifice Pythias' life? Oh, Hermion, it
is you who have gone mad; to tempt me to such dishonor!"

"Dishonor?" she cried, beside herself with
frenzy, her wonted meekness lost in the fierce battling
for the man she loved; against himself. "Dishonor? And what of me? What of Xextus? To
save one's life, all wrong becomes right. The gods
who gave us life have taught us to protect that life
at every sacrifice. It is the voice of Nature itself
that demands it. And all men forgive such a deed,
because all men themselves would do the same thing
in like circumstances. What of Pythias? He is
your friend and mine. Many an hour shall I weep
for his death. But all the hours in life were not
enough for me to weep for yours. Live for me,
Damon! You shall not leave me! What friendship is so precious as is love?"

"I vowed to come back to my punishment."

"And at the altar you vowed to live for me! I
hold you to that vow!"

" Hermion ! "

" You shall not go! I say you shall *not* go. See, my arms are locked about you! To leave me you must hew them away with your sword, for I shall never release you ! "

" Hermion! The hour passes ! "

" Then it shall pass. But you shall remain."

He struggled to break her frantic hold. But her arms were so entwined he could not.

" Mother ! " called a clear, frightened voice from behind them.

Xextus, the woven garland in his hands, stood looking at them in terror.

" Hermion ! " cried Damon in despair. " Loose me! The hour is past. I shall be late, unless —"

" You shall not go ! " she moaned. " Xextus ! Thank the gods you have come back! Kneel beside me here. Pray to your father — pray to him as though he were one of the gods themselves! Pray not to be made an orphan! Pray! Pray not to be left fatherless so soon — so soon! Oh, Damon, my husband, look at us! We are kneeling at your feet! You cannot refuse us. You cannot leave us to die a hundred deaths, just that your friend may live ! "

" No. That my pledged word may live! You are urging me to dishonor. You are bidding me murder Pythias that I may live. Let me go ! "

" No! Never! I —"

Her voice choked in her throat. The tight locked arms fell loose. Overburdened nature could endure no more. Even as Calanthe had done when hope died, Hermion fell back upon the marble and lay there, white as the stone itself, and as unconscious.

Damon knelt beside her. His tears raining down on her pallid upturned face. He pressed his lips to hers; once and yet again. Then, staggering blindly to his feet, he stooped to kiss the weeping Xextus; and fled — fled as for his life.

"Father!" wailed the child. *"Father!"*

"Oh, gods whose faithful servant I have been," groaned Damon as he groped his way, tear-blinded, across the courtyard and to the gate, "have in your tender care my wife and my orphan child. Deal gently with those two who are so gentle! Comfort and strengthen them. For naught save heavenly aid can help them now. Grant that my spirit may return to soften their grief! I ask it, not in reward for aught that I have done, but for what I am to do. For I, a man, go forth to die for my fellow man."

He reeled against the huge sundial that stood just within the gateway of the villa courtyard. The shock of the impact brought him to his senses. He brushed the tear-mists from his eyes with a palsied hand. And his glance fell on the dial. At sight of the late hour he cried aloud as though in mortal pain.

" I have overstayed my allotted time! " he gasped.
" I must ride like the wind or I shall arrive too late!
Gods, lend speed to my horse's feet. For I ride to
my death,— that my friend may live! "

# CHAPTER XXIV

### DAMON'S RIDE

O UT through the gateway to the road sprang Damon.

"Lucullus!" he shouted. "The sun is rushing down the sky. My horse. Is he ready as I bade you have him?"

He halted, mouth open, eyes staring in blank horror.

In the roadway, where he had left the beautiful gray horse, the steed was lying, stone dead, in a wide pool of blood where blue flies buzzed and swarmed. The animal's throat was cut from ear to ear.

Beside the dead horse, stood Lucullus; his dark face impassive as a mask; his eyes fixed on his master. In his hand he held a red-bladed knife.

"Lucullus!" stammered Damon, aghast; his brain whirling.

The slave, his expressionless eyes still on Damon's, opened his lips and spoke. In a heavy, unemotional voice he said:

"My master, in Rome, years agone, you saved my life. As I have but now saved yours. Your horse lies dead. I slew him. But ere I did it, I

drove forth your stabled horses into the forest.
'Twill take a full hour to find them. You cannot
return to Syracuse to die. It is too late to go on
foot. You will kill me for what I have done.
Strike! I shall have perished for you even as you
would have perished for your friend."

" *Gods!* "

The expletive came from Damon's white lips
almost in a yell, as, at last, he comprehended the
fearful thing that had happened.

" Slay me if you will," repeated the slave, dog-
gedly.

" Slay you! " screamed the maddened man. " It
is the least I can do to avenge my friend. Beast that
has robbed me of my honor! "

He leaped like a savage tiger upon the cowering
Lucullus and seized him by the throat.

His left hand buried in the slave's flesh, he whipped
out his sword and poised it for a downward sweep
to cleave the fellow's skull. Then he hesitated.

" A Senator's blade would find ill rest in carrion
like you! " he snarled. " The precipice yonder is
your fitting death."

Dragging his victim along the ground, the infuri-
ated Damon hastened toward a cliff edge, just beyond the villa. As he went, he growled between his
teeth:

" Revenge and sacrifice! Revenge on my violated
pledge! Sacrifice to the red ghost of Pythias that

soars above us, perchance, even now, clamoring to know why I, his friend, left him to die my death. With one thrust over the ledge I'll throw you down to hell; then leap after you and kill my own disgrace."

"Mercy!" pleaded the slave, his stoic courage forsaking him in face of so hideous a death. "Mercy, my master!"

"Mercy?" mocked the insane Damon. "*Mercy?* Aye, the mercy I showed to Pythias when I left him to die in my stead. To Pythias who trusted me and who, to the last, awaited my return! The ax that severed his head from his body has deluged me in his blood. Mercy? Ask mercy of the furies of red hell; — not from me!"

He had reached the cliff edge; an eighty foot sheer drop yawned before him, to the tooth-pointed black rocks in the valley beneath.

Sheathing his sword, Damon gripped the writhing Lucullus by both shoulders and swung him aloft. The slave closed his eyes.

Suddenly, with a shock that drove the breath from his body, he was dashed violently to earth, scarce six inches from the brink of the precipice.

Lucullus started up; wondering at his own escape from the fate ordained for him by the master he had sought to save.

Damon was running at the top of his speed along the cliff edge toward a path that wound its steep way down a milder slope of the precipice to the valley below.

As he had swung the slave aloft, Damon had chanced to spy a mailed horseman cantering along the valley road beneath him. And the sight had filled him with a desperate hope.

To the top of the path he dashed. And down the steep declivity he ran and rolled and fell; clutching at bushes that ripped from their roots at his grasp, clawing at the jutting rocks to steady himself; ever taking chances that threatened life and limb; increasing his speed a pace which, on that hazardous cliffside, was suicidal.

His toga was rent from him by the thorny branches of shrubs. Stones bruised and cut him. Earth and clay grimed his hands and face and garments.

At last he was brought up with a bone-racking jolt on the top of a bowlder that hung fifteen feet above the road. Heedless of life he sprang down; clearing the intervening space and landing in the wayside dust just in front of the amazed horseman, who had watched in wonder his breakneck downward progress from the cliff top.

"Your horse, friend!" called Damon, staggering to his feet, his mouth full of dust. "Your *horse!* At your own price and quickly! I offer fifty ounces of gold for him. 'Tis twenty times his value. Your horse, I say!"

The horse shied violently at the dusty, gesticulating apparation in the road; and the rider, deeming the unkempt and bleeding stranger a lunatic, drew back and would have ridden away.

But Damon was at his side before he could touch spur to the beast. With the strength of a maniac he tore the man from the saddle, and hurled him headlong to earth.

The rider, taken by surprise, fell with a crash of clanking armor. But he was a soldier; toughened in the Carthaginian wars and alert of wit and of body. Scare had he touched ground when he was on his feet again.

His sword flashed from its scabbard and with an oath he rushed on his assailant.

Damon, meantime, had sprung to the bridle of the rearing horse; jerked the brute's head downward and seized the mane, preparatory to vaulting into the saddle.

But now, releasing the steed, he sprang nimbly aside; barely in time to avoid the downward-swishing stroke of the dismounted soldier's heavy sword.

"*Io Triomphe!*" yelled the angry horseman, voicing his war-cry, as he smote again at the unkempt form before him.

But Damon had drawn his own blade; and that of the soldier smote ringingly against it. There was no time for explaining; for argument, for offer of money. The stranger, his martial honor tarnished by the overthrow from his horse, was in no mood for anything save bloodshed.

Back and forth, up and down the dusty road, the two opponents fought; their breath coming hot and fast, their feet stamping in attack, retreat or recovery. Their battling swordblades clanged and whined and whistled the Eternal Hate Song of the Ages.

Foot to foot, eye to eye, blade to blade, they fought; these two who, five minutes earlier, had never seen nor heard of each other, but who now sought to slay.

The soldier fought furiously. But his fury was as nothing to his antagonist's. Damon had no hatred for his foe. But he was mad with eagerness to get away; to mount, to ride at killing speed to Syracuse to rescue his imperiled friend.

This stranger barred his way. Only by slaying the man, apparently, could he hope to pass on. And, only by slaying him right swiftly, could he hope to be on time. Every second of delay weighed against the life of Pythias.

Wherefore, disdaining to guard himself and seeking only to slay ere he should be slain, Damon pressed his opponent with the reckless fierceness of a cornered tiger.

Back, step by step, he forced the soldier who, beholding the other's wild recklessness of life and becoming more and more convinced that he had to do

with a maniac, was sore put to it to defend himself.

Damon beat down the soldier's guard and lunged
swiftly. His sandaled foot slipped in the elusive
dust, and momentarily he was thrown off his balance.

His foe's skilled eye was quick to see the brief
advantage; and his foe's skill as a swordsman was
equally quick to profit by it.

Leaping in, the soldier struck. Damon, recovering himself, shrank aside from the blow, parrying
as he dodged. His sudden avoidance and his intervening sword deflected the soldier's heavily descending blade.

Its edge missed Damon's skull and inflicted a
gash in his left shoulder. Damon, before the soldier could recover from the impetus of that great
stroke, caught the latter's blade on the flat of his
own, and smote downward and to one side.

The trick served. The soldier's sword flew in
air and fell in the roadside bushes. The soldier
stumbled backward, nursing a right arm that was
numb to the shoulder.

Damon sheathed his own blade and with almost
the same gesture, pulled his purse from his belt and
flung it at the other's feet.

"In payment for your steed!" he called, as he
vaulted to the saddle and thundered away toward
Syracuse, without so much as a backward look.

Vaguely he was glad he had not been obliged to slay this foeman against whom he held no hatred. To him the fellow had been but an obstacle — as impersonal as a bowlder or a fallen tree across the road — to be overcome at the least possible waste of time. That he had overcome him without shedding blood was a source of gratification to Damon.

But these and all other thoughts were as mere blurs in his whirling brain. He, the wise, the calm, the icily clear thinker, was in a red swirl of horror. His mind refused its normal functions.

He was possessed and obsessed by one single all-over-powering impulse: — to reach Syracuse in time to redeem his friend's pledged life.

He forced his reeling brain to some momentary semblance of its wonted clearness as the horse bounded down the mountain's lower slopes and into the wide plain that lay between the hill and the city.

Was there a chance he could arrive in time?

The sun had slipped perilously low in the heavens. The shadows were lying in long and weirdly shaped formation along the plain. Sunset was at hand.

When the red sun's rim should touch the crest of the far western mountains, Pythias must die. And the miles of the plain stretched drearily long between the frantic rider and Syracuse.

To the finest edge, Damon had unwittingly prolonged his stay with his wife and son, Hermion's passionate embrace chaining him to his home when he should have been departing.

The slaying of his horse, and his own mad attempt at vengeance upon the too-faithful slave had further delayed him; as had the brief clash at arms with the unknown soldier.

He had wasted time. Time that was not his to waste. And his friend's life might be the forfeit. Thus fiercely did Damon blame himself, in merciless self-arraignment, forgetting that circumstances, and not he, were to blame.

He knew, as a student of human nature, the odd twists of Dionysius' strange nature. He knew the tyrant would keep his word: He would not put Pythias to death one instant before the allotted time. But he would not delay one moment beyond that time.

The whole issue rested with Damon; even as Damon had proposed that it should. And, while Damon raved at his own delay, he could not in justice blame the tyrant for taking him at his word.

In a torture-vision, the scene that must be enacted, burned itself into his soul. He seemed to behold the *agora* with the grim scaffold and grimmer executioner in its center; the silent, morbidly-fascinated throng crowding about the gruesome nucleus.

He seemed to see Pythias — proud, unflinching, his face alight with self-renunciation — led forth from the gloom of the prison into the sunset square and to the scaffold; beside whose block the executioner awaited him, ax in hand.

Pythias! The friend, the more-than-brother, who had trusted in Damon's promise to return and who would gladly lay down life that his comrade might live!

Damon could almost hear the strangled weeping of Calanthe; could see her fresh girlish beauty crushed forever to earth by the fearful tragedy that was to engulf her.

Damon groaned aloud in horror. Frantically he flogged the galloping horse to greater speed. Dully he became aware that this lumbering hack-charger of the army was no match in speed for his own slain horse.

The brute he now bestrode was one of the thousands which army contractors yearly bought up from farmers and from tradesmen and which, after a little veterinary treatment, they sold at huge profit to the government.

Such horses, at a pinch, could be counted upon for a routine march or even for a lumbering cavalry charge. But for a race for life they were usually far out of their element.

The horse was breathing in heaving grunts and, despite Damon's urging, was already beginning to slacken speed. To the rider's urging, the animal no longer responded. His was not the thoroughbred strain that makes the perfect horse kill itself from exertion at the behest of its master.

The beast, bred rather to the plow than to the race course, was spiritless and tired; and saw no reason for tiring itself further.

Damon's sword flashed out. With the flat of the blade he smote the sweating horse across the flanks. The blow raised a weal on the poor animal's skin, but added only a momentary flash of speed to its slackening pace.

And the sun dropped lower and lower. Now it hung scarce a hand-breadth above the western mountains.

Again and again the flogging sword blade rose and fell. And after the first few blows, the horse did not respond by even a brief outburst of speed to the cruel beating. A final frantic stroke, and the hilt turned in Damon's shaking hand. Not the flat but the edge of the blade smote the heaving flank.

The horse staggered, lunged forward and fell; its upper-leg sinew cut.

# CHAPTER XXV

## FOR FRIENDSHIP!

DAMON, wellnigh unseated by the horse's forward plunge, barely saved his leg from being crushed under the falling body. Swinging clear of the great tumbling bulk, he leaped to his feet.

For an instant he stood, as one drugged to stupidity, gazing down at the struggling animal. His last hope was gone. Syracuse was a full five miles away. He was on foot. The sun was making ready to sink behind the black mountain range to westward.

Five miles to go — on foot! And a distance that the fleetest horse could scarce hope to travel in so brief a space of time!

Half subconsciously, he drew his sword's keen edge across the throat of the crippled horse; mercifully ending the poor brute's agony.

As he sheathed his blade, Damon noted that the left side of his torn and muddied tunic was wet with blood. Then for the first time he realized that he had been wounded during his combat with the soldier.

Carelessly, with glazed eyes, he glanced at the flesh wound in his left shoulder. The wound was not dangerous. Yet it was bleeding freely; and the loss of blood was beginning to weaken the man.

His knees shook and his legs felt strangely heavy as he started afoot toward the city. He made no effort to stanch the blood, miserably wishing the wound might have found his heart instead of his shoulder.

Knowing full well the hopelessness of his quest, he nevertheless broke into a shambling run. His sword and embossed sword-belt and scabbard seemed heavy, so feeble was he growing through loss of blood. He cast them behind him in the road.

His sandals weighted his tired feet. He kicked them off and reeled on, barefoot; the sharp stones of the road cutting unheeded into his soles.

"Pythias!" he gasped, chokingly, as he ran. "Pythias!"

And again:

"*Pythias!* Friend who is even now perhaps dying for me! I have failed you. Would to the gods I might have died ere such an hour of shame!"

On, on, he staggered, drunkenly; along the road to Syracuse; sweating, bleeding, dust-choked, dizzy. His mind was clouded. His heart was dead. Yet he moved toward his goal, bitterly hopeless as he knew his journey now to be. Had his feet been hewn away he would have crawled onward upon his knees.

He knew full well there was no chance. Yet, so long as the fiery sun still stood above the mountains he would hasten toward the scaffold with all the weak force he still possessed. After that —

"Gods!" his blackened and cracked lips formed the words that his fear-sanded throat could scarcely voice. "High gods of Olympus! In friendship's holy name I supplicate you! I who never asked a boon for myself! Grant a miracle that shall carry me to Syracuse to die in my friend's stead! Grant it and —"

He staggered blindly against something that blocked his way; and, reeling back from the impact, he sank into the dust.

The shock partly cleared his eyes and his throbbing brain. Looking upward he saw above him a dark faced man clad in snow white; who, seated on a white horse, was gazing down at the fallen Damon in grave wonder.

At sight of the horse, Damon, by a mighty effort, got to his feet. He recognized the steed as a desert Arab of the fleetest breed; even as he recognized the rider as one of the Arabian sheiks who occasionally journey from the far off desert to Syracuse on business of tribal import.

Damon's hand went to his side. But neither purse nor sword hung there. There was no way to bribe or coerce the Arab into letting him have his steed. And he knew himself too weak from loss of blood to grapple the man barehanded.

Even as Damon was rising, the sheik spoke. Eying the disheveled and bleeding Senator, he said slowly:

"Are not you that Damon who was to return to the city to ransom his friend's life? I was in the throng to-day and saw —"

"Yes!" croaked Damon, hoarse, incoherent. "Yes! And I am too late unless — Your steed, Sheik! In Friendship's holy name lend him to me! I will return him and his weight in gold pieces if —"

"In Friendship's name he is yours," returned the Sheik, gravely. "And let there be no talk of pay. Ride to redeem thy pledge!"

Dismounting, as he spoke, he fairly lifted the exhausted Damon to the saddle.

"May heaven thank you as I cannot!" panted Damon, urging the milk white steed into a run.

The blooded horse need no whip nor spur. Across the plain he swept; neck outstretched; tiny feet flying like the hurricane.

The wounded man crouched low in the saddle, his eyes on the sinking sun; praying against all hope, that he might yet be in time.

The swart faced Arab sheik gazed after him.

"May the spirits of the Simoon speed Massoud's feet and bear the gallant man to his hero-death!"

he mused.  " To die as he thus will die shall prove to all future ages that Friendship is holier than all else on earth."

And the westering sun touched the top of the black mountains.

The hour was come.

# CHAPTER XXVI

### THE HEADSMAN

**B**LACK shadows from wall and turret lay
thick across the market square of Syracuse.
In the very midst of the *agora* a hideous
platform has been built.

Around the platform's foot surged and murmured
a vast crowd of men and women. The noise of
shouting, of laughter, of babbling talk, that mark
the presence of a crowd, were wholly absent.

Save for the low murmur of hushed voices, the
throng around the scaffold-foot was silent, void of
life. The faces of its men were white and tense.
More than once the stifled sound of its women's
weeping broke upon the stillness.

The people of Syracuse had come forth into the
*agora* to see a brave man die. From lip to lip sped
low-muttered rumors. One man declared that Damon had returned and was even now about to be led
forth to death. Another whispered that the Senator had been waylaid by Dionysius' assassins and was
even now dead. A third said that Pythias had aban-
doned all hope of his friend's promised return and
was prepared to meet his doom as a hero should.

At this last rumor, a wave of anger swept the crowd. Pythias was their idol. Gladly would hundreds of them have risked life for the dashing young general if, by that risk, he could have been saved.

But, lining the square's edges, stood rank upon rank of Dionysius' picked veterans; full armed; iron of face; ready to sweep the market place empty and to deluge its pavement with blood at the lightest command of their King.

Wherefore, heavy of heart, helpless to strike a blow for their hero, the people stood in tearful or muttering grief, and awaited the drama's next scene.

Even the most casual resident of Syracuse, re-entering the city after an absence, that afternoon, would at once have known that something was much amiss.

Usually, the sunset hour was the gayest of the twenty-four. The fierce heat of the day was then past; the cool breeze was setting in from the Mediterranean; the toil of the masses was over and the time for recreation had begun.

Then it was that from a hundred walled gardens came the soft twanging of lutes and the murmur of song and of laughter. Through the amber light the nightingale's sweet plaint awoke. The fishers' chant arose from the shore as the returning seamen hauled in their brown nets.

Through the alleys of the ilex, white robed lovers strolled arm in arm. Tradesfolk sat pleasantly gos-

siping in front of their shops. Groups of women
and girls loitered beside the public fountain, their
light laughter mingling prettily with the plash of the
water. Children played and shouted in streets and
*agora*. And over all brooded the sweet peace of
the dying day; the beauty of the sunset skies; the
joy of work done and rest begun.

This afternoon the wonted charm and glamour of
the sunset hour were missing. No music or laughter arose. No child shouted; no lover sang his wooing.

Instead, the ominous hush, the heartsick murmur,
the occasional clank of swords or shield or breastplate. A man was to die. A man the city loved.
And the city held its breath in horror and suspense.

And the next move in the grisly drama — the
drama for whose unfolding the populace waited with
fascinated dread — was quick to be made.

The rusty portcullis of the prison at the square's
upper end was raised. The creaking of the grill in
its grooves and the raucous jar of its chains rang
audibly throughout the whole hushed square.

Ten thousand eyes were turned toward the dirty-
brown building.

Through the grim archway, under the raised portcullis, marched six prison guards; each in full armor;
each with sheathed *gladius* at belt and each gripping
a keen pointed *pilum,* which he carried at " guard."

In the midst of this clump of armed men strode

a hideous figure: — a short, squat man, apelike of build; his short legs surmounted by an abnormally muscular trunk from whose shoulders hung arms as long and as sinewy as a gorilla's.

His face was bestial; with small glittering eyes, a grotesquely flattened nose, low forehead, a bristling black beard and close-cropped hair.  His dress consisted of a sleeveless jerkin and short kilt; the costume affected by butchers of that time.

Over his shoulder he carried a long hafted ax with an enormous curved blade; the badge of his calling.

At sight of the sinister dwarfish man, a shudder ran through the crowd, followed by a long sigh of horrified loathing.

Well did everyone there know the newcomer; and, in the streets, women were wont to draw aside their robes as he passed; and even the children would spit at him and hiss.

He was Matho, the public executioner.

Then, as in later and more civilized countries, the public executioner was held in abhorrence and dread by the public at large.  His office was hereditary; descending from father to son.  No one, save outcasts urged thereto by fear, would associate with him.  He was shunned like a leper.

Solitary, embittered, a creature of wholesale hatred, Matho lived out his days; as friendless in the teeming city of Syracuse as he would have been

on a desert island; forbidden even to occupy a house
within the city limits or to drink at a city tavern.

In a little hut-community beyond the gates, he
dwelt; his companions and neighbors, the *paraschites*
(undertakers and embalmers), those accused of
witchcraft and criminals who were in hiding.

Only on occasions when a man must die to satisfy
the law, was Matho allowed to set foot in the *agora*.
And then, only when surrounded by a highly necessary band of bodyguards to protect him from the
hatred of the people.

This afternoon, the thick-packed crowd parted
readily before the advance of Matho and his six
guards. The mass of people parted to make a lane
for them; as one draws back from a slimy serpent.
There was less of fear of the guard in their movement than of aversion to the man who was guarded.

Matho, unhindered, strode through the press; to
the low flight of four steps that led upward to the
platform of the scaffold. In the middle of the platform the headsman's block had been placed. It was
a cylinder of wood whose summit had been hollowed
to allow the neck of a victim to fit into it.

Matho walked over to the block; placed one foot
on it, tested the edge of his ax — and waited.

The sun was touching the western mountains.

# CHAPTER XXVII

**M**EANTIME, within the prison, Calanthe cowered. Refusing all of Creugas' pleas to leave the gloomy place, she had remained on the terrace outside of the door of Pythias' cell.

Recovering from her swoon, she had hastened to the closed and barred door as fast as her faltering steps could bear her. Then, as near as possible to her sweetheart, she had pressed her fair warm body against the cold bars and called aloud to the captor.

Creugas, by entreaties and almost by physical force, had sought to make her come away with him. But her one reply had been:

"After sunset to-day Pythias and I shall be as far apart as are the Earth and the Elysian Fields. For this poor space of time that is left to us, let me be as near to him as I may. It is all that is left to him in life. It is all that will be left to me to remember."

Nor could Creugas' urging shake her resolve. And at last the old man had limped away, mumbling protests against her stubbornness.

Through the long afternoon, as the sun, inch by
inch, dipped toward the western horizon, the girl
had knelt there against the bars, calling now and then
to her prisoned lover; her love words deadened by
the iron of the door.

None molested her.  Perhaps the power of the
signet ring, shown by Creugas to the guard-captain,
prevented the turnkeys or soldiers from ordering her
away.   Perhaps the power of her own heart-broken
love softened their rough hearts and made them leave
her to her grief.

And so the afternoon had dragged by, on leaden
feet.  The  shadows  lengthened  and  the  sunset
breeze drifted in from sea.   And at last the weeping girl felt a hand on her bowed head.

"No.   No!"  she  wailed.  "Not  yet.  Not
yet!"

She looked up to see Creugas bending over her.
Behind him were soldiers.   The men at arms stood
out of earshot at the entrance to the inner corridor
of the prison.   Creugas, if he had accompanied them
thither, had apparently bidden them wait at the ter-
race-end while he spoke with Calanthe.

"Leave me!" implored the girl, recognizing him.
"Leave  me  with  him — alone,  here — until  the
last."

"I have come," began the old man, "to tell
you —"

"There are no tidings that can interest me now,"

she interrupted. " Oh, will you not leave me? Do
not think I am thankless for the service you sought
to render him. Later,— when all is over — I can
thank you, perhaps, as I should. But now I can
think only of my loved one who must die."

" Perhaps he need not die," said Creugas, gently.

" Need not — need not die? " she echoed, incredulous; then: " No, good friend. You are wrong.
He will not consent to escape; even if you can still
save him that way."

" I cannot," returned the old man. " Fortune
never gives twice the same chance to the same man.
To-day, Pythias had his chance. And he hurled it
away from him, for honor's sake. That chance has
flown. See, the ship that awaited him has sailed."

" Then, why do you come here to —? "

" I come to tell you that there is hope for Pythias."

" Hope? What hope can there be? His life
hangs on Damon's return. And Damon cannot return; for did not the assassins of Dionysius lie in wait
for him in the woodland at the mountain-foot and
slay him? "

" No! "

" No? " she cried, trembling all over. " But you
told me —"

" I told you what I myself heard from the tyrant's
own lips. Ten minutes ago I learned Dionysius
changed his plans — he is ever changeable, when the
whim strikes him — and recalled the murderers.

He is resolved not to cog fate's dice, he says; but to let the event shape itself. If Damon returns before the sun has set, Pythias shall live. If he returns not, Pythias dies in his place. But the tyrant has not interfered with Damon's journey. The result is on the knees of the gods."

The girl sprang up; her lassitude gone, her face aglow, her eyes starlike and sparkling.

"Oh, may the gods bring you wealth and bliss!" she cried, impulsively seizing the old man's lean hand and covering it with kisses. "You have brought me to light and air, out of the grave. Pythias will be saved, then!"

"If friendship be so sacred a thing as he and Damon have ever boasted," said Creugas. "If friendship be more to Damon than is Self, then Pythias shall live. If he prefer life rather than *sarifice,* then Pythias dies. All hangs on the weight of Damon's friendship, as weighed against love of life and wife and child. Few could withstand the test, perhaps none."

"None?" she repeated, indignantly. "Have you forgot that for friendship's sake, Pythias this very day did turn his back on life and freedom? Shall Damon do less?"

"That," replied Creugas dryly, "remains to be proven. 'Tis that which the tyrant himself waits in hot impatience to discover. He could not at first believe that friendship was so strong as to make

Pythias yield himself hostage in Damon's stead. Nor, now, can he believe that Damon will be so great a fool as to come back and die when he may remain away and live."

Calanthe scarce heard.  A cloud had crossed the roseate glad hopes that had so suddenly sprung to life within her.  She remembered her own earlier fears lest Damon might not withstand the terrible test; lest Hermion's tears might win him from honor; lest the sight of his adored boy might melt his resolve.

Yet only for an instant did she let her mind dwell on such morbid fears.  The newborn hope was too strong to be long clouded.

With her bare fists she beat upon the iron door of Pythias' cell, shrilling rapturously:

"Pythias!    Pythias,  my  lover,— my  lover! There is hope for you!"

Forgetting that her joyous news could not pierce the thick metal of the door, she cried it over and again.

Steps and the clank of arms sounded behind her. The captain of the guard and a troop of twenty heavy-armed *hopleit* soldiers were advancing toward the cell.

Calanthe's frightened gaze turned instinctively from the oncoming soldiers to the westering sun. The red orb's lower rim was wellnigh kissing the mountain crest.

And again sick fear possessed her. On a mad impulse she threw herself in front of the cell, her arms flung wide across it.

"You shall not take him!" she wept. "Grant him time! Damon may yet come — *will* yet come — to take his place on the scaffold! You reach my lover only across my corpse."

The guard-captain's gnarled face took on a look of irritation. He stepped forward as though to drag the frantic bride away from the cell door.

But Creugas, as if by accident, interposed his body between the girl and the captain. And the sunset rays, touching his uplifted hand, set the signet ring to flashing ominously.

The Captain halted; irresolute; then, choking back his annoyance, said in gruff kindliness:

"Lady, we do not come to take him to his death, — if Damon returns. And there are still some few minutes lacking ere the hour of sunset. We come by orders of his gracious Majesty, the King, to lead the prisoner to the scaffold; there to wait Damon's coming."

"But why —?"

"'Tis at the scaffold, not here in prison, Damon will seek him if he arrives by any chance at the last moment," explained Creugas. "And by going to the scaffold, forthwith, Pythias can behold his friend as he arrives. Were Damon to seek him here at the prison, much time might well be lost in gaining

ingress.   Come, sir!" to the guard-captain, "to
your task.   The lady will not oppose you.   And, by
the authority vested in me, I command that she be
permitted to accompany her husband to the scaffold."

Again, the Captain scowled, and seemed as though
he were about to refuse.   And again Creugas raised
the shining hand that bore the monarch's signet ring.

"As you say!" grumbled the Captain.   "If there
be complaint or rebuke, for so irregular an act, I look
to you to make my peace with the King."

"Do not fear," said Creugas brusquely, "but
make haste.   The King's orders are yet unfulfilled."

The soldier, as though irked at being forced to
take orders from an ill-clad civilian, seemed about to
rebuke the authoritative old man.   But, again, on
second thought, he swallowed his resentment.

He strode to the cell door, unbarred it and flung
it open.

"Come forth!" he ordered.

Pythias, deadly pale, yet his eyes fearless and his
brow calm, stepped out upon the terrace.   As before, his glance swept sea and sky, lingering in brief
dread on the low sun.

Then he saw Calanthe and he stretched out his
arms to her in silence.   She fled to their mighty
refuge and lay close to his breast.

"My sweetheart!" she said softly, her voice

a-thrill with hope. "There is glorious news for you."

"Damon has returned?" asked Pythias, more in sorrow than in hope. "My friend, then, must die?"

"He has not returned," she made reply. "But he may return. The tyrant's order to slay him, as he rode, was countermanded. He was not way-laid."

"Then he will be here."

There was a calm certainty in Pythias's tone.

"May the gods grant it!" prayed Calanthe.

"Come!" ordered the Captain. "You are to await him on the scaffold."

"On the scaffold?" echoed Pythias, recoiling ever so slightly.

"It is the King's command," said the Captain.

"I am ready," answered Pythias, his face and voice as calm as those of a man who fares forth to a feast.

At a word from the Captain, the twenty *hopleits* formed in double rank about the prisoner. Calanthe, clinging to her husband's arm, pressed the closer to him as the armored men hemmed them in. Directly behind Pythias and Calanthe, in the dual hedge of soldiers, stood old Creugas.

"March!" rasped the Captain, drawing his sword and taking his place at the little procession's head.

The soldiers stepped forward as one man, in their

leader's wake, their short heavy swords drawn. In the space between their double ranks walked Pythias and Calanthe, followed closely by Creugas.

In this formation the party moved through the wide door into the prison, along its corridor and across the courtyard to the raised portcullis, where stood four spearmen on guard.

The spearmen saluted, drew aside to let them pass, and then followed them as a rear rank, marching abreast. Behind the departing group, the portcullis clanged down.

Out into the sunset square marched Pythias, his guard in close order around him. At sight of the prisoner a groan as of physical pain went up from the thousands of onlookers that filled the square and the surrounding roofs and windows.

At sight of the captive, all eyes were turned from the scaffold, with its grim form of the executioner standing, ax in hand, beside his block. There was an involuntary general movement toward the man who walked amid his guards; a movement of sympathy, of affection, of fierce pity.

Well it was for the carrying out of Dionysius' orders, that so many and such heavy-armed soldiers had been chosen for the prisoner's escort; else had the crowd torn Pythias free. As it was, the people surged like angry waves on every side of the procession, sweeping up to the very sword-points of the *hopleit* guard.

Through the press, the Captain and his men marched. The people gave back, threateningly and hesitatingly, before their steel clad progress; weeping, murmuring, cursing.

Pythias, his fair head erect, marched gallantly among his captors. The bright eye did not flinch — even at sight of scaffold, block and headsman — nor did the proud step lag.

Firmly, he trod, shoulders back, eyes steady, white brow unruffled. One arm was about Calanthe, supporting her frightened steps. His firm set lips moved only to whisper words of love and good cheer to her; words which old Creugas, hobbling just behind, craned his stringy neck to catch.

And thus, through the helplessly sympathetic crowd, they came at length to the scaffold. At the foot of its steps, the Captain halted.

Creugas drew him aside and whispered earnestly to him for a moment or two. The Captain listened, at first impatiently; but with growing respect. When Creugas had finished, the Captain saluted.

Creugas asked him a question. The Captain answered and Creugas made his way back to Calanthe and Pythias.

" I have ordered the Captain," he said, " to keep sharp lookout for sign of Damon's coming; and to give you every moment that the tyrant's commands will permit."

" Where is Dionysius? " queried Calanthe. " I

had thought he would not miss this chance to gloat over his foe?"

"Trouble yourself no more, then," said Creugas. "He is beholding all. Yet not where the people, should they seek to riot, can harm him."

"Where, then?" asked Pythias, looking around.

"See you the high tower above the prison? Then look closer. Upon its top, do you see three men standing? The parapet shields them and half-conceals them from the crowd."

"I see them. But —"

"The central man of the three, — he with the purple mantle which masks his lower face, — is Dionysius. His companions are Procles and Damocles."

"But, seeing you with us, will he not —"

"Ere he can lay hands on me," said Creugas, "I shall be far beyond his power. Nor will he risk observation by sending orders hither until the crowd has dispersed. The execution is in the hands of the Captain, yonder. He —"

The Captain approached, and motioned Pythias to mount the scaffold. Pythias obeyed; moving with regal trend as though mounting a throne. Calanthe, her arms locked about him, climbed the steps at his side. The officer stepped forward to prevent her. A word from Creugas checked him. And Creugas himself mounted the steps at their heels.

Pythias looked about him; his keen eyes sweeping the crowd that filled the *agora* and blackened the housetops. And, beyond, toward the plain he stared. Nowhere could he see the hurrying figure he sought.

The sun's lower rim touched the mountain top to westward.

# CHAPTER XXVIII

## FRIENDSHIP'S ALTAR

CALANTHE, even more eagerly than Pythias, gazed in every direction for sign of Damon's coming. Out over the plain roved her wide eyes; scanning such patches of the distant road as were visible; — seeking ever for the gray steed and his togaed rider. But the road seemed empty.

Nor, through the crowd, was there sign of Damon shouldering his way forward to save his friend.

" He will not come! " she wept.

And at sight of her tears, a noise of sobbing rose from the crowd. Women wept aloud. Men, in a gust of righteous rage at her grief, jostled forward, hands on knife hilts; threatening, growling, mouthing.

Up to the ring of steel-clad soldiers who surrounded the scaffold, rushed the crowd; only to give back before the bristling line of sword points and spears.

" He will not come! " repeated the heartbroken girl.

"BE BRAVE, MY GLORIOUS WIFE.   ONE LAST KISS."

"DIONYSIUS, TYRANT THOUGH HE BE, WILL NEVER SEVER FRIEND-
SHIP SUCH AS THIS."

"May the gods help him in the misfortune that has befallen him!" said Pythias. "Were it humanly possible, he would be here ere now. He has been slain."

"Perhaps," suggested Creugus, "he suddenly finds his life over-sweet to throw away."

"Old man," rebuked Pythias sternly, "your withered heart has never known true friendship or stirred to the call of honor. Else you would unsay those lying words."

"Creugas!" broke in Calanthe. "You have pointed out Dionysius to me, on yonder tower. Take me to him,— *take* me to him, my friend."

"To what purpose?"

"That I may kneel at his feet and implore of him my lover's life."

"As well kneel to yon sinking sun and bid it stand still," answered Creugas. "There is no mercy in the tyrant. You would but humble yourself in vain, to throw yourself on the mercy of the merciless."

"You shall not do it, my Calanthe," Pythias enjoined. "You shall not kneel to him. I am in the hands of the gods; not of the tyrant."

"But I —"

"It is useless," supplemented Creugas. "Even were there time — which there is not — you could not reach him. For fear of a rising of the people in Pythias' behalf, Dionysius has not only gone to the tower's roof, but he has had the doors behind him barred; and soldiers of his own household guard stands before the doors. No one can pass to him."

"Prisoner," intervened the Captain, coming toward them, "the hour is at hand. Two minutes remain to you to make your peace with the gods."

"I have not waited until my death hour," returned Pythias, "to make my peace on high. I go to my death a brave and stainless soldier. Even as I have sought to teach my followers how to live, so now will I teach them how a true man can die. Calanthe!" he added, turning to the weeping girl, a catch in his own deep voice. "Sweetheart of mine, I shall wait for you at the Gateway of Life. Whenever the time may come, my own, I shall be waiting. For, Elysium will not be Elysium until you share it with me. Death cannot break the golden chain of such love as ours. Be brave, my glorious one. Tears are not for the bride of a soldier. One last kiss — the last of many thousand —"

Their lips met in a long, long embrace. Then —

"Should Damon still live, do not upbraid him," Pythias besought. "He has much to live for. If he be not dead, then have the gods in their wisdom thrown some obstacle in the way of his return. He is not false to me. Be sure of that. Tell him I held him guiltless."

"The hour has fallen," said the officer, laying a heavy hand on Pythias' arm. "Come!"

Shaking off the touch, Pythias gathered the maiden

into his arms and strained her to his heart. Then, gently disengaging her arms that clung so tensely to him, and not daring to look again into her weeping eyes, he turned and walked to the block. Kneeling beside it he laid his head in the grisly hollow that awaited it. Calanthe would have run forward, but the Captain of the guard detained her.

The executioner stepped forward; spat on his calloused palm, balanced the great ax in his grasp and, swinging the weapon on high, awaited the Captain's command to strike.

From the hushed crowd arose a gasp of mortal horror. And, through that gasp, came a cry; — hoarse, spent, yet terrible in its intensity. An instant's pause and then fifty voices from one end of the *agora* took up the cry; and it swelled into a yell of

"*Damon! Damon! Damon!* DAMON!"

The Captain, the word of command trembling on his lips, turned to note the cause of the outcry. The square's eastern end was in wild tumult. The close packed watchers broke up in an eddying mass; an eddy that swirled onward; nearer and ever nearer to the scaffold. And now fifty voices had grown to a thousand; all shrieking:

"Damon!"

The Captain's sharp glance pierced the nearing eddy. He saw all at once that its nucleus was a disheveled man, with blood streaming from a wound in the shoulder and drenching his torn and soiled tunic; a man whose head was bare, and whose gray locks hung loose and disarranged, clotted with blood and dirt; whose ashen face was a mask of torture.

"Hold!" called Creugas, imperiously thrusting aside the headsman's poised ax. "'Tis Damon!"

Calanthe, with a shriek of joy, stared at the approaching man. Weak, staggering drunkenly, Damon was forging ahead, toward the scaffold; helped on in his weak progress by scores of strong arms.

Pythias arose from his knees and ran to the scaffold edge.

"My friend!" he cried brokenly. "My friend! Oh, my *friend!*"

Damon had reached the scaffold's foot. Reeling up the steps, he collapsed, exhausted, at the feet of Pythias; gasping breathlessly:

"You live! You still *live!* Oh, all the gods be praised! I am on time. I could not urge my horse through the thick crowd that walled in the square. I —"

"Damon!" Calanthe was weeping, as she knelt at the wounded man. "Forgive me that I doubted you! Forgive me that I doubted the holy power of friendship!"

"Friendship!" muttered Damon, dazedly.

Then, at the word, a delirium of ecstasy gripped him. Forgot were his fatigue, his wound, his weakness. To his feet he struggled and stood swaying there, glaring wildly out over the tumultuous multitude that shouted itself crazy on every side of him.

"Have I fallen from my horse?" he mumbled, dizzily. "Or has the soldier slain me and am I in the House of the Dead? The gods know I would have died for my friend. And all that mere mortal could do I did. Yet I — I am too late!"

"Damon! My friend! My brother!" cried Pythias, seizing his hands.

The touch lent new life to the delirious man. He stood erect, as though fresh and unwounded; and he laughed aloud in boyish triumph.

"You live!" he exulted. "You *do* live! Then it was not a dream. Yet, there is the block. I stand upon the scaffold. The gods be praised, it is for me — not you! Oh, this is the happiest hour of my life. I am *here!*"

Staggering to the platform's edge, he threw out his arms. Instantly the clamorous crowd grew silent in expectation.

"Friendship triumphs!" cried Damon, his voice ringing forth like a silver clarion. "Friendship triumphs! And I, a Friend, am greater than your King! This scaffold is my throne; — a throne more glorious than Jupiter's own. I am to die. Yet Friendship shall live. Dionysius lives, yet his glory shall die; while mine shall wax ever brighter and

brighter until it has eclipsed the sun itself. *Io Triomphe!*"

A roar from ten thousand throats hysterically
caught up the cry; and walls and hills echoed with
"*Io Triomphe!*"

"Dionysius! Tyrant!" screamed Damon, carried away by the thrill of cheers. "Did ever Syracuse acclaim *you* as now in my person it acclaims
Friendship? When were *you* hailed by shouts like
these? Again, my friends! *Shout!* And let the
noise of your applause rise to high heaven itself!
*Io Triomphe!*"

"*Io Triomphe!*" roared ten thousand voices.

"Tell me!" cried Damon, laughing wildly as he
faced the captain of the guard. "Where is your
tyrant master? Where does he hide? I fain would
look on his defeat and laugh at him."

"Then," spoke a voice behind him, "look — and
laugh!"

Damon's bloodshot eyes turned and met those of
Creugas. And, as he looked, Creugas raised both
hands to his own head and face.

In one gesture he drew away his hands and with
them came the gray hair and beard. A sweep of his
cloak-edge and the disfiguring red blotches and dark
lines were wiped from his cheeks.

"Dionysius!" gasped Calanthe.

"Dionysius!" echoed Damon and Pythias, in one
breath.

" Dionysius," replied the King, his inscrutable
gaze resting on each in turn, " the tyrant on whom
you would fain ' look and laugh.'   What, man? " he
went on, as the three stared upon him aghast, incredulous, spellbound.   " No   laughter?   Yet   I
merit laughter.   For I am become the butt of mine
own jest."

Again his hawk eyes swept them.   And still they
were silent.   To Pythias and to Calanthe, the trans-
formation of the doddering old meddler, Creugas,
into Dionysius himself, was little short of miracu-
lous.   It held them dumb.

Damon, on the other hand, was scarce fit for
speech.   The momentary exaltation had passed; and
weakness and pain surged wave-like over him.   He
had kept his vow.   He had returned to lay down his
life for his friend.   He was in time for the sacrifice.
Nothing else, for the instant, really mattered.   That
the tyrant had suddenly appeared out of space and
confronted him roused scant interest in the exhausted
man's mind.

" Yes," resumed Dionysius, a half-sad smile curving his thin lips, " I am become the butt of mine own
sorry wit.   I pray your heed while I tell in a mere
mouthful of words the tale of the jest.   Pythias, I
have ever envied you: — Your youth, your strength,
your power to make the commons love you.   Aye,
and your power to win this maid.   But most of all
I envied you the one thing which I, with all my wiles

and all my force have never been able to win.   Can
you guess what that is ? "

" Respect ? " queried Pythias, at a venture.

Dionysius winced, ever so little; then forced back
the wry smile to his lips.

" Perhaps Respect were worth the envying," he
made reply.   " And perhaps I have it not; but only
its twin brother, Fear.   Yet it was not of Respect
that I spoke; but of Friendship.   Yes, of that friendship which knitted your soul to Damon's with ropes
of steel; and that I now know must knit it so until the
mortal casket is forever stilled."

He paused, then went on:

" I envied such wondrous Friendship.   I could
inspire fear, flattery, service, and even a cringing reverence.   But even as I greedily filled my purse with
such coins as those, I realized they were of base
metal and that friendship alone is of true gold.   And
Friendship was beyond my winning.   So, like the fox
in the fable of Æsop the Slave, I feigned to scorn
what was above my reach.   I told others — yea, and
I told myself — that Friendship was but an empty
name; that at the first clash with Self-Interest, it
would crumble to nothingness.   Thus did Dionysius,
your King, seek to console himself for what could
never be his.   And thus did he seek to make gratified
ambition take its place; even as men who are starv-
ing chew bits of wood or straw in place of food.

" Then, this day, came an hour when I felt I could

prove, once and forever, how frail a thing is Friendship; and that henceforth I should the less miss its possession. Therefore, I let Damon go free while you stayed in his place, to take on yourself his fate should he not return. I was full sure he would not come back to meet his death. For I knew the love of wife and child are all-powerful. Combined with the love of life, I believed they would burst Friendship's stoutest bonds."

"You believed that — of *me?*" cried Damon, "and yet you let me go?"

"To prove the worthlessness of Friendship was a far dearer wish to me than to glut my vengeance on a foe. So I freed you; with no thought that I should again set eyes on you. But not even yet was I content. I was fain to prove Friendship's weakness in the case of Pythias as well. Wherefore, I spread before him such temptation as I believed no mortal could resist. I played upon every emotion a true man may feel. I offered him freedom, the love of his betrothed, reunion with his loved father, the chance to begin life afresh in other lands. He refused — for Friendship's sake. I told him you were slain and that his sacrifice was futile. Still, in Friendship's name, he would not yield. I sought to shake his resolve by pointing out dangers that awaited Calanthe. In all, he was steadfast. And at last I knew that at least one-half of my experiment had failed. To the very foot of the scaffold I tempted him. And he stood firm. Then, even as I took comfort in the thought that *you* at least had proven false, you returned. The jest is at my expense. You do well to say you wish to laugh at me. For I am beaten. Yet not by any mortal; but by something that is immortal; — by Friendship."

"And now," broke in Damon, "now that you have yourself proven how weak is the strongest monarch, compared with Friendship's power, have done with speaking of that which you can never hope to understand. And turn to that which is within your powers. I am your enemy. I sought to kill you. I am here upon the scaffold to pay my debt. Glut your revenge to the full. Bid your headsman to strike. I am ready."

"To strike?" echoed Dionysius, as if but half-comprehending; then: "When the high gods thwart our puny mortal plans, do we repay them by laying impious hands upon their altars? Nay, we dare not; even if we would. And to-day I am face to face with that which is holier and higher than all the gods of Olympus. I stand before the altar of Friendship. And I dare not defile so sacred a shrine. In slaying you, I would not be ridding myself of a foe. I would be committing sacrilege upon a Deity."

"I am to be imprisoned, then, instead? Far rather would I die. If I am to be parted from those I love, let it be by death, not by a living sepulchre of stone."

"I spoke not of prisons. Friendship cannot be fettered. Peace!" as he raised his hand to check Damon's exclamation of wonder. "Peace until I have issued my commands!"

To the Captain he continued:

"Send forth a herald to proclaim that Damon is pardoned! The 'tyrant' Dionysius gives him back his life. His life and his liberty. Yet not to him, but to Friendship! To that which all my power cannot buy me; nor all his misfortunes snatch from him. He is free!"

THE END